I0627582

To Paradise And Back

By

Bud Fussell

Deep Indigo Books
Published by Indigo Sea Press
Winston-Salem

Deep Indigo Books
Indigo Sea Press
302 Ricks Drive
Winston-Salem, NC 27103

For information regarding bulk purchases of this book,
digital purchase and special discounts, please contact the publisher
at indigoseapress@gmail.com

Cover design by Pan Morelli
Manufactured in the United States of America
ISBN 978-1-63066-553-1

Chapter One

Belmont. Belmont, Alabama. Belmont is well on its way to becoming the recognized playground for all of Northwest Alabama. It is located on the banks of the fifty-thousand-acre Tanisi Lake, pronounced Tan' is ee.

The average high temperature is a comfortable seventy-two point eight degrees and a not too cold low temperature average of fifty one point one. Being able to navigate without having to wear a bulky coat or jacket means a lot to many people.

Nearby Northwest Alabama University, or NAU, known nearly everywhere as a big party school, plays no small part in contributing to the playground recognition that Belmont is known for.

Tanisi Lake was formed by damming up the Tennessee River in the late nineteen thirties, and in the process, it flooded the little town of Laurel Springs, and it took the homes and farms of nearly eighteen hundred people. Not only did those residents receive a very fair price for their property, but they were also given first choice of land around the new lake at a price that was much less than they were paid for their original homes and land, and as a result, most of those people decided to stay. In most cases, the residents were able to buy nicer land than they had had, and as property prices increased for lake property, many of them became pretty well off, financially. In most cases, the ones who farmed, farmed, or if they were businesspeople, they continued in business. If they were retired, then their new property on the lake was wonderful because not only was their land nicer, but they had beautiful views of the water.

The Tennessee Valley Authority or TVA, as it's commonly known, was very cognizant of the fact that flooding Laurel Springs not only uprooted around eighteen hundred families, but it created what many would call a paradise. However, as with all things, time marches on, and hardly anything stays the same, and Lake Tanisi changed as well. Many of the original owners died and left their things to their children or other family members. Some sold their homes to new people moving into the area, and many other changes took place bringing Lake Tanisi and Northwest Alabama up to the present.

The University and Tanisi Dam were built at the same time, creating a huge building atmosphere for the area. When it was completed, many of the workmen went on to other places where they could get work, but some stayed and worked for the TVA and established roots while the University brought in several hundred teachers and professors. While construction on the Dam and University had ended, residential construction picked up, creating a different kind of building boom.

Don Neville was one of the better-known building

contractors, and he had two sons and two daughters, all in their late teens or early twenties. Carol, his youngest daughter and Billy, his oldest son, along with Bobby, Billy's younger brother were all active with the crowd that frequented Lake Tanisi almost on a daily basis during the summer. Sissy, the oldest daughter spent most of her time reading and growing exotic plants and flowers, so she seldom went to the lake with the others.

A lot of college students frequented the lake during the summer as well as high school students, and Donald Lee Mathis was recognized as one of the co-leaders of both groups, however, when the group was made up of mostly the high school age group, Billy was considered the leader.

The TVA had roped off a large swimming area, built restrooms, and put up several picnic tables, all under roof. The area was kept very clean, and it made for a great spot for the local young people, and the vast majority of the ones who were regulars at the picnic area were good people. If on a rare occasion a troublemaker showed up, they would be asked to leave, politely, and if they continued to make trouble, Donald Lee or Billy and some of the others would ask again, and if they still insisted on acting up, they would be physically escorted away from the area.

The Sheriff's Department knew who the troublemakers were and they were thankful that young folks like Billy and Donald Lee and their friends kept order on a daily basis.

Donald Lee was at the top of the age category of most of the kids at the lake. He was twenty-one and an upcoming senior at the University of Alabama, and if he didn't change his mind, he was going to follow his father's footsteps in law enforcement. He and many others in that age group had cut back on their lake activities because now that they were twenty-one years old, they could go to some of the many clubs that were available to them.

Billy was a very outgoing young man, and he had made a name for himself in sports while in high school. He played three sports, and after graduation, he thought he would go to Northwestern Alabama University or NAU as it was known to play linebacker in football, if he could get a scholarship. The NCAA won't let an athlete sign a letter of intent until February after their senior season, but he had become acquainted with the coaches and had made a verbal commitment to them even though he hadn't played his senior season yet. He was not real big as linebackers go, but he was fast and as tough as a pine knot, and the coaches could see that, so a scholarship was likely.

Billy had been dating Sylvia Richardson ever since they were sophomores, and everyone looked for them to get married one day. Billy's best friend was Buddy Russo, and while they double dated a lot, the girls that Buddy went out with were nice girls, but they weren't good friends with Sylvia, and Billy wanted to change that.

One day, Billy told Buddy, "Sylvia's Daddy told her to bring me and you and whoever you want to bring out to their house to ride horses. You wanna go?"

"Yeah. Sounds like fun. When are we supposed to go?"

"Saturday afternoon, and we'll stay for supper."

Nothing else was said at that time. Most all of the kids that were regulars at the lake were friends, but not close, and Billy had definite ideas about who he wanted Buddy to date. He wanted to line him up with somebody that was a good friend of Sylvia's.

On Saturday morning there must have been twenty-five at the lake. Billy was with Sylvia, of course, and Buddy was with Margaret Burns. They were all having a good time swimming and lying in the sun. Billy was watching Margaret, and after a while, when she and another girl got up to go to the rest room, he went over to Buddy.

He asked him, "Have you noticed Hazel this morning?"

"Who?'

"Hazel. Hazel Thompson."

"No. Not really. Why?"

"Well notice her now. She's the best-looking thing out here this morning."

Buddy asked, "Why are you on this Hazel kick. Have you forgotten that Sylvia's lying right over there?"

"I'm not on a Hazel kick. I'm just trying to show

you that there is a doll out here, and I can't believe I'm telling you this, but she wants you to ask her out."

"She does not. You're just carrying on your same old bull crap."

"No, I'm not. I'm telling you the truth. She and Sylvia have been talking, and she told Sylvia that she wishes you would ask her to do something, sometime."

Buddy answered, "I don't really know her. I know she's really good looking, though."

"She is that. You're crazy if you don't ask her. Look, I told you the other day that Sylvia's parents want us to come out to their place this afternoon to ride horses, and they said you could bring someone with you if you want to. They're going to cook out at supper time, and I think you'd have a good time. Sylvia's Dad is a hoot. Why don't to go with us?"

Sounds like fun, but I don't know if Margaret would want to go or not. I can ask her."

Billy said, "I'm not believing this. Look, Ace, I'm not talking about you taking Margaret. I'm talking about you taking Hazel. She really wants you to ask her, so what do you say?"

"I still think you're pulling my leg. I don't even hardly know her."

"You don't have to know her, and I'm not pulling your leg. Just ask Sylvia. They've been talking. Why don't you take Margaret home and ask Hazel if she'd like to go with you out to the Richardson's this afternoon. I don't think you'll regret it."

"How am I going to work that? I'm with Margaret this morning."

"Just tell Margaret you need to leave and then take her home. I'll get Sylvia to set things up for you with Hazel. All you'll have to do is go pick her up and bring her out to the Richardson's. We'll have a lot of fun."

In a few minutes, while Buddy was lying on the blanket with Margaret, Billy yelled for him to come over to where he and Sylvia were. He told Margaret, "I wonder what he wants. I guess I'll go see. I'll be back in a couple of minutes," and he got up and went over to Billy who was out of earshot of where he and Margaret were lying."

"What do you need, padna?"

Billy said, "Hold on just a second," and he told Sylvia to go over and get Hazel, which she did. When they got back to where she and Billy had their blanket, Sylvia told her to sit down for a minute, and she did. Then, Billy told her, "Hazel, Sylvia's parents want us to come out to their place this afternoon to ride horses and they're going to cook out. They want us to bring you and Buddy. Would you like to go?"

She looked at Buddy and asked, "Are you going, Buddy?"

And Buddy, beaming, said, "I am if you are."

Then she said, "Then, I guess we'll both be there. Thanks for the invitation. What time?"

"I'm not sure. I'll have to ask Mom, and I'll call you."

"Okay, sounds like a lot of fun," and she got up and went back to where she had been lying, and before she got back on her quilt, she turned around and went back to Sylvia and said, "Syl, if I'm not home when you call, call back. I've got some errands to run, and I don't want to miss you."

"Okay. You know where I live don't you?"

"Yeah, I know."

"Don't you want Buddy to pick you up?"

"This first time, I'll drive. If there's a second time, he can probably pick me up."

Sylvia said, "I know there will be a second time and a third, and no telling how many more, but you do it the way you want to, Girlfriend."

In about forty-five minutes or an hour, Billy and Sylvia and Buddy and Margaret picked up their blankets and left. Hazel was with a girl named Gail, and when they saw the others leave, they left as well.

Sylvia's parents said they should be at their house around three o'clock if they wanted to have plenty of time to ride before supper. Billy didn't have a car and neither did Buddy, but Buddy's Mother was good to let him use her's whenever he wanted to, so he picked Billy up, and they went to the Richardson's together.

On the way out there, Buddy asked Billy, "Did I tell you about the run-in I had with Eddie Edwards and his henchmen the other day?"

"No. What happened?"

"Well, I was coming out of Margaret's house last Tuesday when I ran into Eddie and four of his buddies when I got out to the street. Before I could do anything, Eddie said, "Buddy, I don't want you to see Margaret anymore, okay?"

"I said, what do you mean?"

"He said, Margaret is my girl, and I don't want you to see her anymore."

"I told him that if Margaret didn't want me to see her, then she will have to tell me herself," and he and the other four started closing the circle.

"He said, this is the last I'm going to tell you."

"I was afraid they were going to jump me and I was kinda scared because there were five of them and I was by myself, but I managed to tell him one more time that if Margaret didn't want to see me anymore, she will have to be the one to tell me, and not him, and I brushed by one of his buddies and got in the car and left."

Billy didn't like that, and he said, "I wish you had called me. We would have gone out to Eddie's and straightened him out."

"Do you know him?"

"Yeah, and he's a first-class jerk. He wouldn't have said anything if he had been by himself. He has to have a gang around him in order to try and look like a big man."

"Well, I'm glad you put me onto Hazel, Maybe I won't have to get my butt kicked if I start dating her."

"I'd say you won't," and then they came to the Richardson's house and got out and went in."

Sylvia's Dad was named Fred, and everybody

called him Fred R. After everyone got there, he suggested they go to the barn and pick out a horse they wanted to ride. Hazel and Buddy hadn't ridden that much, and they didn't know which horse they wanted, and Fred R picked one out for each of them, assuring them the horse he picked for them was gentle. Billy hadn't ridden that much either, but he was so full of B S, anyone would think he was probably born on a horse. He insisted on saddling his, and Fred R knew he didn't know how, but he let him try, anyway. He did pretty good, but failed to tighten the cinch tight enough, and rather that say anything to him, Fred R just walked over and made like he was checking all the horses, and when he came to Billy's he just tightened the cinch, and nobody knew the difference.

It was about three or four miles around the Richardson farm, and the foursome rode on *slow* the whole way. When they got back to the house, Fred R had lit the grill and was waiting for the charcoal to get hot enough. He asked how many burgers each one wanted and the girls each said one, and Billy and Buddy both said two. Fred R and his wife both ate one. Betty, Sylvia's Mother, had fixed a huge salad as well as baked beans and deviled eggs, so nobody went hungry. They topped the huge meal off with a freezer of homemade vanilla ice cream. Buddy had the best time he had had since he could remember, and he could tell that Hazel was having fun, too.

After supper, the women cleaned up and after the

pace sort of died down, Sylvia came in the den with two blankets. She said, "Wanna go out to the grapevines? And threw one of the blankets to Hazel."

Hazel and Buddy wondered what she meant by going out to the grapevines, but neither one said anything. They just followed Billy and Sylvia out to the back yard where there was a fairly large group of grapevines, all held up by what looked like aluminum conduit. Buddy asked, "What kind of grapes are these, Sylvia?"

"I think Daddy said they're concord grapes. Pick some and eat them. They're delicious."

It had been a beautiful day and the evening carried that out. The moon was not quite full, but it was large and bright, and it seemed as if every star in the sky was out. Sylvia and Billy picked out a spot they liked and spread their blanket. While they were spreading their blanket, Hazel and Buddy spread theirs. Although it was getting dark, the foursome lay on their blankets under the light coming from the house. All four were lying on their backs, talking, and every minute or so one or more of them would reach up and pick some grapes to eat while they talked.

The conversation was about several things; the lake, the end of summer and other things, and at one point, Sylvia asked, "Has anybody met the Fryes yet?"

Hazel asked, "Who?"

"The Fryes: two brothers and a sister. Their daddy is going to be the new head man at Southern Mills.

The sister is Mary, and the two brothers are Freddy and David."

Billy asked, "Are they our ages?"

She said, "I'm not sure. I heard that the boys are in college, and the girl is a senior in high school."

"Where do they go to college, NAU?"

"I heard that one is going to go to Alabama and one to Auburn. Word is, the oldest is transferring from Miami of Ohio to Alabama, and the other one is just a freshman."

Hazel said, "Are you sure their names are Frye? I heard somewhere that the man who is the head of Southern Mills is named Von Steen or Von Stein or something like that."

Sylvia said, "I think Frye is right. Maybe they're his stepchildren."

Buddy said, "Maybe they are."

The two couples stayed until around nine-thirty, and Hazel said she had to go. They all got up and picked up their blankets and went into the house. Billy and Buddy decided to leave as well, and they told Betty and Fred R what a good time they had. Buddy walked Hazel to her car, and while his heart was beating like crazy, he made a move toward her to kiss her, and to his delight, she was very receptive to him, and they had a very nice kiss. They made a date for the next night after the Richardson's had invited them to do so, in fact; they saw each other every night for most of the rest of the summer.

Sometimes, they would go to a movie or a ball

game or a gospel singing or something else, and it looked as if the love bug had bitten them both.

One night when the four were going to be at the Richardson's, Buddy had to work late, and he didn't get there until after the other three were already there. It was a hot night and Billy had his shirt off when Buddy got there, so Buddy took his shirt off. In a little while, Fred R winked at Billy and asked, "Billy, did you show Buddy that new Jenny we got today," and Billy said, "No sir, I haven't. Wanna see it, Buddy?"

Buddy said, "Yeah, I'd like to," so the two of them went outside in the dark to see the new jenny. It was a particularly dark night, and one could hardly see their hand in front of their face, but they eased on out further, and Buddy said, I can't see anything, Billy," and Billy said, "I know. It's not much farther. You should be just about there," and about that time, Buddy walked up against an electric fence with his bare chest, and after the initial shock, he yelled and said, "Billy Neville, I'll get you for this. You just wait," and Billy had to wipe tears from his eyes, he was laughing so hard.

By then, Sylvia, Hazel, Sylvia's Mama, Betty, and Fred R had slipped out on the porch, and they all got a huge laugh at Buddy's expense, but Buddy was still too shocked to laugh.

Hazel and Buddy were made to feel just like one of the Richardson's own children, and they felt totally at home whenever they were out there.

The days of summer were beginning to slow

down, and football practice was about to begin. Billy and Buddy both played football and would soon have their activities at the lake and with their girls seriously altered. Billy and Sylvia were so serious, the changes wouldn't affect them, and while Buddy and Hazel really enjoyed being with each other, they weren't nearly as serious, in fact; their relationship was beginning to have cracks in it.

Hazel was a year older than Buddy and had already graduated from high school and was working in the office at a large insurance company in Huntsville. They were still seeing each other, but it was easy to see that things weren't the same between them as they were two or three weeks ago. She couldn't get off work to go to the lake with the others except for the weekends, and that sort of stuck in her craw. She could still go out at night, and that helped, but things just weren't the same.

One Saturday, all the kids were at the lake, and that time, the three Frye kids were there. Billy, being very outgoing, spotted them as soon as they got there and went over and introduced himself to them.

He went to Mary first, and said, "Hi. I'm Billy Neville," and she said, "I'm Mary Frye."

Billy then asked her, "Are these your brothers?"

She said, "Yeah, this one is David, and the one lying face-down over there is Freddy."

David stood up and held out his hand to Billy and said, "Hi. I'm glad to meet you."

Freddy, on the other hand, didn't get up. He just

turned his head toward Billy and held up his hand and said, "Hi," then turned his head away again, as if he had no interest in him.

The longer Billy stood there and talked to them, he determined that David was really the spokesman for the three. He decided that David was outgoing and had a good personality, that Mary was very nice, but she was bashful and not very outgoing, and that Freddy could be a troublemaker and needed watching.

Chapter Two

While Billy was at the Richardson's one night, Fred R. asked him, "Where are you going to be at lunchtime tomorrow?"

"I've got to be in town tomorrow. My mom and I went down to Caudles the other day and bought some clothes for me to wear this year, and I've got to go pick them up."

"I thought I heard you tell Sylvia that you were going to be in town tomorrow. I've got to be there tomorrow for a meeting at the bank. I thought if you would like, I'd be happy to buy your lunch."

"That sounds good. Yeah, I'd like that. When and where?"

"Do you like the Steak and Shake?"

"I love the Steak and Shake."

"Good, why don't I meet you there at twelve thirty?"

"Great. I'll be there."

"Okay, I'll look forward to it," and with that, Fred R. went into another part of the house where Betty was, and Billy went to find Sylvia.

Sylvia asked him when he found her, "What were you and Daddy talking about?"

"Oh nothing. He just asked me if I would like to meet him for lunch tomorrow."

"Are you going to?"

"Yeah, I told him I would."

"Why is he meeting you?"

"No reason, I guess. He said he had a meeting downtown tomorrow," and smiling, he said, "I guess he just wants people to see him in the company of a good-looking guy."

Sylvia smiled back and asked, "Maybe he does. I guess he's going to meet you at the restaurant, right?"

"You're a smart A., do you know that?"

She just smiled bigger. It was getting late, and Billy said he needed to go, so he kissed her goodbye and left.

The next day, Fred R. and Billy met at the Steak and Shake as planned. As they went up to order, Fred R told Billy to go ahead and order first. Billy said, "I want a cheeseburger, large fry, and a chocolate milkshake and please put mustard on the cheeseburger."

Fred R. told the guy taking their order, "I'll take the same thing."

He asked, "You want mustard on your cheeseburger, too?"

He said, "Yes, please," and then he told Billy, "I didn't know anybody else liked mustard on their cheeseburgers except me."

Billy said, "Yeah, I like mustard on just about everything."

While they were eating, Billy said, "Did you say you had a meeting this morning?"

"Yeah, at the bank."

"At the bank? Sylvia said you own part of the bank. Is she right?"

"Yeah, she's right if you consider being a minority stockholder a part owner."

"Well, I do. I definitely consider being a stockholder a part owner; no matter how much stock you own."

"Well, I don't have much say-so in things. The meeting this morning was pretty much a 'get acquainted' thing. A fellow named George Cochran is a native of Belmont, and he left here several years ago and went up north to college. After he got out of college, he went to work for somebody, and at some point, he invented something: I'm not sure just what, but whatever it was made him a multi-multi-millionaire. George is getting up in years now, and he decided that he and his wife, Coco, would move back to Belmont, and he bought majority interest in Northwest Bank. Our meeting this morning was so we could get acquainted with him."

"Did you like him?"

"As much as I could tell from one meeting, he seemed like a nice guy, but I think his wife is a different story."

"Why do you say that?"

"Because I don't think I saw her smile even one time this morning, and if someone said something to her, it was almost like she wanted to bite their head off. Of course, that was my first time seeing her, and she might be a very lovely lady once you get to know her," and after a short pause, he said, "But I seriously doubt it."

The two guys finished their lunch and engaged in quite a bit of small talk before Fred R said, "Billy, I need to go. I have some things I need to do this afternoon, but it has been a real pleasure having lunch with you. Are you coming to the house tonight?"

"Yes sir, I think so. I haven't talked to Sylvia, so I don't know what our plans are, but I'll say I'll be there. Thank you for lunch."

"You bet. See ya. Oh, I almost forgot; did you know William Overby?"

"Yes sir, I do. Why, is something wrong?"

"He died last night."

"Oh, I'm sorry to hear that. He was a nice man."

"I don't know whether they will have the viewing tonight or tomorrow night, but Betty and I will be going whenever it is, so if we're not at home when you get there tonight, that's where we'll be."

Shortly after Billy got to the Richardson's, Fred R and Betty came in from visiting the funeral home, and while they were sad over the death of Bill Overby, they were on an emotional high because of the funeral home's new host, D. W. Handy.

Betty told Sylvia, "Honey, we met the nicest man tonight."

"Who was he," Sylvia asked.

"His name is D.W. Handy, and he's a host at the funeral home. When you walk into the funeral home, feeling sad and down, he greets you and something about his personality makes you feel so much better."

Fred R said, "You know, grieving over a friend or family member is never a pleasant thing, but if you're able to encounter someone like him, things seem to be so much better."

Billy asked, "Where did this guy come from?"

"I asked him that and he said he left Pulaski, Tennessee and came to Belmont about three months ago. Bobby Pearson is a close friend of his. He and Bobby met in college, and Bobby talked him into coming to work at the funeral home. The elder Bob Pearson is ready to retire and young Bobby will take over the home, and he wanted D.W. to come work with him."

Soon, it seemed as if D.W. was everywhere. Being single, he ate nearly all his meals out, and it seemed as though he ate at a different restaurant each time he went out. He began attending the Belmont United Methodist Church and became a faithful attendee. It didn't matter what the season was for sports; he was always at the games if he wasn't working. Word was that he was a four-sport letterman at Pulaski High.

Football season was getting ready to start, and Billy and Buddy and the rest of the team were anxious to start. It had been a great summer, but after so long with not much to do, things were beginning to get a little boring.

After a three-week preseason, Belmont was finally ready to play their first game, and the stands were packed. Billy and Buddy both played great, and after the game, several people had gathered outside Belmont's locker room to speak to the players when they came out after showering and changing into their street clothes.

Buddy's parents, Helen and Henry, were out there and showered compliments on all the players, especially Buddy and Billy, but Billy's parents weren't there. Henry asked Fred R about it, and Fred R told him that they never went to any of their children's games or anything else that they participated in, but since Billy and Sylvia had been dating, Fred R and Betty made sure that they attended everything that Billy was involved in.

While everyone was milling around and shaking hands and talking, Billy noticed a fellow that he didn't recognize talking to many of the players and parents, and he wondered who he was. In a little bit, after his and Buddy's parents left them, the fellow came over to them and introduced himself.

"Hi, I'm D.W. Handy. You guys played a terrific game tonight. Billy, when you hit that guy on third down to end their drive was something that should have been filmed. It was beautiful."

"Thanks. I've got to say it felt good."

"I bet it did."

Billy said, "I've heard a lot about you, Mr. Handy, and I'm glad to finally meet you."

"I'm glad to finally meet you, too. I've heard about you as well, and I'm just D.W.; not Mr. Handy, okay?"

"Okay, D.W."

After that first game, D.W. was at nearly all the rest of the games, and if he missed, it was because he was working.

Billy and Buddy pretty much lost contact with D.W., except for when he would come to their games and show up outside the locker room to compliment them and the rest of the team. Occasionally, his name would be mentioned after a funeral had been held for someone they knew. One thing stood out about him and funerals, and that was how beautiful he could sing. Someone found out that he could sing and they asked him to sing at their relative's service. From then on, he was asked to sing at several other funerals because of his beautiful voice. Word got around about him, and because of his warm, comfortable demeanor and his voice, several people had their deceased loved ones brought to Pearson's rather than to other funeral homes that they would normally go to.

One day, in the middle of January, George Cochran passed away and Coco chose Pearson's for his services. Neither George or Coco had any family, and the only people who went to the funeral home were friends of George's, and there weren't that many of them. Coco had no friends because of the way she was, so the visitation was very light, and it carried on to George's funeral the next day.

The day of the funeral was the coldest day of the year up to that day, and it was really icy, even in the middle of the day. The handful of people that showed up were miserable and could hardly wait until the preacher said the final prayer, so they could leave and get warm. D.W. couldn't help but feel sorry for Coco. She had worn a nice suit and a mink stole, but it wasn't nearly enough for that cold day. D.W., being the gentleman that he was, went over to her at the cemetery, took his coat off, and wrapped it around her. Even then, she didn't smile, but she did say, "Thank you, young man. I'm afraid you'll get cold."

"No problem, Mrs. Cochran. I just don't want you to get too cold. It might not be good for you."

"Well, thank you again, young man."

"You're very welcome", D.W. said.

The service ended and everyone rushed to their cars to turn their heaters on. D.W. got in the flower van to warm up, and before he knew it, the family's car, with Coco in it, left to take her home, and she still had his jacket. He thought, *well darn. I wanted to help the lady, but I thought she would give my coat back before she left. Oh well, I'll go out to her house and get it when I finish this afternoon.*

Later that afternoon, when he finished up at the funeral home, he left to go to pick up his jacket at Coco Cochran's. Her house was located several miles outside of town on a beautiful property overlooking Lake Tanisi. The house was huge. D.W. estimated that it had at least six thousand square feet; an awfully lot for two people.

He rang the doorbell, and after what seemed like

forever, Coco opened the door. She didn't say anything; she just stood there. D.W. finally said, "Mrs. Cochran, I forgot to get my jacket back when the service was over, so I came to get it."

She said, "Oh, that's right. Come in and I'll get it for you."

He followed her into what he supposed was the den. It was large with dark paneling, and one wall was almost totally a bookcase, completely full of books. She said, "Have a seat, and I'll get your jacket."

He sat in one of the comfortable leather chairs and looked around from his seat while he waited on her to bring his jacket. Finally, she came back into the room holding his jacket, and he stood up and reached out to get it. "Thank you, Mrs. Cochran. Again, I'm very sorry about the loss of your husband. I guess I had better go."

"Thank you, young man. If you have time, sit back down. I'd like to talk to you for a moment."

"Yes ma'am. I have time, and my name is D.W. I hope you'll call me that."

"Okay, D.W. What does D.W. stand for?"

"Donald Wayne. Donald Wayne Handy, but I prefer D.W. My dad called me that when I was just a boy, and it sort of stuck."

Coco said, "Well. I like D.W. D.W., I think you did a wonderful job singing at George's funeral today, and I want to thank you."

"Thank you, Mrs. Cochran. I'm glad it pleased you."

She went on and asked, "D.W., are you a native of Belmont?"

"No ma'am. I'm from Pulaski, Tennessee."

"Well, tell me a little bit about yourself. I think I would like to get to know you."

D.W. told her everything he could think of, beginning when he was a small child all the way up to where he was today.

She said, "That's very interesting. It sounds as if you've had a full life so far."

"Yes ma'am, I have."

The conversation slowed down, and neither of them could think of much more to say, so D.W. said, "Well, I guess I had better be going. It's going to be your dinner time shortly."

Coco said, "I wish you didn't have to go. I've enjoyed getting to know you, and I hate eating by myself. Some of George's friends have brought food over for me, and I certainly can't eat it all. Would you like to stay and eat with me?"

He had skipped lunch and was really hungry. He knew that most of the time, funeral food was delicious, so he said, "Are you sure?

She said, "I'm sure. Now that I have someone to eat with, I'm hungry, and I feel like you are, and I would like to have you. Will you stay?"

"Mrs. Cochran, I'd be happy to stay. You're right. I'm starving. I haven't had anything since a biscuit at breakfast."

Coco said, "Good. D.W., since it looks as if we're

going to be friends, I wish you would call me Coco. Will you do that?"

"I sure will, Coco. I don't like being so formal, do you?"

"Not at all. Thank you, D.W. George and I usually ate our meals in the kitchen unless we had some formal company. Will the kitchen be alright with you?"

"It definitely will."

"Okay, then. Let's see what we have." She began pulling food out of the fridge, and there was no way the two of them could eat it all.

D.W. said, "Boy oh boy, Coco. This looks delicious. I haven't eaten this much food all week."

"Well, help yourself. Do you want to fix your plate or would you rather I do it. George always wanted to fix his own."

"I'm like George. I prefer to fix my own."

They both fixed their plates with a wide variety of food, and Coco insisted that D.W. microwave his first. After both their plates were hot, they sat down to eat, and it was great. In a little bit Coco said, "Save room for dessert. There's blackberry cobbler and banana pudding. Do you like either of those?"

"They're my two favorite desserts," D.W. said.

The pair seemed to enjoy each other's company, and they really enjoyed the food. D.W. began getting a little antsy, and almost immediately when they finished eating, he told Coco that he had to go.

Surprisingly enough, coming from Coco, she

walked him to the door, and with a big smile, she said, "D.W. you just don't know how much I've enjoyed spending this time with you. You know how I don't like to eat alone, and you're alone as well, so we should get together often and have dinner. I've been told that I'm a pretty good cook, and if I could encourage you to come over, we can have some pretty good meals together. I'll buy the food, and all you'll have to do is come eat with me. This will help my loneliness and help your pocketbook as well. Do you think we might could do this?"

"I'm sure we can. The only thing is that I'm pretty busy at work in the evenings, and I like to support our schools by going to their ballgames. This only leaves a couple of nights a week."

She said, "D.W., I'll take whatever I can get, okay? Is there any other time this week that we might get together?"

"I don't know, Coco. I'll have to call you tomorrow."

To say D.W. was confused by the evening he had just spent with Coco Cochran would be a huge understatement. Before that night, he had only known her by reputation, and that wasn't good. He had heard that she was a true sourpuss and didn't know how to smile or be congenial to others, but when he got ready to leave after they had had their dinner, she smiled, and it showed all over her face. He decided right then that she might not be such a bad person after all. After these thoughts, he told himself, *I think when I call her tomorrow, I'll tell her that we can get together any time she wants to as long as I'm free.* By the time he got his thoughts sorted out, he arrived at his apartment complex and went in to watch TV for a little while before bed.

The next day, at lunchtime, he called Coco. When she answered, he said, "Coco, D.W. How are you today?"

"I'm fine, D.W. I'm starting to go through George's things, and I'm already seeing that I'm going to have to have a lot of help, especially with the finances. George was a wealthy man, and I think he left everything to me, and I don't have any idea what all these papers and things mean. Do you know any financial people, personally, that I might can get to help me?"

"Coco, I know a couple, but I don't know where their expertise lies. Before you call anybody, would you mind if I come over and see what you've got, and maybe, between the two of us, we can decide which one will be the best to do what you need."

"Would you do that for me, D.W.?"

He said, "I would love to help you, Coco. I'm free tonight and can come to your house when I leave work, if you want me to."

"I would like that. Could you eat some more leftovers? As you know, I still have plenty of food that people brought in."

"That sounds good to me. I loved those meatballs and scalloped potatoes." Kidding, he said, "You didn't eat the rest of that banana pudding, did you?"

She said, "No, I'm saving that for you. Besides, I like blackberry cobbler better, anyway."

When she said that, he thought he detected a little lightheartedness in her voice. He said, "Great. Is five thirty too early?"

"Oh no. Five thirty will be good."

"Okay, I'll see you then."

D.W. left the funeral home at four thirty and went to his apartment to freshen up before he went to Coco's. When he got to her house, it was right at five thirty, and she must have been looking for him because before he could ring the bell, she opened the door, and said, "Hi, D.W. Come in."

He went in and they engaged in the usual unimportant small talk, and in a few minutes, Coco asked, "Are you hungry?"

He said, "Yes ma'am, I sure am," and they went into the kitchen where Coco had already taken the food out of the fridge.

After they had sat down and were eating, Coco said, "D.W., I'm very anxious to get George's things straightened out, especially the things having to do with money. You see, George took care of all that, and I never had much money for myself. Don't get me wrong. George gave me anything I wanted and needed, but since he took care of everything, he didn't think it was necessary for me to have a big bank account, and now that he's gone, I only have a few dollars in my account, and I need to know how to get some more. George was rich, and I'm sure he wouldn't want me to run out of money."

"Coco, I'm sure George had an attorney. Do you know who it is?"

"No. I don't know anything about any of his business."

"Okay then. When we finish eating, you can show me what you have, and maybe we can figure out what has to be done. In the meantime, if you need a little money, I can let you have some, and you can pay me back whenever you can."

"Thank you so much for that very sweet offer, but I have enough to hold me until I can get George's released."

"Okay. If you're sure."

They went into what was George's office and in addition to his desk and other furniture, there was a good sized safe. D.W. said, "Show me what you have and don't understand, and I'll see if I can help you."

She picked up a large stack of papers, including some ledgers and legal papers. D.W. asked, "Do you know the combination of the safe?"

"No."

"Well, let's see if we can find something with the combination on it," and he began going through the drawers in the desk. After taking out several things, he found a small notebook, and on the inside cover was written five seemingly unconnected numbers, and he told himself, *this has to be it.*

He took the notebook to the desk and tried the numbers, and voila, the door opened. He said, "Coco,

I think this is what we're looking for." There were quite a few legal binders with financial institutions' names on them, and one common denominator that he found was the name of Andrew Cagle, Attorney at Law, under the name Cagle and Cagle, PLLC.

"Well, here's George's attorney," D.W. said.

Coco said, "Oh, you found him. Good."

D.W. told her, "Coco, I'm sure Mr. Cagle is aware of George's passing and is more than likely waiting for you to contact him. Do you want to call him, or would you like for me to? I'm sure he can work with you on all of George's business dealings and finances as well."

"Would you mind, D.W.? I can go see him whenever he wants me to."

D.W. took the number from one of the legal forms and dialed Andrew Cagle. When he got Andrew on the phone, he explained who he was and explained that he was helping Mrs. George Cochran with her things and asked if Coco could make an appointment with him very soon.

Andrew asked him to hold for a minute, and then he came back on and asked if two o'clock the day after tomorrow would work for her. He held the phone away from his ear and asked Coco, "Mr. Cagle say he can see you day after tomorrow at two o'clock. Is that good for you?"

Coco said, "Yes, that will be fine, if you can go with me."

That surprised him, but after a brief pause, he said, "Yeah, I'll go with you. I'm sure Pearson's will let me off since it's you." He held the phone back up to his ear and told Andrew that they would see him then.

The day was Tuesday when D.W. called Andrew, which meant he and Coco would meet with Andrew on Thursday. He got to Coco's at one thirty, and they drove her luxurious Lexus LS500 to Andrew's office. D.W. had never driven a car as luxurious as that one, and he hated to get out when they arrived at Andrew's.

When they first began talking after getting into Andrew's office, Coco had to explain her relationship with D.W., and D.W. tried his best to make a good impression on Andrew because he was already harboring some thoughts about himself and Coco's money, just in case the opportunity presented itself, sometime.

George's holdings were extensive, and it took quite a while to cover everything. Their meeting began at two, and at five they were still going. Finally, at a quarter to six, Andrew said, "Well, Mrs. Cochran, I think we've covered just about everything. Again, I'm very sorry about George. If you find there's anything else that I can do to help you, please don't hesitate to call me. D.W., it was a genuine pleasure meeting you, and I'm glad you're going to be helping Mrs. Cochran because she's going to need someone she can trust to help her look after her holdings. After all, thirteen million plus dollars is a sizeable estate, and I'm very glad that she decided to make you her Power of Attorney. That should make things a little easier for her.

Chapter Three

Six Months Later

As expected, Billy was offered a football scholarship to NAU, and the plans were for him to do big things, however, during recruiting season, the coaches were able to recruit some huge, fast, and quick linebackers, and when the season opened, the three starting linebackers did not include Billy. Two of them were veteran players and the other was one of the players recruited over the summer. Billy's ego was seriously injured, and he didn't know if he would continue to work so hard and not be a starter or not. He got to play some, but his size hindered him. He weighed two hundred and five pounds and the other linebackers weighed in excess of two-twenty, plus, they were all over six-two, and Billy was not quite six feet; he measured five-eleven and a half. While two o five and nearly six feet is a good sized man, it's small when compared to men on a football team, who most of the time weighed between two fifty and three hundred pounds and were anywhere from six two to six six or six seven.

Billy was fast and quick, but so were the other larger men, and since he was pretty sure he wasn't going to get any bigger, he decided not to go back out the next season. He worked really hard, and he thought that even though he worked hard, he didn't get to play that much, and he thought that it just wasn't worth it.

The linebacker coach as well as the head coach tried to talk him out of quitting, but when he made up his mind to do something, usually, there was no talking him out of it. Besides, he had other things on his mind. He and Sylvia had set a date in June for their wedding, and he had that coming up as well as trying to find a job that would support a new wife.

Sylvia had been able to get a job at the Marshall Space Flight Center where Hazel now worked, and Hazel still dated Buddy, occasionally, but the four of them didn't spend as much time together as they used to. Hazel had found some guy at her new job and went out with him some, so Buddy was no longer the one man in her life.

The four of them still spent time at Sylvia's parent's farm and still had a lot of fun out there, but since they had all gotten older, it wasn't quite the same, even though all of them, except possibly Hazel, wished it was. Fred R still cooked out when they came, and it was still good. Billy and Sylvia still acted the same. But Hazel seemed to be more withdrawn no matter how hard Buddy tried to make their time together a lot of fun. They were both going to be in the wedding, and each one secretly thought that that might be the last time they would see each other as a dating couple.

Billy had talked to Don, his dad, after he had decided to quit football at NAU, and Don thought he had convinced him to stay in school, but the closer the wedding got, the more determined he was to quit school and go to work fulltime.

Don was a prominent builder in the area and one day Billy had a serious talk with him and told him that he was going to drop out of school and would like to come to work with him, building houses and things. When he was in school, he had worked Saturdays and summers for him, so a hammer and saw weren't strangers to him. Don said one day that "Billy's already a better builder than I am," and Billy reminded him of that during their talk.

Finally, Don said, "Okay, Billy, I can see that I'm not going to be able to talk you out of it, so I guess you can come with me, Now, I would like for you to finish this semester, so if you should decide to go back to school sometime, you would at least have that much completed."

"Okay, Dad. I'll do that."

After their talk, Billy was free for the day, so he thought he would go to the Steak and Shake and have lunch. He felt as if a load had been lifted off his shoulders, and he really loaded up on food. After he had finished eating, and before he left the restaurant he looked up and saw D.W. Handy coming in the door. He waited until D.W. ordered, and when he was looking for a table, he called out to him. D.W. looked over and saw him, and Billy said, "Come over and sit with me."

He sat down with Billy and said, "Billy, I'm really

glad to see you. I've been pretty tied up most Saturdays and haven't been able to get to many games. Have you had a good year?"

"Not too good, I'm afraid, D.W. They brought some gorillas in and played them instead of me. I just have left my dad where I told him that I'm quitting football and school, and that I want to go to work for him."

"Man, I hate to hear that. I thought you would at least be all-conference this year."

"I just couldn't compete with guys that are bigger, faster, and quicker than me. I got to play some, but to me it's just not worth having to work like a dog and then not getting to start."

"I can understand that," D.W. said.

Billy continued. "You know, football season was over in November, and workouts began the next week, so really, football is a year round thing. I'm just not prepared to work that hard for such a small payback, so I'll just go to work for Dad and build some beautiful houses." He smiled and asked, "Want me to build you a beautiful house, D.W.?"

D.W. replied, "I bet you could do it. Are you still going with Sylvia?"

"Yeah, and we're going to get married in June. I'll send you an invitation."

"Great. I'll look for it."

Billy asked, "Are you still working at the funeral home?"

He said, "Yeah, plus I'm sort of working part-time

for Mrs. George Cochran. Do you know her?"

"No, but I've heard the name. Didn't her husband work at one of the banks?"

"Yeah, but he didn't work there. He owned controlling interest in it."

Billy asked, "What do you do for her?"

"Anything she wants me to. She's in her late seventies, and she doesn't want to drive anymore, so I take her places. I pay her bills, do her banking, and look after just about everything in her life. It's a pretty plush job, and the pay is great. Boy, is the pay great. I make more working for her part time than I do working full time at the funeral home."

"Why don't you quit the funeral home and work fulltime for her?"

"That would be nice, but think about it, Billy. Mrs. Cochran is seventy-eight years old, and of course, she could live to be a hundred, but that's not likely, and let's say she lives another four or five years and then passes. Then, I would be out of a job, and I don't want to do that, so I'll just keep doing what I'm doing for as long as it lasts. Besides, Mrs. Cochran, or Coco as I call her, is very generous, and she encourages me to help her in some of her philanthropic projects," and half-joking, he said, "I keep hoping she'll make me one of her charities, sometime."

"What do you do to help her?" Billy asked.

"Well, Coco is not able to do a lot of things, herself, anymore, but she still wants to help people, and do you know what a Power of Attorney is?"

"No, that's a new one on me."

"A Power of Attorney is when someone authorizes someone else to act for them because of their poor health or something like that. The person that needs the act done has to have an attorney draw up papers and everyone has to sign them, and then the person designated to act for that person can legally do things, such as signing their checks or contracts and things like that."

"Oh, I see."

"Billy, do you go to church?"

"Yeah, I go to White Oak Baptist with Sylvia and her family. Why?"

"Well, I go to Belmont First United Methodist, and the preacher is going to make a really big announcement next Sunday, and it involves me. I'd love for you and Sylvia to come over there, Sunday, if you would like."

"What kind of announcement is he going to make?"

"Well, I don't want to say right now. I want you to be surprised. Of course, you certainly don't have to come, but it would mean s lot to me to have you guys there. I think a couple more of my buddies are going to be there. If you don't come, it'll be okay. You'll probably hear about it, later."

Billy said, "Well, if it means that much to you, we'll be there."

They finished their lunch and conversation, and Billy said, "D.W., I've got to go. I've got a lot to do this afternoon. If nothing happens, I'll probably see you Sunday."

"Okay, Kid. I'll look for you. Enjoyed the lunch. See ya."

Billy, then ran a couple of errands and went home. After he talked to his mom for a while, he decided to call Buddy. After Buddy answered, they talked for several minutes about things that had absolutely no importance, and in a few minutes, Billy said, "Guess who I had lunch with today."

Buddy said, "I have no idea. Who?"

"D.W. Handy. I hadn't seen D.W. in quite a while, and I ran into him at the Steak and Shake. Did you know that he's working with that rich widow on the side?"

"Yeah, he told me the last time I saw him. That's a strange situation if you ask me. Did he ask you to come to his Church Sunday?" Buddy said.

"Yeah, he did." Billy asked. "What's that all about; do you have any idea?"

"Not a clue, but I told him I'd be there."

"I did, too, so I guess we'll find out Sunday. Are you still dating Hazel?"

"No, I haven't seen her in quite a while."

Billy said, "Aw Man, I thought you two would stay together from now on."

Buddy said, "I would have liked to, but she just seemed to lose interest in me. I figure she's probably rubbing shoulders with some of those dudes that she works with in Huntsville and thinks they're more exciting than I am. I don't know, padna, she acted really cool the last time I talked to her, so I made up my mind not to call her anymore."

When they finished talking, Billy laid down and took a nap, and when he woke up, his mom had supper ready. He ate a quick bite and then showered and got ready to go to see Sylvia for their regular, nightly visit.

During the evening, he told Sylvia about D.W.'s invitation to them to come to his Church next Sunday, and Billy said, "I told D.W. I would be there, and I hope you'll go with me. Will you?"

"You know I will, but that's a long way from here. Why don't I just meet you there, and maybe, after Church, we can go somewhere and grab some lunch."

"That sounds great," and then he told Sylvia and her parents what D.W. had told him about working with Coco Cochran and how he helps her with her business and other things that she is involved with, as well as her philanthropies.

After Billy told them that, he noticed that Fred R. didn't have anything to say about it; he just had a look on his face as though he was in some kind of deep thought.

Sylvia didn't know how long it would take to get from her house to the Church, so she left in plenty of time in order to not be late meeting Billy. She got there several minutes early, and there were several empty places in the parking lot. She pulled into a spot where there were three spaces together, and she took the middle space in hopes that one of them on either side would still be empty when Billy got there.

Billy had the same thought as Sylvia about leaving home early in order to not be late, and as luck would have it, he got one of the spots right next to Sylvia.

They both got out of their cars and went into the Church. It was a typical Methodist Church in terms of its layout, and it looked to be large enough to hold three hundred and fifty to four hundred in the sanctuary. Billy and Sylvia went about two thirds down the center aisle and took seats on the end of an empty row.

In three or four minutes, Buddy came in and when he saw Billy and Sylvia, he went down to sit with them. They noticed that D.W. had come in from the front and sat down on the second row. He looked around and when he saw them, he smiled and gave a small wave. By then, it was almost time for Church to start, and even though people were still coming in, the Pastor began making announcements, and after the announcements, the congregation sang two hymns. After the two hymns, some men took up the offering, and after the offering, a man came to the podium and sang "I Can Only Imagine."

When he finished singing, he took a seat in the choir, and the Pastor came to the podium. He had a large smile on his face, and before he began his sermon, he said, "Church, this morning I want to tell you something that is going to make you very happy. As you all know, we have been hoping to be able to build a new Family Life Center here at the Church, but it seems that every time we would get within reach of breaking ground, the price of building materials would go up, and the house and grounds committee would pull back and wait for a better time.

"Recently, one of our faithful members invited me to have lunch with him, and we talked about this, and he told me that God had laid it on his heart to give us enough money, not only to break ground, but to pay a sizeable amount on the debt. I normally don't give the names of people who contribute to the Church, but this gift is so important, the gentleman that is making our Family Life Center possible gave me permission to use his name.

"I'm beyond happy to tell you this morning that Mr. D.W. Handy has made a donation of one-hundred thousand dollars to use for the Lord's work. D.W., would you please stand?"

D.W. stood up, and the congregation applauded. The Pastor then said, "D.W., on behalf of our Lord, I want to thank you for your generosity," and then he said, "Folks after the close of the service, I'm sure you will want to come by and speak to D.W. and thank him for this wonderful gift." He then opened his Bible and began his sermon.

Billy and Buddy looked at each other, and Buddy lipped the word WOW.

After the service, and after they spoke to the Pastor and talked to D.W. for a couple of minutes, the trio stopped outside the Church to talk for a little bit.

Billy asked Buddy, "Where did D.W. get all that money?"

"I don't know, but I know he's spending a fortune. Have you seen what he's driving?"

"No. What is it?"

Buddy said, "A Shelby Cobra. I don't know what he paid for it, but I looked them up, and they run for between eighty and a hundred and thirty thousand dollars. One of the vintage Shelby's sold at auction a while back for seven point two five million. Can you believe that?"

Billy said, "If he gave the Church a hundred thousand, and let's say he paid a hundred thousand for his car; where did he get it?"

Buddy said, "I don't know, but I heard he bought Jolene Fuller a new Jeep Wagoneer. Those three items alone amount to a quarter million dollars or more, and there's no telling what else he's done."

"You're kidding," Billy said. "I think you and I need to start hanging around D.W. I'd like to have a new F-150. He must have a golden goose somewhere."

Buddy said, "You'd think so. I'd like to get a new Tundra. Maybe I should hint a little the next time I see him."

Billy said, "Let me know if it works."

"I will. What are you guys going to do this afternoon; anything exciting?"

Sylvia said, "I don't know what Billy's going to do, but I've got to wash and iron some clothes to wear to work next week."

Buddy said, "I didn't know you had a job. Where are you working?"

"In Huntsville. I'm working at the same company that Hazel works for; just in a different department. If I see her tomorrow, I'll tell her I saw you. Anything you want me to tell her?"

"No. I guess not. Listen, I need to go. It was great seeing both of you. If I'm ever able to find a squeeze that will go out with me, why don't the four of us go out to eat sometime?"

"Billy said, "That sounds great, but padna, you know you don't have to have somebody with you in order to come around."

"I'll keep that in mind. I wish things were like the way they used to be, but time rolls on, doesn't it?"

As they were leaving, Sylvia turned around and yelled at Buddy. "Buddy, come here a minute, will you?"

She and Buddy walked toward each other, and when they met, she said, "Buddy, I don't know why I didn't think of it before, but there's a girl that works with me that I think would be perfect for you, if you're interested."

"I'm always interested in perfect women," he said. "Tell me more."

"Well, her name is Sally Jo Presnell, and she lives here in Belmont. She's our age, and she is really a sweet person. She has a great personality, and as far as I know, she isn't dating anyone. Are you interested?"

"Absolutely. Lead me to her."

"Tell you what. She works in the same department that I do, and I will see her tomorrow. I'll tell her about you and see if she's interested in meeting you. If she is, I'll get you her number, and you can give her a call. How does that sound?"

"It sounds great. Just let me know."

Buddy was excited after his conversation with Sylvia, and he thought about the possibility of meeting Sally Jo all the way home, and he hoped to hear something the next day.

The next day, he was really busy at work and didn't have time to think about it very much, but on the way home, he thought hard about it. He just knew Sylvia would call with Sally Jo's number, but unfortunately, it didn't happen, and he went to bed disappointed.

The next morning, he got up and went to work, and throughout the morning, he thought about getting together with Sally Jo if she accepted his invitation, but first, he had to hear from Sylvia in order to get her number.

When lunchtime came, he went to his car to eat his sandwich and relax a few minutes. While he was eating, his cell phone rang, and it was Sylvia. "Hey, Gal. What's up?"

She said, "I called Billy to get your number, and he said he thought it would be alright if I called you; that you were probably on your lunch break. The reason I'm calling is to tell you that I talked to Sally

Jo, and she wanted me to give you her number. She's anxious to hear from you. You're going to like her, Buddy; I just know it. Will you call her?"

"I will. I'll call her just as soon as I get home this afternoon. Will that be a good time?

"We have to work 'til five-o'clock, and she has a pretty long drive, so why don't you wait until around six to call, and I'm sure she will be home by then. Here's her number."

"Great." He wrote down the number and said, "I'll call her at six o'clock. Thanks a lot for getting her number for me."

"You bet. I'll tell her you're going to call her at six. I hope things will work out for you two."

"Me too. Thanks again, Syl." He went back to work after he finished his lunch and could hardly wait until time to go home so he could call Sally Jo.

Finally, it was time to quit work for the day, and Buddy lost no time going to his car and heading home. His hours were from seven 'til three-thirty, and he was home by a little before four o'clock; two hours before he could call Sally Jo. He didn't know what he was going to do for two hours because time seemed to be moving at half-time while he waited for six o'clock to get there. He thought he would take a shower, and then, he took a powernap, and at last, it was time to make his call.

He dialed the number that Sylvia gave him, and to his disappointment, he got Sally Jo's voice mail. He debated with himself for a few second about what to do, and finally, he left a message. He said, "Hey Sally Jo. This is Buddy Russo. Sylvia Richardson said I should call you around six o'clock, but I guess you're not home yet. I'll call you later, or if you want to call me before I call you back, I'll be really happy to hear from you. You can call me at this number. Thanks. Bye."

No sooner had he hung up until his phone rang. The I.D. said Sally Jo.

He answered, and instead of saying Hello, he said, "Sally Jo. Hey."

Sally Jo said, "I'm sorry I missed a while ago, but I left my phone on the front seat of my can, and by the time I heard it and got to it, you had already hung up. Sorry."

"That's okay. I was just afraid I might miss you, and the way Sylvia has talked about you, I sure didn't want to miss you. Did you have a good day?"

"Yeah. It was good. How about yours?"

"It was good, especially this afternoon. Sylvia called me during lunch with your number, and I've thought about calling you all afternoon."

"That's the way it was for me, too. She told me that she had talked to you, and that you were going to call me this afternoon."

"I hope you were as excited as I was."

She said, "I was excited, but I was also nervous."

"Listen, you don't ever have to be nervous about me. I'm just plain old Buddy, and I don't think I could make anyone nervous if I tried. Sally Jo, the way

Sylvia has talked about you, I think we should meet. What do you think?"

"I guess we should. When do you want to?"

"Is tonight too soon?"

"No. I guess not. Do you want to come over here?"

"That would be great. Give me your address, and I'll be there whenever you say, or here's another idea. Give me your address, and I'll come pick you up, and we'll go get a pizza. Does that interest you?"

"It does. I went shopping and didn't have any lunch, and I'm starving. Pizza sounds really good to me. Let's do that. I'll text you my address, okay?"

"Okay. What time?"

"I'm ready now."

"Great. I'll be there as soon as I can." He was glad he had already showered, so all he had to do was put on a clean pair of jeans and a nice golf shirt, and he was ready. He received her text shortly after they talked, and he programmed the address into his GPS and he was off. He didn't know where her street was, but the GPS said he would arrive in eleven minutes, so he knew she wasn't too far, and sure enough, in eleven minutes he pulled up to what he hoped was her house.

He got out of the car and walked to the door, and before he could ring the bell, the door opened. There stood as the song says, '*a vision of loveliness*'. He had been used to Hazel Thompson, who was a beautiful girl, but in his mind, he thought Sally Jo was about the prettiest thing he had ever seen.

He said, "Hi", and she said, "Hi. Come in for a minute before we go."

As soon as he got inside, she said, "Come into the den, and meet my parents."

He followed her into the den and there sat a very attractive couple, and Buddy spoke to each of them, and then Sally Jo said, "Buddy, this is my mother, Kathy, and my dad, Joe. Mother and Daddy, this is Buddy Russo. Buddy is a friend of my friend, Sylvia."

Buddy spoke again and said, "I'm sure glad to meet you both. Sally Jo and I are going to get a pizza. Would you all like to go with us? I haven't told Sally Jo yet, but there's a new pizza place called Coppolas, that's supposed to be outstanding, and I thought we'd go there tonight. If you'd like to go with us", we'd be glad to have you."

Joe said, "No, thank you. Not tonight. You kids go on and have a good time. Maybe we can all go together another time, but thanks a million for asking us. I don't think any of Sally Jo's dates have ever invited us to go anywhere with them.

After a couple more minutes of talk, Buddy looked at Sally Jo and asked, "Ready to go?"

She answered, "I'm ready," and they walked out to Buddy's car.

When they arrived at Coppolas, the parking lot was full, and they had to park quite a way from the entrance. They waited for a table when they got inside, and Buddy noticed how loud it was. He mentioned it to Sally Jo, and she agreed with him.

He asked, "Would you like to go somewhere else?" and she said, "Well, since we're here, we might as well stay here. I'm anxious to see if their pizza is as good as your friends say it is."

Just then, someone took them to another dining room in the back and seated them. Their location was not nearly as loud as the area where they first came in, and Buddy said, "This is much better isn't it? I think we can talk back here."

She said, "Yeah, this is fine."

Buddy asked, "Do you want to share a large, or would you like to have your own?"

"I can't eat that much. If it's alright with you, let's just share one."

"What kind do you like?"

"I like them all. You decide and order what you want."

Just then the waitress came to take their order, and Buddy said, "We'll have a large meat-lovers and two plates, please," and looking at Sally Jo, he asked" What do you want to drink?"

She said, "I'll just have water," and he told the waitress, "We'll have two waters."

While they were waiting on their pizza, Buddy couldn't help but notice how pretty Sally Jo was, and he asked, "Why haven't we run across each other before now, Sally Jo? You didn't go to Belmont High did you?"

"No. We've only lived here for a little over a year."

"Where did you come from?"

"Pulaski, Tennessee."

"Really? I have a friend here that's from Pulaski. His name is D.W. Handy. You probably don't know him. He's older than we are. I'm twenty-three, and I'm guessing that you're about the same. Am I close?"

She said, "You guessed right."

Buddy said, "Well, Sally Jo, tell me a little about yourself."

"Well, there's not much to tell. I was born in Pulaski and graduated from Pulaski High, and after high school, I went to Giles Community College for two years. Right before I was to finish GCC, my dad decided that we were going to move down here, so here I am. Now, tell me about Buddy Russo."

Before Buddy could say anything, their pizza came, and they each got a piece and began eating. He talked while he ate and started out by saying, "I was born here, went to school here, played sports in school, and have a lot of friends that I still hang around with. My best friend is Billy Neville, Sylvia's fiancé. Have you met Billy?"

"No, but I want to. Sylvia says he's a real character."

"He is. Tell you what. Sylvia lives with her parents on a farm outside of Belmont, and Billy and I spend a lot of time out there. Her parents are great folks and we're always welcome. Maybe, if you'd like to, we can go out there sometime. I think you'd really like her mother and daddy. Sometimes, we ride horses, and Fred R., Sylvia's dad, cooks out, and we always have a great time. Would you like to go with me sometime?"

"I sure would. Just let me know when."

They talked at length about Billy and Sylvia and their upcoming wedding, and Buddy told her about the group that still goes to the lake when it's warm enough. They seemed to be very much at ease with each other, and all at once it was after nine o'clock.

Buddy said, "Sally Jo, I sure have enjoyed tonight. You're good company, the pizza was good, I liked your folks, and it seems as if all is right with the world, and I hope you had a good time as well."

"I did, and I hope we can do it again sometime."

Buddy said, "Does that mean I can see you again?"

"It does, and I hope it won't be long," she said.

"Do you think tomorrow night is too soon?"

"Not for me. What do you want to do?"

"I don't know. Let me think about it tomorrow. To be honest with you, I'd be happy if we just sat somewhere and talked, but I wouldn't do you that way. We'll do something."

"Buddy, I would love to just sit and talk. I'd like to get to know you better. You could come over to my house. I know Mother and Daddy would like that. They would like a chance to get to know you, and I think you all will like each other. They normally go upstairs fairly early and watch TV, and we would have the whole downstairs. That is, if you would like to do that."

"I can't think of anything I'd like better. Just tell me when. Oh, would you mind if I make a quick call?"

"No, go ahead."

When they got to the car, Buddy got his phone and punched in a number. In a few seconds, he said, "Billy, just want to tell you that I just had pizza with the most beautiful woman in Belmont, and she says I can see her again. Whatta ya think about that?"

It's unclear what Billy said, but he was apparently happy. Buddy then asked, "Is Sylvia around? If she is, let me talk to her for a minute."

He waited a few seconds, and then she picked up, and he said, "Syl, I just want to thank you for putting Sally Jo and me together. We just finished eating pizza and talking, and if it was as much fun for her as it was for me, it was a great night. She's sitting here just a smiling. I won't keep you. I just wanted to thank you. Next time I see you, I'm going to give you one of my famous Buddy hugs. Okay, Honey. Good night and thanks again."

When he hung up, Sally Jo said, "I'm really flattered, Buddy. I did have as much fun as you did, and I can't wait until we can get together again." She picked up his hand and kissed it. "Sylvia told me that you're sweet, and I believe it."

He said, "I think we had better go, don't you? Five o'clock will be here early in the morning."

"Yeah. I have to get up early, too.:

They went straight from Coppolas to Sally Jo's house, and Buddy walked her to the door. They both wanted to kiss goodnight, but thought they better not, since it's so early in their relationship, but as Buddy turned to go to the car, Sally Jo asked, "What do I have to do to get one of those famous Buddy Hugs?"

He turned and gave her a huge, tight hug, and said, "Nothing. You earned one by just going out with me. I'll see you tomorrow night. Sleep tight."

On his way home, Buddy was in a major state of euphoria. Hazel was always fun when they were together, but there was something about Sally Jo, other than her beauty, that really rang his bell, and he couldn't wait to see her again tomorrow night.

Not long after he got home, Billy called. He asked Buddy, "Were you pleased with Sally Jo?"

"Absolutely."

"When are you going out with her again?"

"Tomorrow night."

"Good, because Fred R wants the two of you to come out there tomorrow night. He's going to cook burgers and dogs."

Buddy asked, "How did Fred R know I was with Sally Jo tonight?"

"Sylvia told him and Betty after you called us earlier. Fred's tickled because he was hoping you would find a good replacement for Hazel. He hasn't liked the way she has been treating you, and Sylvia convinced him that Sally Jo may be the one for you. Sally Jo called her about a minute after you left her, and by the way Sylvia said she talked, you hit a grand slam home run tonight, padna. I'm really happy for you."

Buddy said, "She told me that she hasn't met you yet, and I can't wait to see your face when you meet her. Boy, is she pretty."

"I'm anxious to see her. Look, try to get a good night's sleep, and I'll see you tomorrow night."

"Okay. Good night."

Chapter Four

Sally Jo was able to get off at four-thirty, so she could get home and get ready for Buddy to pick her up and get to the Richardson's by six thirty. Sylvia had told her not to rush; that they never ate at the time when her daddy said they would, but Sally Jo wanted to be on time, especially since this would be her first trip out there.

Buddy arrived at six o'clock, and they drove the thirty minutes to Fred R and Betty's. The way they welcomed Sally Jo, one would think she had been a longtime friend instead of being a first time visitor.

Billy was already there when they got there, and when Buddy introduced him to Sally Jo, he was careful to look at Billy's face. Being known for his good natured wise cracks, Sally Jo immediately disarmed him with her beauty and classy demeanor. She said, "I'm so glad to finally meet you. Sylvia talks about you a lot, and last night, Buddy told me what a special friend you are."

All Billy could do was smile and say, "I'm glad to meet you, too."

Sylvia said, "Come on, you guys. Let me show Sally Jo around a little." She yelled at Fred R, "Daddy, how long before we eat?"

"About twenty minutes."

"Okay."

As they walked around outside, Buddy and Sally Jo were side by side, and at one point, Sally Jo took Buddy's hand, and in a couple of second, their fingers intertwined. Buddy could hardly contain himself; he was so happy.

Sylvia took them to see the horses, the barn, and most of the other things that farms have, and then it was time to go in and have supper. Buddy hated to turn loose of Sally Jo's hand, but since she was the one who initiated the original move, he felt like she would be receptive when he made the next move.

Fred R outdid himself with the barbeque. He cooked baby back ribs and chicken wings, along with tater tots and slaw and his homemade barbeque sauce. Everybody ate until they were stuffed, and Sally Jo commented, "I'm sure glad I found you, Fred R. I think this was the best barbeque I ever had. Thank you and Betty for having me."

Fred R answered, "Sally Jo, we're tickled to have you. Betty and I are very happy that you and Buddy found each other." He looked at Buddy, and with a big smile, said, "Now Buddy, don't mess up."

Betty said, "Fred R, you shouldn't say something like that to Buddy. He's not going to mess up anything."

"Buddy knows I was just joshing him. Sally Jo don't pay any attention to me. We go on like that all the time. Buddy is one of my favorite people, and I would never say anything to hurt him."

With that, they all got up from the table, and Fred R and the guys took care of the grill and leftover meat while the three women did the dishes and cleaned up the kitchen. After spending a little time with the young folks, Betty and Fred R excused themselves and went into their room and watched TV, leaving the two couples alone in the den, where Sally Jo quickly became one of the group.

A little after nine, Buddy said they needed to go; that he had to get up early the next morning, and Sally Jo agreed. They said their goodbyes to everyone, and they all hugged except Billy and Buddy didn't hug each other. They just did a fist pump.

On the way home, Buddy asked, "Well, what did you think of my friends?"

"I really liked them. They made me feel as if I belonged."

"Do you think you would like to keep seeing some of us; meaning me?"

She asked, "Do you want to keep seeing me?"

He answered, "Honey, I know this is just the second time we've seen each other, but I hope and pray that you'll want to see and be with me as much as I want to be with you. As far as I'm concerned, I would like to spend the rest of my life with you."

"Are you serious?"

He said, "As serious as a heart attack. I know two days are not many, but I think this might be a God thing. I just hope my saying this doesn't run you off."

"Run me off? As long as you want me, I'll be here. You said you think it might be a God thing. Are you a Christian?"

"I am. Are you?"

"Yes, and you know what?"

"What?"

Ever since I was a little girl, my parents have prayed that God would someday let me meet somebody that was a Christian and lead a Christian life. After being in Belmont for just a year, he sends me you, so I, too, think this is a God thing."

Buddy asked, "Are you happy about that?"

She said, "I'm absolutely thrilled."

"So what do we do now?" he asked.

"Are we crazy? We haven't even kissed."

He said, "Well, I'm going to take care of that just as soon as we get to your house."

"Really? Want me to help? If you want me to help, I don't mind."

In a few minutes, they pulled into Sally Jo's driveway, and Buddy was good to his word. They turned toward each other, and with little hesitation, they kissed for about twenty or twenty five seconds. Sally Jo said, "What about that?"

Buddy answered, "It was wonderful. Wanna do it again?"

She made an "unhhunh" sound, and they grabbed each other again. They kissed passionately, and then Sally Jo said, "I think I had better go in. When will I see you again?"

"How about tomorrow night?"

"I was hoping you would say that. You want to come over here and spends some time with Mother and Daddy and me?"

"I'd like that. What time do you all eat? I won't come until you're through."

"We usually eat around six thirty, but you can come whenever you want to."

"Okay. I'll try to be here about a quarter after seven."

They gave each other a smack on the lips, and she got out of the car and waited on Buddy to get around to her side and walk her in. They gave each other another smack, and she went in.

The next day at work was a 'crusher' for Buddy. There was first one problem, and then no sooner had it been taken care of than another problem popped up. It seemed as if the entire day was like that, and he couldn't wait for it to end. He was in such a foul mood when he got off, he thought to himself, *I can't go see Sally Jo like this. Maybe, if I call her, she can soothe my mood a little,* and sure enough, by the time he hung up, things seemed a lot better.

He went home and cleaned up, and his mother had fixed meatloaf (his favorite), and he had a great meal. He helped with the dishes, and at seven o'clock, he left for Sally Jo's.

Again, he was warmly welcomed into Sally Jo's family's home, and he was immediately put at ease. He expected to be questioned when he got there because after all, he was dating their daughter, and they had the right to know something about the person taking her out, but the questions and answers came easy and were in no way offensive.

After about an hour of conversation, Joe asked, "Buddy, what do you do for a living?"

Buddy replied, "I work at Southern Mills."

"What do you do there?"

"Actually, I'm in training. Hopefully, I'll be able to learn the entire business, and they have promised that I'll have a real good job when I'm through."

"How did you get into that?"

"Well, my dad helped me get the job. He's been there for several years, and I guess his boss likes me because he seems to be always trying to help me."

"You mean Charles Nichols?"

"Yes sir. Do you know him?"

"I do; in fact, he's one of the main reasons we moved to Belmont. You see, I'm a manufacturer's representative, and Southern Mills is my largest account. Charles has become one of my closest friends. You said your dad works there. What's his name?"

"Henry Russo."

"Henry Russo. Of course, the head of Quality Control. I guess I didn't put your names together. I don't know Henry well, but we've been in a couple of the same meetings. He seems like he's real sharp. Buddy, what do you hope to be, once you've learned everything about the business?"

"I really don't know. I've always wanted to be a salesman, but Southern doesn't really have a sales force. They make stuff for other manufacturers, and it's so consistent, there's not really any need for a sales force. Mr. Nichols and a couple of other people apparently look after that part of the business, so if I stay with them, I guess I'll just have to be content to not be a salesman."

Joe said, "You know Charlie Nichols is about to retire, don't you?"

"No sir. I haven't heard that."

Then Joe asked, "Which would you rather do, stay in the mill if you were given a good job or go in sales?"

"Well, if I had a chance to get into some kind of sales job where I could make some good money, I'd do that, but from what I hear, it's really hard to get into a good sales job, especially if you don't have any experience. I think I would make somebody a good rep if I just had a chance, though."

Joe said, "From the limited time I've known you, I think you would do okay in sales. You seem to be aggressive, and you have the personality that a salesman needs. Maybe you'll be able to find something before long. I hope you don't take this wrong, but have you talked to God about it?"

"Yes sir, I have."

When Buddy's and Joe's conversation slowed down, Joe said, "Kathy, it's time for us to go upstairs. Shark Tank is coming on, and we need to get out of these kid's hair. Buddy, it has been nice talking to you, and I hope you'll come around some more. Don't worry, you'll find what you want. Just put it in

God's hands, and He'll work it out for you."

"Thank you, Mr. Presnell. God and I are on pretty good terms."

"Atta boy," and with that, he and Kathy left Buddy with Sally Jo.

She was sitting on the sofa, and when her parents went upstairs, Buddy got up and moved to the sofa and sat down next to her. He took her hand, intertwined their fingers, and picked up her hand and kissed it.

She asked, "What did you think of my parents?"

"I really did like them. I'd like to spend more time with your daddy."

They talked for a while and sandwiched a kiss or two in between sentences, and all too soon, it was time for the evening to be over.

Buddy said, "Sweetie, I had better go. Would you like to go out and eat tomorrow night?"

"I'd love to. Where do you think we'll go?"

"Have you ever been to Ryan's? To me, it's the best in town."

"Let's do that."

She walked him to the door and kissed him goodnight. He left and headed home."

The next day was Friday, and they both were ready for it. It was a good day at work for them both, and it was also payday. The last three nights had been unbelievable, and neither could hardly wait for the end of the day.

They didn't exactly dress up when they went to

Ryan's, but they took a little more pain about their appearance. They got a table next to the wall overlooking Lake Tanisi, and that just added to the atmosphere. The menu was large, and it took Sally Jo a while to decide. Buddy already knew what he wanted. When the waiter came to take their order, Sally Jo still wasn't ready, but Buddy ordered some fried dill pickles as an appetizer, and when the waiter brought them, she was ready to order.

While they waited on their food, Buddy heard somebody in back of him say, "Hey Buddy."

He turned, and it was D.W. Handy and Jolene Fuller. "Hi, D.W. How're you doing?"

"I'm fine. Do you know Jolene?"

"Yeah, I know Jolene. How are you, Jolene?"

"I'm good. It's good to see you, Buddy."

Buddy then introduced Sally Jo to the couple. "Jolene, D.W., this is my friend, Sally Jo Presnell. Sally Jo, this is Jolene Fuller and D.W. Handy."

They all told each other it was nice to meet them.

Buddy asked, "Would y'all like to sit with us?"

D.W. answered, "We'd like to, but we're meeting Bobby Pearson and his wife, but thank you, anyway. Maybe we can do it another time." As they were walking away, D.W. turned and said, "Sally Jo, it was great meeting you."

Not long after their meeting Jolene and D.W., their food came, and they thoroughly enjoyed it. Buddy asked, "What would you like to do when we finish?"

"I don't have anything in mind. We can do whatever you want to."

"Why don't we go by the theaters and see what movies are playing?"

"Okay. That sounds good."

Even though ten movies were on, the couple didn't want to see any of them, so Sally Jo suggested that they go back to her house, and that was fine with Buddy.

On their way, Buddy asked, "Do you like pecan pie?"

"I love it."

"Do you have room for a piece?"

"I always have room for pecan pie."

"Let's stop by The Sweet Tooth. It's on the way, and they have outstanding pecan pie." Sally Jo agreed, so that's what they did.

When they got to the little dessert shop, it was nearly full, but they were able to find a table, and they both ordered warm pecan pie with vanilla ice cream, and it was the perfect cap to their perfect evening.

On the way to Sally Jo's house, Buddy was full of superlatives about their date. They went in the house, and Joe and Kathy had already gone upstairs. They sat on the loveseat in front of the TV and held hands with an occasional kiss mixed in.

Buddy said, "Well, SJ, we've got nearly a week behind us. Do you want to try for two?"

She said, "Or three, or four, or a thousand."

"A thousand? Boy, that sounds good to me. Do

you not think you will get tired of me before then?"

"Buddy-roe, I don't think I'll ever get tired of you. What about you? Do you think you will tire of me?"

"Not in a million years. You know what?"

"What?"

"I wish we were married right now."

"Are you serious?"

"I'm very serious. Does that scare you?"

"It doesn't scare me at all. I would have said yes if you had asked me the night we went to get pizza."

"You're kidding."

"I'm not kidding. Ever since that night, I've been thinking and hoping that someday you and I could make the decision to spend our lives together."

"How do you think your parents would like having me as a son-in-law?"

"I think they would be thrilled. Of course, they don't really know you yet, but I'm sure when you spend more time with them, they'll come to love you the way I do."

Her statement sent minor shock waves through him, and he asked, "Did you say you love me?"

"I did. Does that surprise you?"

"Sort of. I wasn't expecting it."

"Do you have anything to say?"

He knew what she was wanting him to say, but instead, when she asked him if he had anything to say, he smiled and said, "About what?"

She frowned and said, "About what. About me telling you I love you. That's about what."

Again, he smiled and said, "Oh about that." He thought, *I'm about to make her mad. I'd better quit kidding.* Then he said, "Honey, you just can't imagine how much I love you. I never thought it would be possible in this short a time, but it looks as if you've got your hooks in me good, and I hope you never take 'em out. Now, I've got a question for you. What do we do now? You haven't even met my parents yet. Not that you have to meet them, but I think it would only be right that you know them, at least a little, before we make the big move. Also, when are we going to tell your parents?"

"Now, I'm going to be silly and ask you a silly question. What big move?"

His mouth flew open, and he was speechless for a minute, and then he asked her, "What are you talking about?"

She smiled at him and said, "You know, it sounds as if you're talking about getting married, and I'm definitely open to that, but you haven't asked me yet. Is that the big move you were talking about?"

The question caught him by surprise, and he didn't know just what to say, and then he smiled and said "You're a real smart A--. Do you know that?

She laughed and said, "I've been called that before, but is that the big move?"

"Yes, Miss Smart A, that's the big move, and you're right. I've been talking like things are already settled about our marriage, and I haven't even asked you yet. I've been thinking about that, and I was hoping to have an ultra-romantic night, but since I opened my mouth too soon, and you caught me, would you mind if I asked you now?"

Smiling, she asked, "Ask me what?"

He said, "Stop it. I'm trying to be serious."

Her big grin changed into a very slight smile, and she said, "Okay, I'm serious, too. Now, what were you going to ask me?"

With a very serious look on his face, he said, "This is not the kind of mood I was looking for, but I guess it will have to do." He cleared his throat and said, "Sally Jo, I know we have only known each other for a week, but I already know that I love you more than anything else in the world. I believe that God has brought you to me, and that you are supposed to be mine, so if you love me half as much as I love you, I hope you will do me the honor of being my wife. Will you?"

She didn't answer. She just grabbed him and gave him a huge kiss. After the kiss, he asked, "Does that mean yes?"

She said, "Yes, yes, yes. I, too, think God is the one who put us together. I will love being your wife."

"They kissed again, and being facetious, Buddy said, "Well, I guess now we can start planning the big move, can't we?"

Sally Jo asked, "Now, who is the smart a--?"

He said, "Okay, now let's get serious. When are we going to let you meet my parents?"

She couldn't help but smile with a huge grin, and

she said, "Now that we're going to start planning the *big move*, I think the sooner, the better, don't you?"

He tried to overlook her smart alec answer, and asked, "Why don't we go out to my house tomorrow afternoon and let you meet them, and if all goes well, maybe we can take them out to eat tomorrow night; not for a fancy meal, but maybe a burger or pizza or something like that. They love that kind of food. What do you think?"

By then, she was over her smartness, and she said, "That sounds great. Maybe we can go back to Coppolas."

"That what I was thinking. I'll ask them when I get home tonight, and if they don't have other plans, we'll do it. Now when are we going to tell both sets of parents about the *big move*?"

Sally Jo asked, "Do they know each other?"

"I don't know about our mothers, but I know our daddies do. Daddy works at Southern, and your daddy calls on them, and your daddy said they have been in meetings together."

"That's great. Why don't we take all four of them out to eat, sometime, and tell them all at one time. Maybe we can take 'em to Ryans."

"They should like that, but you and I had better start saving our money, so we can pay the check," he said, kiddingly.

Then, she asked, "When are we going to tell them? Should we wait until we have been dating longer, or should we shock 'em right away?"

"What do you think?"

"Well, I think we should decide when we're going to get married, first, and then tell them in plenty of time to make plans. Do you want a big wedding?"

"Honey, that will have to be up to you. As long as we can get married, I don't care. If you want a big wedding, that's okay with me, but I think I would feel just as married if we went to a Justice of the Peace."

"Well, I don't want to go to a Justice of the Peace, but I don't want a huge wedding, either. If we go medium sized and send maybe a hundred and fifty or two hundred invitations, that will be big enough for me. I know people who have sent six or seven hundred invitations to their wedding, and to me, that's ridiculous."

Buddy said, "Billy and Sylvia are getting married in June, and I would rather wait until after that, but anytime after June suits me fine."

"Are you going to be in their wedding?"

"Yeah."

"How about sometime in September or October?"

"That's a long time away, Sally Jo."

"I know it is, but think about it. The heat in July and August is almost unbearable down here, and I know the Church is air conditioned, but think down the road to our anniversaries. We might want to go somewhere on one or more of our anniversaries, and if the weather is too hot, we won't want to do anything except sit inside with the AC. In September or October, the temperature is much better, and to me, that would be a much better time."

"Good thinking. Let's go with September, and if it suits you, we'll tell our parents sometime in June. The only things bad about that is, you won't be able to wear a ring until then. Does that bother you?"

"As long as I know you're mine, it doesn't bother me at all."

"Okay. Now that we have some sort of plan, we don't have to be in any hurry to tell them, but I would still like to get both sets of parents together, so when we do tell them about our engagement, it won't come as such a shock."

"I agree. Do you still want to introduce me to your mother and daddy tomorrow?"

"Yeah, I'd like to."

When he got home, his parents were still up, and he asked them if they had any plans for the next afternoon, and they both said they didn't, so he said, "Well, I've been dating a girl that I really do like, and I'd like to bring her over so ya'll can meet her. "

Henry said, "Boy, she must be pretty special. You've never intentionally brought any of your girls to meet us, and now, to bring one just to meet us must be very important. I'm anxious to meet her. What's her name?"

"Sally Jo Presnell."

Buddy's daddy said, "Cute name."

Buddy said, "Cute girl. I hope you like her. She's very special."

Chapter Five

Buddy picked Sally Jo up a little after two on Saturday afternoon, and they went to his house, so Sally Jo could meet Helen and Henry, his parents. As they were walking from the car to the house, Henry opened the front door and said, "Ya'll come in. Sally Jo, I'm Henry, and the pretty lady behind me is Helen. We're sure glad to meet you."

Sally Jo said, "Thank you. I'm glad to meet you, too. Buddy has told me a lot about you."

Helen led them into the den where they sat down, Helen and Henry in their recliners and Buddy and Sally Jo on the long sofa.

Henry said, "Buddy, you didn't tell us how pretty Sally Jo is. I can certainly see why you would want to be around her," and Sally Jo said, "Thank you, sir."

Then Henry said, "Sally Jo, we're sure glad to have you visit us. Are you from Belmont?"

"No Sir. I'm from Pulaski, Tennessee. My dad does a lot of business with Southern Mills, and about a year ago, he decided we should move down here, since he has to spend so much time at Southern."

Henry said, "Hmm, Presnell. Are you Joe Presnell's daughter?"

"Yes sir, I am."

"Well how about that? I know Joe. He's a great guy."

"Thank you."

He said, "I'm guessing that you're about Buddy's age. Do you work?"

"Yes sir, I work in Huntsville. You know Billy Neville's girlfriend, Sylvia, don't you?"

"Yes, I know Sylvia."

"Well, I work with her, and she's the one who put Buddy and me together."

He smiled and asked, "Have you forgiven her for that?"

"Yes sir. I have not only forgiven her, but I feel as if I owe her a huge debt."

"Wow. Buddy, I can see why you think she's special."

When a break in the conversation came, Helen asked, "Sally Jo, would you like a coke or something?"

"Oh, no ma'am. I'm good."

Soon, the get acquainted questions were over and a normal conversation started, especially between Sally Jo and Helen. Buddy watched as they interacted, and he was so pleased with Sally Jo's ease with his mother. They could almost be like sisters instead of a daughter and future mother-in-law. Time just flew by, and when Buddy looked at his watch, it was almost five-thirty, and he said, "Sally Jo and I are going to get a burger or a pizza. Why don't ya'll come with us?"

Helen said, "You kids don't want us hanging around. You all go on and have a good time."

Sally Jo said, "No Ma'am, you're wrong about that. We would really like it if you would come with us. Will you?"

Helen said, "Henry, what you think?"

Henry said, "It sounds good to me. Where are we going; to get pizza or a burger?"

"Which ever you want. Mother, which would you rather have?"

"It doesn't really matter. I like both, but I think tonight, I would rather have a burger."

Buddy said, "You like the Steak & Shake don't you?"

She said, "Yeah, it's one of my favorites."

"Okay, we'll go to the Steak & Shake. Are ya'll hungry?"

Henry said, "I'm starved. Your mother had me working in the yard this morning, and I worked through lunch."

"Good. Let's drive both cars, and Sally Jo and I will go to her house from there."

"Sounds like a plan. Are you ready?" Everybody said they were, so they left.

When they got to the Steak & Shake, Buddy insisted that he pay the check, and while they were waiting for their food, Buddy looked up and guess what? There was D.W. Handy.

D.W. said, "Buddy, it looks as though we have the same brain waves. They seem to take us to the same places at the same time, don't they?"

"Yeah, they do. D.W., do you know my parents?"

D.W. said, "Not really, but I've seen them a lot. I used to see them outside the locker room when they would be there to see you after a football game. How are you folks tonight?"

Henry said, "Yes, I remember seeing you several times. I'm Henry Russo, and this is my wife, Helen."

D.W. said, "It's nice meeting you. I'm D.W. Handy. Buddy, I see you have this pretty lady with you again," and then he looked at Sally Jo and said, "We met at Ryan's the other night, remember?"

She said, "I sure do. It's nice to see you again."

They talked about absolutely nothing important for the next couple of minutes, and then their food came; first D.W.'s, and then Buddy's. D.W. said, "It was very nice meeting you, and Buddy and Sally Jo, it was good to see you again. We should get together one night."

Buddy said, "Good to see you, too. We'll do it."

While they were eating, Henry asked Buddy, "Son, who is D.W. Handy, and what does he do for a living?"

"I don't really know who he is. He moved to Belmont when I was in high school and worked at Pearson Funeral Home. He and Bobby Pearson went to college together and became good friends. He used to come to all the football games, and I think he went to basketball and baseball games as well. I hear that he sings at a lot of funerals, and did you know George Cochran?"

"The banker? Yeah, I knew of him, but I didn't

know him personally."

"Well, when Mr. Cochran died, D.W. helped Mrs. Cochran with a lot of things, and then he started working for her when he wasn't working at the funeral home. She must pay him a huge amount the way he spends money."

"Such as?"

"Well, he bought himself a Shelby Cobra, and those cars run anywhere from eighty to a hundred and thirty thousand dollars. He bought the girl he's dating a new Jeep Wagoneer, and a few weeks ago, he gave his Church a hundred thousand dollars for their building fund. I'm sure he has bought more than that, and I feel sure Bobby Pearson isn't paying him that mush working in the funeral home.

"Are you sure he gave his Church that much, or is it just a rumor?"

"It's not a rumor, Daddy. I was there, at his Church, when the pastor made the announcement and recognized him. He gave a hundred thousand dollars."

Henry, being a practical and conservative man didn't say much. He just said, "That's interesting."

D.W. wasn't mentioned anymore that night. The balance of the time was spent talking about different things, such as Sally Jo's interests, her parents, her hopes for the future and generally just things of interest for the others.

After a while the conversation sort of wound down, and Henry said, "Folks, this has been very nice. I appreciate the delicious meal, and I think that now, I should go home and loosen my belt. Sally Jo, it has been an absolute joy getting to know you, and I hope we'll see you again and get to be with you."

Sally Jo responded with, "Thank you so much. I have really enjoyed today, and I hope we can do this again." Helen gave her a hug, and they all left.

On the way back to Sally Jo's, Buddy asked, "What did you think of my parents? Did you like them?"

"Oh yeah. I really did like them. They're so easy to be around."

"Do you think they'll make good in-laws?"

"Of course, today's the first time I've seen them, but from what I saw, I think they'll be perfect in-laws. You must take after your daddy. You're both so sweet."

It was still early when they got back to Sally Jo's, and she invited Buddy in for a little while. Her parents were still up, and as they had become used to doing, Buddy and Joe clowned around with each other. In a few minutes, Kathy asked them where they had been.

Sally Jo answered, "I met Buddy's mother and daddy, and we went to the Steak & Shake and had a really good time."

Joe chimed in and said to Sally Jo, "So you met your in-laws, did you?"

Sally Jo and Buddy looked at each other and smiled, Then Sally Jo answered, "Yes sir. I met 'em, and they were really nice to me. I like 'em a lot," and then she looked back at Buddy and smiled again.

Then Joe said, "It looks as if you two love-birds are getting kinda serious," and neither one said anything.

Then, in a second, Buddy joked, "I tried to take her away tonight, but she wouldn't go, so that shows you how serious we are."

That sort of diffused the subject, and nothing else was said about it. Instead, Joe told about his day, and lamented that he was usually off on Saturday, but Southern was having some sort of a problem with one of his products, and he spent a large part of the day on the phone trying to solve it. He said, "One of these days, I'm going to hire me an assistant to take care of some of these things. I'm just getting too big to be able to handle everything myself." He laughed and asked, "You want a job, Buddy?"

Buddy didn't say anything, but deep down, he thought how much he would like to have a job working with Joe.

For the next month or so, Sally Jo and Buddy continued their relationship. They were with each other nearly every night with just an occasional break. Most of the time, they just went to her house or maybe his house. Sometimes, they would go to the Richardson's to be with Sylvia and Billy, and a couple of times, Joe and Kathy went out with them for pizza. Helen cooked a couple of times, and Sally Jo really enjoyed her dinners. The more they were with each other, the stronger their love grew.

Buddy almost stopped packing his lunch every day. Instead, he would grab a sandwich somewhere. He liked the Steak & Shake and the Krystal better than anywhere else, so that's where he went most of the time. D.W. Handy must have like the Steak & Shake nearly as much because he and Buddy ran into each other real often. Depending on when they got there depended on where they sat. If they got there at about the same time, they would sit together, If not, they would sit by themselves.

One day, when they were sitting together at lunch, Buddy said, "You know, Billy Neville and Sylvia Richardson are going to get married in about three weeks."

"I know. Billy called me and asked if I would sing at the wedding."

"Are you going to?"

"I'm afraid so. I told him that I thought he could get somebody with a better voice than me, but he said that he and Sylvia wanted me, so I told him I would. I hope they're not disappointed."

"I'm sure they won't be."

D.W. asked Buddy, "When are you and Sally Jo going to get married?"

"Sally Jo and me? That's not in the cards right now."

"You're pulling my leg. I've seen the way ya'll look at each other. You can't look that loving and not think about getting married."

Buddy was afraid that if he confided in D.W., it might be spread around, so he tried to get the subject off him and Sally Jo by asking, "Do you and Jolene have any plans to marry?"

"Heavens no. We're just good friends, besides I'm a confirmed bachelor."

Buddy said, "Yeah, right. I've seen the way you two look at each other as well, so don't hand me that confirmed bachelor garbage. I know ya'll must have at least talked about it."

"Why don't we change the subject," D.W. asked.

"Let's do," Buddy said. "D.W., are you still working for Mrs. Cochran?"

"You mean the old battle axe? Yeah, I'm still her right hand boy."

"You sound as though you don't like it. She pays good, doesn't she?"

"I shouldn't have said that. She treats me like a king, and she gives me anything I want. It's just that she's such a crabby old woman. You know the book of Proverbs says that it's better to live in the corner of an attic than in a beautiful home with a cranky, quarrelsome woman. Of course, I'm not living with her, but she sure is a cranky, quarrelsome woman."

"You can overlook that if she treats you so well, can't you?"

"Yeah, that's why I'm still there, but sometimes it's hard."

Buddy said, "She's rich isn't she?"

"Yeah, she's got millions."

"Won't she share with you?"

"Not hardly, but she does take good care of me, so I guess I shouldn't complain."

"If you ever need a helper, call me."

He smiled and said, "Okay, I will."

Buddy said, "D.W., I've enjoyed this, but I need to go. I've got a lot to do this afternoon."

D.W. said, "I need to go, too. Listen, why don't you and Sally Jo go eat with us one night. I'll tell Coco that I want to take out one of my friends, and she'll want to pay for it. Maybe we can go to Ryan's."

"That sounds good. Just give me a call when you're ready."

"Okay, Pal. Have a great afternoon."

"You, too."

Three Months Later

Sally Jo and Buddy were at Shoneys one night, and while they were there, Buddy said, "I think it's about time, isn't it?"

"Time for what," she asked.

"I think it's time we announce our engagement and tell our parents, don't you?"

"Really? I've been hoping you would be ready pretty soon. Yeah, I think it's time. When do you want to do it?"

"Tell you what. Let's take our parents out to eat one night and tell them while we have all four of them together. Our mothers will know how to go about getting it in the paper. Does that sound alright?"

"Yeah, it sounds good. When do you want to tell them?"

"As soon as possible. How about Saturday? I'll ask Mother and Daddy when I get home tonight. I doubt if they have anything planned. Do you think your folks will go with us Saturday?"

"I'll bet they will. They will go anywhere, anytime with you. I'll ask them." Then she said, "I'm so excited."

"I'm excited, too. I know they'll ask us when the wedding will be and a hundred other questions. Will you know what to tell them?"

"I have no idea. I think we need to decide on a date before we tell them, and then we can play the rest of it by ear. We talked about September one time. Does that still interest you?"

"Yeah. September sounds good. Have you got a calendar?"

He took out his billfold, and he had a small calendar. He handed it to her and said, "There are thirty days on there. Pick one."

She asked, "Do you want to get married on a Saturday or a Sunday"

He said, "I think a Saturday."

"Okay. We'll get married on September twenty second. That will be the first day of fall, and the weather should be beautiful. Is that alright?"

"Perfect."

Sally Jo asked Buddy, "Why did you decide to do this tonight?"

"Well, first, as you know, I didn't want to have any conflict with Billy and Sylvia's wedding, and Honey, I haven't said anything about this, but I'm not very happy with my job, and I would like to find something else. I didn't want to say anything in case I got another job because if I did go to work somewhere else, I would be concentrating on trying to get established with it, and it would be hard to keep my mind on planning a wedding. Today, I decided that if I do or don't get another job, it's not fair to you to keep you hanging about our wedding, so I thought we should go ahead and make the announcement."

"I didn't know you are unhappy with your job. What do you want to do?"

"I guess I'm not actually unhappy with it. It's just not what I want to do for the rest of my life. I have a hard time seeing me going to work every day, doing the same thing over and over and not having any excitement in my life. Don't worry. I'm not going to give up what I have until something better comes along. I would like to get into some kind of sales job, but good ones are few and far between. Besides, Mr. Nichols, our head man is retiring, and I don't know what is going to happen. They might not even want me anymore."

"Don't worry, Sweetie, the right thing will come along when you least expect it. Have you talked to God about it?"

"I have."

"You know He'll take care of you, don't you?"

"I know. Are you through eating?"

"Yeah."

"What do you want to do?"

"Nothing, really. Today has been a hard day. I wouldn't mind going back to the house, unless there's something you want to do."

"I'm tired, too. That suits me, and we'll call it an early night, if you want to."

"Let's don't make it too early because I want to spend as much time with you as I can."

They went to her house and sat in the den in front of the TV. It wasn't long until Sally Jo caught Buddy dozing, and she spoke softly to him and said, "Honey, why don't you go on home. You're worn out, and we'll see each other tomorrow night." She kissed him on the cheek, and he got up and went home."

Saturday

Buddy and Sally Jo were both excited and nervous about the upcoming evening, and what was going to happen. Buddy had been thinking for a while that he hadn't given Sally Jo a ring, so the day after they decided to announce their engagement, he went to a jewelry store and bought what he thought was a beautiful diamond. The lady at the store sort of helped him make up his mind. Now, he had to find the right time to give it to her, and he wanted to do it before they went out with their parents that night, so he called and told her he was going to pick her up, and they were going to get an ice cream cone. She agreed, and he went to get her.

At Kay's Ice Cream Parlor, they both had a cone with two scoops: hers chocolate and his strawberry. After they finished, they went to his car and for a couple of minutes, they just sat there. Sally Jo wondered why he didn't start the engine.

In another minute or so, Buddy turned to her and said, "Sally Jo, Honey, we've been talking about getting married for a while now, and tonight, we're finally going to announce it. I want everything to be perfect for you, and if you're going to be engaged, you need an engagement ring."

He reached in the console and took out a small box and opened it. He said, "I hope you love me just half as much as I love you. I know I've already asked you to marry me, but I want to ask you again, just to be sure. Sweetheart, will you marry me?"

She nearly yelled, "YES, YES, I'll marry you. I love you so much," and he slipped the ring on her finger. She just went on about how beautiful it was and said, "I can't wait to show it to Mother and your mother tonight, when we make the announcement."

He said, "That reminds me; are we going to tell them before dinner or after?"

"Let's tell them before, so I can wear my ring while we eat. Are you going to be the one to tell them?"

He said, "If you want me to. Would you rather tell them?"

"No, no. I doubt I could get the words out. You tell them."

"Okay, during the appetizers."

"Yeah, I thought we would have shrimp cocktails. I think everybody likes them."

"Boy, that sounds expensive. Are you sure?"

"Yeah, this is a special night. How many more times do you plan to announce your engagement?"

She didn't say anything.

Buddy had made reservations at Coach's, a fine restaurant owned by two retired Belmont High School coaches. He had played for both coaches when he was in school, Coach Mayfield in Football and Coach Lewis in Baseball. The reservations were for seven o'clock, and the group drove three cars. Sally Jo rode with her parents, Buddy's folks together, and Buddy alone. The thinking was that after dinner, Sally Jo and Buddy would be together, and both sets of parents would have their cars. He had planned the evening perfectly.

When they entered the restaurant, the first person they saw was Coach Mayfield, and he warmly welcomed Buddy. He always liked Buddy because he was one of his better players and always worked hard. A hostess showed them to their table, which was in a semi-secluded part of the dining room where the atmosphere was outstanding.

Since none of them drank, that part was left off, and they went straight to the appetizers, and Buddy took over. He told the waitress, "We'll have six shrimp cocktails." He looked around the table and asked, "Is that alright with everybody?" They all agreed that it was.

They all talked while they waited on the appetizers, and in a few minutes, Buddy and Sally Jo nodded to each other, and then Buddy said, "Folks, Sally Jo and I have something we would like to tell you. As you all know, we have been dating exclusively with each other for the last several months, and we have decided that we want to take it to the next level and get married.

"We don't know if any of you suspected anything or not, and we tried our best to keep it secret until tonight because we were afraid you might not like it because it is so soon, but we love each other dearly, and this is what we want to do. Talking about being so soon, you won't believe this, but Sally Jo said she was ready to marry me the first time we met and went out for pizza, and I felt it a couple of days later. We both feel that God has brought us together and will bless our marriage, and we hope ya'll feel the same way. Now, Sally Jo, why don't you show them your ring?"

Anticipating that, she had her little purse in her lap, and all she had to do was open it and take out the ring. She put it on and held out her hand, showing it to Kathy first, and then to Joe. Next she held it over to Helen and then Henry. They all went on over it, even the daddies. Joe was sitting next to Kathy, who was sitting next to Sally Jo, and then Buddy, so he got up and went around the two women and shook hands with Buddy.

Their waitress must have seen something going on

and held up their appetizers until the excitement died down a little. As Joe was shaking Buddy's hand, she brought the shrimp cocktail, and as they began to eat, Coach Mayfield came by and said, "It sounds as if something exciting is going on over here," and Buddy said, "Coach, I just gave my girl a ring."

"Great, Buddy." He looked at Sally Jo and asked, "Is this pretty lady the lucky girl?"

Buddy said, "Yes sir, it is," and then he introduced him to Sally Jo and her parents. Coach already knew Helen and Henry.

He said to Buddy, "Congratulations. I know you'll be happy," and then he told Sally Jo and the rest of the table, "You're getting a great guy. I coached him for four years, and in my estimation, he is what I would call a 'top notch' young man. Congrats, again," and he left the table.

So far, there had been a tremendous amount of excitement, and they hadn't even had their dinner yet. In the midst of everything, the waitress brought their food, and Joe and Henry and Buddy tore into theirs as though they hadn't had anything to eat for a long time. The ladies had changed their seats around, so that Sally Jo was in the middle of the two mothers. Their food just sat there because they were so busy talking and making future plans. In about ten minutes, Joe said, "Ladies, I know you've got more important things on your mind right now, but you should eat before your food gets any colder," and each one began to eat a little; not too much because they were all too excited to eat.

At nine-thirty, two and a half hours after they got to the restaurant, they finally got up to leave, and Buddy said, "Since this is Sally Jo's and my party, this is my treat, and I hope you've enjoyed it all. We want you to know that we love you."

There was the usual argument between Joe, Henry, and Buddy about who was going to pay the bill, and Buddy finally prevailed. They went to the register to pay, and the lady at the register said, "Your bill has already been taken care of."

Buddy asked, "Who did that?" and she answered, "Mr. Mayfield. He said to tell you congratulations, and to have a happy life."

Joe said, "You must have been some kind of a ball player for your coach to do something like this," and Buddy said, "I was okay, I guess."

And Henry said, "I've always liked him. Now I see why. "Then he said to Buddy, "Son, thank you for tonight. Your mother and I think you're getting a wonderful girl. We'll see you when you get home."

Kathy hugged him and said, Buddy, I can't wait for you to be my son-in-law," and he said, "I can't wait, either."

Both sets of parents said goodbye to each other and left to go home. Sally Jo and Buddy went to her house.

On the way, he asked, "Well, how do you think it went tonight?"

"I think it went wonderfully well. I don't think

anything could have pleased my parents more, especially Daddy, than to be getting you as their son-in-law. They both love you so much."

"That's the way it is with my parents as well, so I guess it was a good night."

They arrived at Sally Jo's and kissed before they got out of the car. When they got in the house, Buddy only stayed a few minutes because he was worn out and wanted to get home. He had had a grueling day, making sure everything was planned out just right for the big night. The physical part was not too bad, but the stress and mental part was tough, and stress will take its toll on a person.

As soon as he had gone, Sally Jo called Sylvia. "Hello."

"Sylvia, Sally Jo. How ya doing?"

"Hey Sally Jo, what's up?"

"I just wanted to tell you that Buddy gave me a ring tonight."

"Really, well congratulations. I've been wondering when he was going to do it. Tell me about it."

"Sylvia, we've known we were going to get married ever since the second time we saw each other. I knew it the first time I met him, when we went out for pizza, and he said he knew it by the second time we went out."

"Why didn't you tell anybody?"

"Because we were afraid out parents would be against it if we told them we were going to get married after only two dates, so we decided to wait and tell them when we were ready to make a public announcement."

"Did you tell them tonight?"

"Yeah, we made a big production out of it. We took Mother and Daddy and Buddy's parents out to Coach's restaurant and told them all at the same time over dinner, and it was wonderful. Our parents seemed to be very happy."

Sylvia said, "Coach's Restaurant" That's Coach Lewis and Coach Mayfield's place, isn't it?"

"That's what Buddy said. I met Coach Mayfield tonight, and Coach Lewis wasn't there, so I still don't know him, but the restaurant is really nice. Have you been there?"

"Not yet. They've only been open a few months, but I'm anxious to try it."

"Why don't you and Billy go with us one night. We're anxious to go out there again."

"We definitely will. I'll talk to Billy, and I'll call you, or tell you at work"

"Sounds good. Look, it's late, and I'll let you go. I just wanted to tell you about Buddy and me. I guess I'll see you at work, Monday. Good night."

"Good night."

Chapter Six

A Month Later

Right after lunch on Monday, Buddy's phone rang while he was at work. This never happened, and it alarmed him a little because he thought something must be wrong to make someone call him at work. The caller I.D. showed it was Joe Presnell, and that scared him even more.

He answered and sure enough, it was Joe. Joe said, "Buddy, I hate to call you at work, but I talked to your dad, and he said he thought it would be alright. I'm calling because I want to talk to you about something, and I didn't want to take the chance that you might not be coming to my house tonight. Are you coming out?"

"Yes sir, I'm planning on it. Sally Jo talked about going to the Steak & Shake for a burger and shake, but we can do that later."

"Later would be good. If you don't mind, come by the house first, and then, I'll buy your supper when y'all go."

"Okay, is there a special time when you want to see me?"

"No, just whenever you get there"

"Okay, I'll see you tonight."

After he hung up, he wondered, *I wonder what he wants to talk to me about. I don't know of anything that I've done wrong. Sally Jo and I are okay as far as I know. I wonder what he wants.* He finished out the day and wondered what Joe wanted the rest of the afternoon. He went home and took a shower and changed clothes. Sally Jo normally got home a little before six, so he waited to give her time to clean up and change clothes before he went over there.

When he got there, Joe and Kathy were just finishing their supper. Buddy went into the kitchen where they were eating and spoke to them and told them he just wanted to say "Hello." Joe told him that he would be through in a minute, and he would be in the den in a little bit, and they would talk.

He went into the den and sat down with Sally Jo, and in a few minutes, Joe came into the room. When he came in, Sally Jo got up and went into the kitchen where her mother was cleaning up. She said, "I'll go help Mother. I know you two want to talk."

After she left the room, Joe asked Buddy, "Can you see why I love her so much? She can even read my thoughts."

Then he turned his thoughts to why he wanted to talk to Buddy. He asked, "Did you have a good day at work today?"

Buddy answered, "Yes sir. It was good."

Joe began, "Buddy, the reason I wanted to talk to you is to see if you might like to do something that I'm going to tell you about. You know that I work a lot with Southern Mills, but I'm not certain that you know what I do. Do you?"

"No sir. Not really."

Joe said, "I know you've seen the hundreds of bales of cotton in that huge warehouse at Southern. Well, I'm the one who sold those to them."

Buddy interrupted and asked, "Where do you get that cotton?"

"Different places, actually. Around the cotton growing states in the south, there are cotton co-ops that sell cotton for the farmers in their areas, and I buy that cotton and sell it to different yarn mills, such as Southern. In some areas where the farms are so huge, I buy the cotton direct from them. Now, I guess you're wondering why I'm telling you all this. Well, here's the reason.

"I feel that I've pretty much reached my full potential in the raw material part of the yarn business, and I've had several inquiries about selling the yarn for the mills that I sell the cotton to, and Southern is one of them If I get into yarn sales, which I'm going to do, I'm not going to be able to handle it by myself, and I'm going to have to get someone to come in with me and help me sell it. I remember you telling me the first or second time I ever saw you that you would like to get into sales at some point, and I wanted to see if you might have an interest in working with me to set up a new company and sell yarn to hosiery mills and thread to clothing manufacturers. This can be a gold mine, if you work at it. Do you think you might be interested in something like this?"

"Mr. Presnell, this would be a dream come true.

Are you sure you want to have someone like me, who has never sold anything?"

"Well, you sold yourself to me, and you sold yourself to my daughter, and neither of us is an easy target. Here's something else, Buddy. I know your situation at Southern, and I know your dad works there and would like to see you follow in his footsteps by getting into management at the company, but it's not in sales, and that's what you said you want to do. I firmly believe that if you're going to be happy in life, your occupation will have to be something you enjoy. Otherwise, you'll always be wishing you were doing something else. Selling yarn and thread may not be what's going to make you happy, but having been in sales for the years that I have, I can't help but feel that you would be happy.

"I talked to Henry about this before I called you earlier today, and he confirmed what I said about his desire for you, but he also said, he knew you wouldn't be happy going to work every morning and going home every afternoon every day for the rest of your life, and when I told him what I had in mind, he urged me to be sure and talk to you."

Buddy said, "You talked to Daddy about this?"

"I did, and he talked like you're doing what I'm talking about would not only make you happy, but it would make him happy, knowing that you're happy."

"Let me ask you this," Mr. Presnell. "As you know, Sally Jo and I are going to get married in September, and I have to be sure I'm going to make enough for us to live on. I know this is a startup, and it won't be generating much income for a while, so do you think I'll be able to make enough to live on?"

"I'm sure you will. Let me explain. The thread company will be new, and you're right. There won't be much coming in until we can get it going good, but the yarn sales will just be a spinoff of the business I have now, and there's plenty coming in for all of us to live comfortably. If the thread company takes off the way I think it will, I'll probably have you selling more thread than yarn, and I might set you up with a draw, if you decide you want to come with me. Do you know what a draw is?"

"No sir. I don't have any idea."

"A draw is used when someone works on commission. Let's say you're on a thousand dollar draw. That means you'll get a thousand dollars the first of the month or whenever we set it up, and you sell enough to make three thousand dollars commission that month. When payday comes, you would get the three thousand dollar commission less the one thousand dollar draw, or two thousand dollars. Do you understand how that works?"

"Yes sir. A draw is just an advance on the commission."

"Exactly. It's just something to run you until payday. Buddy, what are your thoughts about what I've told you? Do you think you would like to give it a try?"

"I really do think I'd like to do it. Are you talking

about starting soon?"

"Yeah, but I think you should work out a notice for Southern, if they want you to. When you tell them you're leaving and offer to work out a two week notice, they might tell you okay, or they might say that since you're just training, you can go ahead and leave. Whenever they say, I'm ready, and there's one more thing. If we're going to be working together, I hope you'll call me Joe instead of Mr. Presnell."

Buddy broke into a huge smile and said, "Okay, Joe."

"And call my wife Kathy, okay?"

"Okay, Joe."

Joe said, "Oh, I nearly forgot. Buddy, if you come with me and like it and do as well as I think you will, at some point, I want to set you up as partner, and we'll split everything that comes in. That could be phenomenal, and we could both get rich."

"I like that word."

"Me too. Let's do it. Whatta ya say?"

"I say I'm going to make you glad that you brought me in."

Joe asked, "Do you have any question?"

Yes sir, I have one."

"What is it?"

"I'm sure a job like I'm going to have will have some travelling to it. Do you have a feel for how much I'll be out of town overnight?"

"You're right. There will be traveling, and some of it will be overnight, but you won't be out of town every night. I can't tell you right now just how much you'll be gone, but my educated guess is that you may be gone three or four nights one week a month, and then from zero to one or two nights the other three weeks. It will all depend on your accounts and how many there are. I've been doing this for years, and the nights away just tend to make you appreciate being home all the more. Once you get established, then you'll pretty much be your own boss, and if something important comes up on a week that you're supposed to be gone, you'll have the flexibility to adjust your schedule. The important thing is to cover your accounts. Anything else?"

"No, not now, but I'm sure I'll need plenty of help when I get started."

"When do you think you'll tell Southern you're leaving?"

"Tomorrow."

"Good boy. The sooner, the better. Call me and let me know what they say. Why don't you go in the other room and get my daughter right now and take her somewhere to eat? I'm sure she's hungry."

"I'll do that. I'm hungry, too."

They had originally planned to go to the Steak & Shake before Joe interrupted their plan, so now, even though they're later than planned, they still went to get their burger and shake.

After they ordered, and while they were waiting for their food, Sally Jo asked, "What did Daddy want to talk to you about?"

"He didn't tell you?"

"No, he doesn't tell me much. What did he want?"

"Did he tell you that he's expanding his business, and is going to be selling thread as well as yarn, and he offered me a chance to come work with him."

"Wow! Are you going to?"

"I sure am. I'm going to tell Southern tomorrow."

She was so thrilled at the news that she did a little dance, standing right there in line.

"Do you know much about his business?"

"No, I know absolutely nothing about it, but I know he does well, and since you're marrying me, he must be sure that you'll do well, too."

"That's what I was thinking."

Just as they were about to pick up their food, someone said, "Buddy," and they turned around and it was D.W. Handy, by himself. They spoke to him, and since he was alone, Buddy said, "When you get your food, why don't you come sit with us?"

"Thanks. I will."

After D.W. joined them with only a milkshake, he asked, "What are you guys up to?"

Buddy answered, "We haven't been up to much, but tonight we're sort of celebrating some great news. You're actually the first person to hear this."

"I'm flattered. Tell me."

Buddy said, "As you know, I've been working at Southern Mills, and tonight, Sally Jo's daddy asked me to come work with him selling yarn and thread, and I'm going to do it."

"I guess you'll be traveling, won't you?"

"I'll be traveling some, which means I'll probably have to get another car. Mine has a lot of miles, and I don't want to get to Atlanta or Chattanooga or some out of the way place and have car trouble."

"What are you going to get?"

"I don't know. I haven't thought about it until this minute. I'll probably have to carry samples with me, so I'll have to get something large enough for that. Sally Jo, does your daddy carry a lot of samples with him?"

"Not too many, but right now, he's only selling stuff to make yarn, but I'd say when he starts selling yarn as well as thread, he'll have to carry a lot more."

D.W. asked again, "What kind of vehicle would you say you will have to have if you carry a lot of samples?"

"D.W. I really don't know. If I have to carry a lot, I'd say that I'll have to get something like a Suburban or Yukon or something that size, but they're so expensive, I know I won't be able to get a new one. If I can get my lady here to go with me, I'll probably go car shopping Saturday."

D.W. said, "Speaking of Saturday, would you guys like to go out with Jolene and me Saturday night?"

Buddy said, "That sounds good," and he asked Sally Jo. She said she would like to. "Where are we going?"

"Have you ever been to The Lighthouse out on

Lake Tanisi? Jolene and I have fallen in love with that place, and I think you'll like it."

"Good. Let's go there. Does that suit you, Honey?"

"Yeah. I've heard about it, but I've never been there. I'm anxious to try it."

"Great. We'll meet you out there at seven o'clock. Is that alright?"

They said it was, and since they were finished, they got up, said their goodbyes and left.

On their way back to Sally Jo's, she asked, "Do you think you'll like working with Daddy?"

"I think so. He seems to be not too hard to get along with, and as long as he treats me right, I'll like working with him. I'm going to turn my notice in to Southern in the morning, and we'll see what happens."

"If they tell you to just go ahead and leave, when will you start with Daddy?"

"They'll probably tell me that, since I'm just a trainee, and if they do, then I'll call your daddy and tell him, and hopefully, he'll not want me until the first of next week, but if he does, then I'll start whenever he says."

True to his word, Buddy went to his superior the next morning and turned in his notice. He told him, "Mr. Parker, I want to thank you for all you have done for me since I've been in your training program, but I'm afraid I'm going to have to leave you, and I want to give you my two-week's notice."

"Really? Why are you leaving? We'll miss you around here. Have you got another job?"

"Yes sir. You may know that my real desire has been to get into sales, somewhere. Well, my fiancé's dad is a sales representative, and he is expanding his business, and he asked me if I would like to come into his business with him."

"Did you say fiancée?

"Yes sir. I did."

"Well, congratulations. Do I know her?"

"I don't know, but I think you know her dad. Her dad is Joe Presnell, the guy who sells you most of your cotton."

"Joe Presnell. Well, I'll be darn. I didn't know Joe had a daughter."

"Yes sir, he does. Her name is Sally Jo, and she's the light of my life."

"So, you're going to work with Joe. Buddy, that should be a good move for you. Joe is a great salesman. Did you say he's expanding his business? What's he going to do?"

"He's going to continue what he's doing, but instead of just selling raw cotton, he's going to start selling yarn, and he's picking up a thread line. By the way he talks, I'll probably be selling mostly thread. I'm really excited about it."

"I wish you well, Buddy. I'm sure you'll do well, and since you're going to be working with Joe, I'll probably be seeing you from time to time, and listen, since you're a trainee, and we don't have to train another person to replace you, I think that if you'll just work to the end of this week to tie up any loose ends that you have, you won't need to stay here for two weeks. Buddy, we'll miss you, but I know you'll do well in your new endeavor. Thanks for offering the notice."

He left Mr. Parker's office and went straight to his dad's office. "Well Daddy, I just gave Steve Parker my notice."

"Really? What did he say?"

"Not much. He wished me well. I offered to work out a two-week notice, but he said since they don't have to train a replacement for me, that he would like for me to work the rest of this week, and then I can leave. He was real nice."

"When will you start with Joe?"

"I'm not sure. I've got to call him. I'd say next week. Did I tell you that I might try to buy another car?"

"What are you getting?"

"I don't know. I haven't looked at anything yet, but I think I'll need to get one because I'm going to have to travel quite a bit, and my old car has got a lot of miles."

"Well, I hope you won't go into a lot of debt. Cars are awfully high right now."

"I know, but I think I'm going to have to have something. I'll probably look for something a year or two old."

"I think you'd be wise to do that."

Buddy asked Henry, "Before I go back to work, could I make a quick call on your phone?"

Henry said he could, so he dialed Joe's number. When he answered, Buddy said, "Joe, I just wanted you to know that I turned my notice in to Southern a few minutes ago."

"What did they tell you?"

"They were very nice and said I wouldn't have to work out two weeks, but they would like for me to finish out this week, and I said I would."

"That's fine. Does that mean you can start with me next week?"

"Yes sir."

"Good. I'll see you. I'm sure you'll be at the house some this week, won't you?"

"I'm sure I will be. See ya."

Before he left Henry's office, Henry said, "Your mother said she would like for you and Sally Jo to eat supper with us tonight. Do you have plans?"

"None that I know of. What's she having?"

"I don't know, but since she asked you to come, I'm sure she's fixing something you like."

"Okay, we'll be there, but Sally Jo doesn't get home until close to six, so it might be six thirty or after before we can get there."

"That's alright. Just come as soon as you can."

Dinner was delicious that night, and Buddy noticed that every time Sally Jo is around his mother and daddy, they become closer, and that pleased him. After dinner they stayed until time for Sally Jo to go home, and then Buddy took her. On the way to her house, she told Buddy that the next time they went to his and his parents house, that she would drive, and that would keep him from having to make the round trip to her house just to take her home. He protested slightly, but deep down, that sounded good to him.

The next night, they went shopping for some nice clothes for him to wear when he called on customers, and he was amazed at how much they cost, but with Sally Jo's help, they found some nice-looking things, and even though they were more expensive than he wanted to pay, he bought them, mainly to please her. He knew she had good taste and wouldn't want him wearing something that was not professional looking.

The following night, they didn't see each other. Sally Jo didn't feel well, and Buddy welcomed the chance to rest.

Friday night was when they were to meet D.W. and Jolene at the Lighthouse. Previously they agreed to meet at seven o'clock, and Sally Jo and Buddy got there promptly at seven. D.W. and Jolene had already arrived and were waiting for them inside. They greeted each other, and almost immediately the hostess showed them to their table. Talk was light while they studied the menu, and Sally Jo asked Jolene, "What are you going to get?"

She said, "I think I'm going to try their stuffed flounder. I had scallops the last time we were here, and they were delicious, so I'm hoping the stuffed flounder will be just as good."

"What are you going to have?" Buddy asked D.W.

"I think I'm going to have the scallops. I tasted one of Jolene's last time, and that's what I want tonight."

The waitress came for their order, and in addition to what D.W. and Jolene had said what they were going to order, Sally Jo ordered the stuffed flounder, and Buddy ordered a fried shrimp and scallops' combination. While they waited for their food, D.W. said, "Buddy, you said you were going car shopping tomorrow. Are you still going?"

"Yeah, I hope I can find something I can afford."

"If you could buy your number one choice, what would it be?"

Buddy answered, "I would really like to have a Suburban or a Ford Expedition, but unless I can find a really good buy on a used one, I won't be able to get either one of those. I don't want to have a car payment if I can help it, and I don't know if I have enough savings to pay cash for something really nice. I'll probably just have to buy something that I won't really want in order to have a good traveling vehicle, but who knows? I'll just have to shop and see what I can find."

After the car talk, the conversation revolved to other things, but mainly to Coco Cochran and D.W.'s relationship with her. At one point, he said, "I am so lucky to have found Coco. You know, after her husband died, I helped her with a lot of things, and she has been extremely generous to me in return. In fact, she just recently gave me *Carte Blanche* on all her holdings. She told me that she knew she wouldn't live long enough to spend all her money and insisted that I not want for anything. If I wanted something, go ahead and get it. It was alright with her."

Buddy and Sally Jo looked at each other, and they both had the same feeling: something's fishy about this, but they didn't say anything. They just went on about how wonderful it would be for someone to do something like that for them.

Soon, the conversations ran out, and Buddy said, "Folks this has been great, and I hope we can do it again pretty soon. To me, the seafood here is just as good as it is at the coast, and I'm going to come back real soon. Jolene, it was great getting to know you better, and D.W., are you sure we can't take care of the check?"

"No, no. My benefactor told me to do this and to enjoy ourselves. I've enjoyed it as well. Sally Jo, it was nice getting to know you better, and Buddy, good luck on your automobile search tomorrow. If you find something, call me and let me know what it is."

"Will do. Ya'll have a great rest of the evening."

Sally Jo said a few final words to Jolene, and they left.

On the way to Sally Jo's, Buddy said, "Boy, that seafood was good wasn't it?"

She said, "I think that was probably the best stuffed flounder I've ever had. I may have the scallops next time I go there."

"What did you think about Jolene and D.W.?"

"I liked them a lot, but I got the idea that D.W. was kind of a blow hard. That story he told about Coco Cochran, and how she's sharing her fortune with him was a little over the top. Did you believe him?"

"About half-way. It seemed pretty much out there, but I've seen some of the things he's done, and I can't say he was exaggerating. After that hundred thousand dollars he gave to his Church, I won't put anything past him. Maybe I should get acquainted with Coco."

"Maybe you should."

"Are you still going with me car shopping tomorrow?"

"Yeah. What time?"

"I was thinking about ten o'clock. Is that too early?"

"No, that's fine."

When they got to her house, they both got out of the car, and he walked her to the door, but didn't go in. They kissed goodnight, and he went home.

Chapter Seven

At ten the next morning, Buddy was chomping at the bit, ready to find himself a new car. He was in a great mood, and when he got to Sally Jo's, he went in, and Joe and Kathy were still having coffee. They offered him a cup, which he declined, and they talked for a few minutes before he and Sally Jo left. Joe wanted to know what they were going to do, and when Buddy told him he was going car shopping, Joe didn't encourage him, but he didn't discourage him, either.

On the way to the car, Buddy said, "I think we'll start at the Chevrolet dealers. Maybe they'll have some nice, used Suburbans."

When they got to the Chevrolet store, they began walking around the outside where a lot of new cars were parked. Buddy spotted some Suburbans, and when he got to them and looked at the price on the stickers, he knew immediately that he couldn't afford one, no matter what kind of deal they offered.

Then, he looked for some used Suburbans, but couldn't find any. He saw a man who looked like a salesman, and he asked him where the used Suburbans were, and the man said they didn't have any. He said they sold used ones as fast as they came in because of the prices of the new ones.

Next, they went to the Ford dealer, and the same

thing. They had two Expeditions, but unless a person was rich, they couldn't afford one. No used ones there either.

He had his heart set on either a Suburban or an Exhibition, and was disappointed when he couldn't even find a used one.

When they got in the car, he told Sally Jo, "This sucks. I might not be able to find a car, after all."

She said, "You said one time, something about a Yukon. Are you still interested in one of those?"

"Thank you, Honey. I forgot about the Yukon. That's a GMC, and I think that dealer is in with the Dodge and Chryslers. Let's go see if they have any."

At the GMC dealer, he struck out. They didn't even have any new Yukons, so he told Sally Jo, "We may as well go home. I'll check again in a week or two, and if I begin traveling within the next week or so, maybe I can find something at a dealer where I will be."

"That sounds like a good idea. Let's go get some lunch. You want to?"

"Yeah. Maybe that will cheer me up. Where do you want to go?"

"How about the Krystal?"

"Good choice."

In between bites, Buddy asked Sally Jo, "Is there anything special you would like to do this afternoon?"

"No. Do you have anything you want to do?"

"No. I thought we would probably be riding

around in my new car, but that's out."

She said, "Buddy, if we're going out tonight, why don't you take me home now? I've really got a lot to do to get my clothes ready for next week. I've got several things to iron as well as other things to do, so if you don't care, why don't you do that."

"Okay, if that's what you want. What do you want to do tonight?"

"How about a movie?"

"Okay. Call me afterwhile."

He let her out at the street, and he headed home, with the intentions of mowing the grass, but when he got home, Henry had already mowed and was running the weed eater. They waved at each other, and Buddy went in the house. He had eaten six Krystal hamburgers, but he still wanted something else. He looked in the fridge and found a cold fried chicken thigh and wing, and he made quick work of them. When his daddy came into the house, he wanted to know if he had found a car, and Buddy said, "No sir. I was looking for an SUV and immediately found out that I can't afford a new one, and I don't know if I can afford a used one or not because none of the dealers I went to had any. I asked one salesman at the Chevrolet store if they had any used Suburbans, and he said they didn't. He said they sold used ones immediately, and most of the time, when a friend of someone that buys a new one finds out they're going to buy one, they make a deal with the dealer before the used one comes in. I don't know what I'm going to do because I don't know how long my old Bronco will last with me traveling a lot."

Henry said, "That's unbelievable. Maybe you can find something in one of the towns you will be traveling to. I'm sure there's something out there, somewhere that's just for you, so just try to have patience, and I feel you'll find one."

"I'll try, but Daddy, it's hard to have patience when you need something, and nobody has what you're looking for."

"I know but trust me. The right thing will turn up."

After the brief encounter with Henry, Buddy went to his room and took a nap. He slept until four thirty, and when he woke up he called Sally Jo, and they decided that each would eat supper at home and then go to the nine o'clock movie. Buddy told her that he would probably be through with supper around seven o'clock, and he might be over to her house around seven fifteen or seven thirty.

Before they went to the movie, Kathy said, "Buddy, I'm glad you're here. You know, your wedding is only two months away. Has Helen said much about it. Of course, she won't have as much to do as I will, but I think it's time we start some of the preliminary planning, such as coming up with a menu, making sure the Church date is open, and other things like that, and she might want to be included in it. When you see her, you can mention that I talked to you, and she might want to call me."

"Okay, I'll tell her."

When it was time to go, Sally Jo and Buddy left for the movie. Since it was Saturday, neither one had to worry about getting home too late. The movie was over at eleven o'clock, and although it hadn't been too long since they had had dinner, they decided to go to the Sweet Tooth for dessert.

Buddy told Sally Jo, "Honey, your mother got me to thinking before we left about our wedding. You know, I've been excited about marrying you, but I don't think the actual wedding was ever a reality until tonight, when your mother said we need to start planning and doing some of the preliminaries. That made it become a reality. Do you feel that way?"

"A little, maybe, but the wedding has always been a reality for me, even though it was going to be a long time before it happened."

"Well, it really hit home for me tonight. I thought about it all through the movie, and do you know the main thing I thought about?"

"What?"

"I thought about where are we going to live. Have you thought about that?"

"Yeah. I figured that we would just fine a cute apartment somewhere when the time came. It would be nice if it was on the Huntsville side of Belmont, so I wouldn't have to drive so far to work."

"You know what? It's going to be here before we know it, and I think we need to get busy and do some important things, such as finding a place to live, and furniture, and things like that before the wedding, and we don't have a place to live or a bed to sleep in."

Buddy smiled and said, "Or other things."

She smiled and reaffirmed. She said, "Or other things "

Buddy said, "Would you like to ride around tomorrow afternoon and see what there are in the way of apartments?"

"Yeah, I would like to. I'm beginning to get excited now."

"Okay. We'll do it. We'll go to Church first, and then go look around."

They finished their dessert, and then went home. The next morning, Buddy called and asked her if he could come and go to Church with her and her family, and of course she said yes.

After Church, they went to a Mexican Restaurant for lunch, and afterwards, Buddy and Sally Jo left her parents and went to look at apartments. They had a couple of real estate booklets that Buddy had picked up, somewhere, that had several listings, so those places were where they went first. Of course, they were all locked, except for one, that was an 'open house,' and they knew from its location that it wasn't a place they would be interested in. They spent most of the afternoon driving around and looking, and they saw a couple that might be worth going to see. Buddy asked her, "We liked two. Do you like them well enough for me to call the realtor tomorrow?"

"Yeah, I especially liked the town house that overlooked the pool."

"Okay, I'll call tomorrow and try to set up an appointment. Can you go tomorrow night after work?"

"Yeah. Go ahead and try to set it up."

They got to Sally Jo's around suppertime, and Kathy and Joe invited Buddy to come in for a sandwich. He stayed until time to go home around nine thirty, and each time he was around them for any length of time, they got closer to each other.

The following week was to be his last at Southern, and being the responsible person that he was, he worked just as hard as he would have, had he not been leaving. At three o'clock, Thursday afternoon, his boss came to where he was and said, "Buddy, are you still starting your new job Monday?"

"Yes sir, I am."

"Well, I'm going to give you a parting gift. When you finish up here in a few minutes, you can consider this your last day, and you won't have to come back tomorrow, and you'll get paid for tomorrow just as if you worked."

"Thank you, sir. This will let me have a long weekend, Thank you."

When he got off, he went to his daddy's office and said, "Well, Daddy, I'm no longer working here as of about ten minutes ago."

"You're through? This isn't Friday."

"I know, but they gave me tomorrow off with pay. That was nice of them, wasn't it?"

"Yeah, it was. They've always liked you. That

might come in handy sometime."

First thing the next morning, Buddy called the realtor about the apartment that he and Sally Jo liked, and the man agreed to meet them later that afternoon at six fifteen. He was getting excited just thinking about the possibility of getting his own place to live. He had always lived with his mother and daddy just like Sally Jo had always lived with her parents, so if they got the apartment, it would be a learning experience for both of them. He called her to tell her about the appointment, and they were to meet at the apartment later that day.

That afternoon, they met the realtor and went through the apartment. It was actually a town house with a large living, dining, and kitchen on the lower level. The kitchen and dining area were separated by a bar that served as a table if chairs were placed under it. The upstairs had two bedrooms and two baths, with a balcony off the master that was approximately six by fifteen feet, overlooking the nice pool.

Sally Jo really liked it and told Buddy she wanted it, so he told Jack, the realtor. They had already been told the amount of rent, but they needed to know how much deposit they would have to put down. When they gave all the information to Jack, Buddy asked him if he would be working the next day, since it was Saturday, and he said he would be. He told Buddy that when they came in to sign the lease, they would need to fill out an application for a credit report. He assured them that there would be nothing to it. The application was nothing more than a formality, but the head of the real estate company said they have to get one.

When they left Jack, they decided to go to Old Smoky's Bar B Q to eat before they went to her house. Since they were both driving, they met there. and while they were eating, they had a chance to talk about what they needed to do next, and they both agreed that getting some furniture should be next on their agenda. They finished their ribs and left for her house to tell Joe and Kathy about the apartment and to get some advice on filling out a credit application.

Buddy talked to Joe over the weekend, and Joe told him to come to his house at eight thirty, Monday morning. Joe's house was where he worked out of until he and Buddy could find a suitable office for their new business setup.

Buddy was at Joe's promptly at eight thirty, and Joe invited him in for a cup of coffee before they went out.

Joe told him, "Ever since you said you wanted to come in with me, I've been scouting around for office space. Also, I want to name our new company something other than Presnell Sales, and I'd your input on a name. Buddy, I'm approaching this whole new business as if we've been partners for years, and all the things we're going to do will show you just how much confidence I have in you, but if you're getting cold feet and want to back out, now is the time to do it. You're absolutely sure this is what you want to do? If not, tell me now."

"Joe, I've never been any surer of anything, and I can't wait to get started. I'm anxious to make you glad that you brought me into the business, and I'm anxious to make you proud of your son-in-law."

"Okay, then. Let's get started."

The first order of business was to look at some of the offices that Joe had looked at before. Joe said, "I've looked at I don't know how many office spaces, and I've narrowed them down to three or four, so let's go see them first."

The first two were nice, but each one had some drawback that either Joe or Buddy didn't like. Number three was really nice, with two offices and a nice sized reception area. One office was quite a bit larger than the other, and Joe didn't like that. He wanted both offices to be equal in size, plus, it only had one restroom, and he felt there should be two.

The fourth one they went to see was just what both of them liked a lot. First, the location was excellent. It was on the ground floor of a much larger building, with the utilities included in the rent. The interior had two large offices plus a space that could be used as a sample or conference room. It had a large area for a receptionist, and later, if they decided they needed two girls, there was room, and last but not least, there were two nice sized restrooms.

Joe asked, "Whatta ya think, Buddy?"

"I think out of the four we've seen; this is the one I like best. What do you think?"

"I like it best, too. If it's okay with you, we'll take it."

The agent who showed them the office was the one to handle the paperwork for the lease, and Joe told him to go ahead and do what he had to do, and he and Buddy would be back late in the afternoon to sign it and pay the first and last month's rent.

"Now, we'll have to get some furniture. I've been thinking about using my old desk, but with a new office and all the other furniture, new, do you think a new desk would be in order?"

Buddy said, "I think a new desk would definitely be in order."

The first store they went to advertised name brands at low prices, but they couldn't find what they wanted, so they went to T.H. Layne, the most recognized office furniture store in the area. The nicest saleslady, Ruth Wood waited on them, and after Joe explained what they were doing, she took them to see just what he had in mind. He asked Buddy, "What do you think?"

"Is it between these two groups?"

"I think so. Ruth, do you have any other groups that would fit into what we told you, without breaking the bank"

"No sir. These are the only two where everything matches."

Buddy said, "I think I like this one best."

Joe said, "Good. That's my choice as well. Okay, Miss Ruth, sharpen your pencil and let's see if we can come up with enough money to pay for all this."

She led them up to the office and sat down to a calculator and began to feed it numbers. In a minute, she came up with a figure and showed the tape to Joe.

He looked at it and whistled and asked," Is this the best you can do, Ruth? We just need a place to work, not a place to live."

She took the tape back and said, "Let me see," and she began to figure some more. When she finished, she tore out a new tape and handed it to Joe. "Joe, this is the best I can do. I knocked fifteen percent off everything, and you should be pleased with this."

He looked it over and was satisfied with the total. The fifteen percent amounted to over eighteen hundred dollars. He said, "Okay, we'll take this group. When can you deliver it?"

"We should be able to get it out to you first thing in the morning. Is that alright?"

"Perfect. Oh yeah, Do you have any four drawer file cabinets that won't break us"

"I do," and she showed them some file cabinets.

He picked out two that had locks on them and told her, "We'll take these two

When they finished picking out the furniture, they went to the realtor's office to take care of the paperwork for the office space they rented. Joe said, "You know, we've spent most of the day on the offices and we still haven't decided on a name. Let me call Kathy to see if she's cooking, and if she is, you can eat with us, and we can try to come up with something. Is that alright with you?"

"That's fine with me."

Kathy said she was cooking and would love to have Buddy eat with them, so that's what they did, but before they went to Joe's, they went back by the new offices and mentally arranged the furniture that was to be delivered the next day.

Buddy was very happy to go to their house for dinner because he could see Sally Jo earlier than usual. Joe and Buddy did their usual kidding around at dinner, and before they all finished, Joe told Kathy and Sally Jo that he would like for them to give their input on coming up with a name for the new business.

After the dishes were done, Kathy and Sally Jo went into the den where Joe and Buddy were, and Kathy said, "So you want Sally Jo and I to come up with a name for your new company?"

"No, I just want ya'll to help us decide on one. It would be great if you could come up with something that would really hit home, but I think it's going to take all four of us. Now, as ya'll know, the present name is PRESNELL SALES, which is good," but looking at Buddy and smiling, "I'm going to bring this character in with me, and I'm afraid if I don't include his name, some way, he'll get his feelings hurt."

Buddy said, acting serious, "I think I've got just the name. I don't know why I didn't think of it before."

Before he could say anymore, Kathy asked,

"What is it, Buddy?"

Still serious, he said, "Buddy Russo and Friend Sales Company."

Sally Jo and Kathy both laughed.

Joe said, "Yeah, right. You may be onto something there, Buddy. I think I'll just change our present name to Presnell and Friend Sales. How's that?" Not a word. Finally, he said, "Okay, guys. enough playing. This is serious stuff. We have to come up with a name or else I'm going to have to hang on to Presnell Sales, and speaking of Presnell Sales, I'm not going to change that name for my cotton business. It's already established, and people are familiar with it, and I don't want to change anything there. Buddy, you'll still be working with me at Presnell Sales, but the new company is where I want a new name. Okay, I'm open to suggestions."

Everyone began to throw out suggested names: J & B Sales, Joe and Buddy Sales, Presnell Thread and Yarn, North Alabama Thread and Yarn Co, Belmont Textile Supply, Belmont Thread and Yarn Co., Ideal Thread and Yarn, Quality Thread and Yarn, Dixie Yarn and Thread Co., Industrial Thread and Yarn Co., Commercial Thread and Yarn Co.

If a name sounded good to Joe, he would write it down to see how it looked in writing. He liked Ideal Thread and Yarn and Industrial Thread and Yarn more than the others, and he said he wanted to mull it over for a day or so before he made the final decision. He also wanted to consult with Buddy, one on one.

As it always does, time just flew by, and it was time for Buddy to go home. He told Kathy how much he enjoyed dinner and asked Joe what time and where was he to come in the morning. Joe said, "Since they're bringing the furniture in the morning, just meet me at the office about nine o'clock. Sally Jo said, "I'll walk you to your car."

He always hated to leave her, but he was tired and was actually glad it was time to leave. They talked for a few minutes, and he said he had better go. They kissed goodnight, and he left.

The next morning, he arrived at the office promptly at nine, and Joe was already there. He opened the door and went in, and Joe had brought coffee for them both. He took his cup and thanked Joe, and they stood drinking their coffee because there was no furniture in the office yet. Joe said, "Here's your key. I forgot to give it to you yesterday."

When Joe gave him his own key, he felt a warm and fuzzy feeling come over him. Now that he had his own key, he felt that he was actually a part of Joe's business.

Standing in a bare room began to get tiresome, and Joe said, "You know what? We forgot about buying chairs. Let me see if I can catch the truck before it leaves." He took out his phone and told it to call T.H. Layne. When someone answered, he asked to speak to Ruth Wood, and when she answered, he said. "Good morning, Ruth. Joe Presnell here. Listen, I forgot to buy chairs when I was at your place yesterday. If the truck hasn't left yet to bring our furniture, how about holding them until I can get there to buy some chairs. I'll be there in ten minutes. Bye."

He hung up and said, "Come on, Buddy. The truck's ready to leave, and we need to get there asap. Ruth is going to try and catch them. Come on. We'll take my car."

They rushed to the store and hurriedly picked out a desk chair for each of them plus a chair, suitable for a receptionist. Two guys came up and pushed the chairs back to the loading dock, with Ruth's help and loaded them on the truck while Joe and Buddy returned to the car and headed back to the office.

In just a few minutes after they got back, the truck came with the furniture. As they unloaded it, Joe directed them where to put each piece. After it was all in place, and the truck left, Joe and Buddy walked through each room and then back to Joe's office, where he sat down at his desk. Buddy was left standing, and Joe said, "I guess we still didn't get enough stuff, did we?" And then he asked, "Well, what do you think?"

"I think we're about ready to do business, don't you?"

"Yeah, I think so, but there are still a few little things to do, plus one big one."

"What?" Buddy asked.

"We still don't have a name, but I thought of one

after you left, last night that I would like for us to use. It is the name of an old line thread company that's no longer in business, and if you agree, it's the name we'll use. It's Signal Thread and Yarn Company. What do you think about it?"

"I love it."

"Well, if we're going to use Signal, I need to do several things immediately."

Buddy asked, "What do you have to do? Is there anything I can do?"

"No, not right now. First thing is, we have to get telephones hooked up. I've got to call a sign painter to come and paint the name on our front door, and I have to design some business forms and then, find a printer to print them. Tomorrow, we'll go see the thread manufacturer that I've been talking with and pick their brain about thread. I know most things about yarn, but I'm sort of lost when it comes to thread, and that's where you're going to become an expert. Tell you what. It's almost lunchtime, so why don't we go get something to eat and hit these things hard when we get back? Is that okay with you?"

"It is. I'm kinda hungry."

Joe asked, "Where do you want to go?"

"Anywhere is fine with me. The Steak & Shake is where I go most of the time, if I don't go to the Krystal."

"Okay, the Steak & Shake it is. You wanna drive?"

While they were eating, Buddy looked up, and

who was walking his way other than D.W. Handy. "Hey, Buddy," D.W. said. "Mind if I join you? The place is packed."

Buddy couldn't say anything else but "No, sit down." After he was seated, Buddy said, "D.W., this is Joe Presnell, Sally Jo's dad."

They shook hands and told each other that they were glad to meet.

Buddy said to D.W., "D.W., I'm coming into business with Joe, selling thread and yarn."

"That's right. You told me you were going to do it when you and Sally Jo ate with us last week. You were going car-shopping the day after we ate. Did you find one?"

"No. I'm still looking. When I start traveling, I'll check with some dealers in the towns where I'll be, and maybe I can find something."

D.W. said, "You will. I've just got a good feeling about it."

Not too much else was said. They all just concentrated on their eating. D.W. finished first, and said, "Well, guys, this has been nice, but I've got to go. We have a service at four o'clock, and I have to go over my songs again. Joe, it was a real pleasure meeting you, and Buddy, remember what I said. I've got a really good feeling about a car for you. Oh yeah, would you and Sally Jo like to go to the Lighthouse again?"

"I would. Have Jolene call Sally Jo."

"Okay. Again, it's great to see you guys."

When he left, Joe asked, "Buddy, who is that guy?"

"D.W.? Bobby Pearson brought him to Belmont to work in Pearson Funeral Home after they graduated from college together. He immediately became a hit with people because of his charisma and good singing voice. A man named George Cochran, the controlling stockholder in one of the banks, died. He was a multimillionaire and left no one but his wife. D.W. handled his funeral and helped his wife with her business, and she liked him so much, she persuaded him to work for her all the time when he wasn't working at the funeral home. She has so much confidence in him that she gave him her Power of Attorney and almost complete control of her affairs.

"She apparently pays him a fortune because he has given a fortune away. He gave his girlfriend a new Jeep Grand Wagoneer. He gave his Church a hundred thousand dollars for their building fund and no telling what else he has given away. I know of two other people who he gave cars to."

"When he first moved here, he came to all our football games as well as other sports, and that's how I got acquainted with him. I've seen him many times and about a week or so ago, Sally Jo and I went to the Lighthouse with him and his girl, Jolene. We enjoyed being with them and would like to do it again."

"Do you think he's on the up and up?"

"Well, I've never heard anybody say anything against him, and unless he does something to hurt me,

I'm going to be his friend."

"He sounds worthy to be your friend. We had better go. It's after one, and we have a lot to do this afternoon. Why don't we go by T.H. Layne's and see if we can find some guest chairs? There might not be anybody that will come in, but if they do, we have to have somewhere for them to sit.

Ruth Wood had just returned from lunch, herself, and Joe asked to see her. In a minute, she got to him, and he told her that he needed some chairs for visitors to sit in, and did she have any good buys on that kind of chair.

"You're here at the perfect time, Joe. We have a group that has been discontinued, and I can let you have them for a steal. How many do you need?"

Joe looked at Buddy, and they said a few words to each other, and then he said, "Three."

Ruth asked loudly, "Three? You must not be planning to have any visitors. Do you really think three chairs will be enough?"

Joe said, "I think so. We're just a small sales office, and Buddy and I will be going to them, rather than them coming to us. Three chairs should be enough."

"Okay. Whatever you say, but let me throw this out to you. Let's say that you or Buddy has called on a potentially large customer without closing the deal, and then they decide they want to buy from you, and they want to come to your office to place the order and set things up. In all probability, there will be more than one person, so what are you going to let them do? Have one sit and one stand?"

Joe laughed, and said, "You're a great salesman, Ruth. How many do you suggest?"

"For you and Buddy, and the receptionist, I recommend two for each one of you, Then, if one of you has, say three guests, you can always move a couple of chairs around. Do you want me to send you six? We might can get them to you later this afternoon."

"Whoa, Kemosabe," Joe said. You haven't even told me how much they are."

That time, she didn't go to her calculator. She had a pad and pen in one of her pockets, and she figured it up right there.

Joe said, "I thought you said they were discontinued. These prices don't sound like it."

"They are," and she gave them the original price and then the sale price, and Joe could readily see the difference.

"Okay, Miss Sales Whiz. Bring 'em on. This office is costing a whole lot more than I was expecting. I hope this is all the furniture we have to buy." He signed the sales order and they left.

Thank goodness for cell phones. Since they didn't have phone service yet, Joe asked his cell phone the number for the telephone company, and it not only gave him the number, it dialed it, and he ordered one line for three phones.

They couldn't go to the thread manufacturer the

next day because they had to wait for the telephone people to come and hook them up to the outside world. The sign painter was also scheduled for the next day. In the meantime, Joe designed what he wanted in printed forms and went to the printer the next day and left Buddy there to wait on the people who were coming.

The rest of the week was spent getting the business set up and ready to begin selling. Buddy and Joe had an appointment in Chattanooga, Tennessee on Tuesday with Shepherd Apparel, one of the largest sportswear manufacturers in the world.

Shepherd Apparel was not only the largest sportswear manufacturer, but they made the 'Fin' line of socks, which was huge, and Joe thought that if they could just get their foot in the door, he would see to it that Signal's quality and service would be so good, Shepherd couldn't afford not to eventually make them one of their most important resources.

He felt confident about it because Roger Nichols, the yarn buyer, used to be the cotton buyer at Southern, and Joe had sold him millions of pounds of cotton in the past. He and Roger became good friends during that time, and Roger not only promised to possibly buy from him, he said he would put in a good word for him to Dan Hughes, the thread buyer.

Chapter Eight

Jolene Fuller made reservations at The Lighthouse restaurant for six thirty, Saturday night after talking to Sally Jo on Wednesday. Then, on Saturday afternoon, she called Sally Jo and said D.W. had gotten tied up on something and wanted to know if seven thirty would be alright, if she could move their reservation back an hour. Sally Jo called Buddy, and that was fine with him.

He and Sally Jo got to the Lighthouse at seven twenty, and Jolene and D.W. were standing outside, waiting for them. They went in and were seated at a table with a beautiful view of Lake Tanisi the way they did the last time they were there. They all ordered, and the food was just as good as it was the first time they came. They all ate and then stayed and talked for a few minutes before leaving. Sally Jo noticed that Jolene was giddy and almost smiling the whole time they were eating, and sometimes her actions and comments were almost silly. Sally Jo tried to figure out what was going on with her, and then it dawned on her: She and D.W. were about to get engaged. She kept waiting on her or D.W. to say something but they never did, and in a few minutes, D.W. asked, "Are y'all ready to go?"

When they got outside to the parking lot, D.W. said, "How about walking over here with us. There's something I want to show you. Sally Jo thought, *I knew something was up. This must be what she's been so giddy about.*

They walked a little way and stopped in front of a group of cars, including a beautiful, shiny, white Suburban. D.W. asked, "This is pretty, isn't it?"

Buddy answered and said, "It really is. This is what I first looked at the other day, but the sticker price told me I couldn't afford it, and they didn't have any used ones. Is this yours, D.W.?"

D.W. answered, "No. It's yours."

"What did you say?"

"I said it's yours. I bought it for you, so you won't have any worries when you travel. This is my wedding gift to you and Sally Jo."

Before Buddy could say anything, Sally Jo grabbed D.W. and gave him a huge hug and said, "Thank you."

While she was hugging D.W., Buddy was hugging Jolene. Then, they switched: Buddy hugged D.W., and Sally Jo hugged Jolene.

Buddy said, "D.W., I don't know what to say. How in the world could you do this?"

"Remember when we were talking a while back, and I told you how Coco wants me to do things for people. I was telling her about you, and how you're one of my favorite people. I was telling her how you were going to start traveling, and how your car had so many miles on it, you were uneasy about driving it on long trips. After she heard this, she told me to go out and get you a nice car. I heard you say that you would like to have a Suburban, so I thought I would get you one, compliments of Coco Cochran."

He said, "I absolutely cannot believe this. This is so expensive. If you'll give me her phone number, I'll call and thank her."

D.W. said, "No, no, don't do that. She can't hear the phone; her hearing is so bad. I'll tell her how grateful you are. You might want to write a short thank you note, and I'll take it to her, and don't worry about the cost. There's a lot more where that came from."

He remotely unlocked the door and went around to the passenger's side and opened the glove compartment, and took out some papers. He handed them to Buddy, one at a time, and said, "Here's the Bill of Sale, the Application for title, and other things. I gave the dealer your phone number, so when the title comes in, they will call you. You can go by there next week and they will have the license tags for you. You said you're going to Chattanooga, Tuesday, and it'll be alright if you drive up there with the temporary tags. Finally, you're going to have to take Jolene and me home because we drove your car here, if that's alright."

"Alright? Padna, I'll drive you anywhere you want to go, after what you've done. I really don't know how to thank you or what to say."

"D.W. said, "The words thank you are enough."

Buddy said, "Thank you."

D.W. said, "You're welcome."

They all piled into the Suburban, with Buddy driving, and D.W. said, "Buddy, take us to my place and I'll take Jolene home."

Buddy said, "10-4. Man, this thing drives like a dream. Are you sure you want to do this, D.W.?"

"I'm sure. Just forget about where it came from and enjoy it."

"You know what, Buddy?"

"What?"

"It's got enough room for a half dozen kids."

Before Buddy could answer, Sally Jo said, "Right."

D.W. lived in an apartment in downtown Belmont, and Buddy let them out there. They all said how much they enjoyed The Lighthouse, and Buddy said, "The next time it's on me. " He thanked D.W. one more time, and they left.

On the way to Sally Jo's, she said, "I can't wait for Daddy to see this. He's gonna flip."

When they got to her house, the lights were still on in Kathy and Joe's room, and she said to Buddy, "You wait here, and let me go get Mother and Daddy."

They came out and when they saw the SUV, they didn't say anything at first, and then Sally Jo said, "Look what Buddy's friend gave him tonight."

Joe asked, "What are you talking about?"

She said, "Buddy's friend, D.W., gave him this car. Isn't it beautiful?"

Joe asked, "Buddy, why would he do something like this? Do you think he might have stolen it?"

"No sir. I've got all the paperwork that goes with it. I've got the bill of sale, the title application, and other stuff. Do you remember when we saw him at the Steak & Shake the other day, and he said he had a good feeling about me getting a car? Well, it looks like this was his good feeling." Buddy handed over the Bill of Sale from the dealer where it showed the purchaser as Coco Cochran. The signature was Coco Cochran by D.W. Handy, POA, and then he showed him the paperwork showing the vehicle being transferred from Coco Cochran to H.T. (Buddy) Russo.

"Are you going to keep it," Joe asked.

"Yes sir. I plan to, unless I find out something illegal or something else is wrong. This is not the first car he has given away in the last year or so. This is the fourth one that I know of, and there could be more, so yes sir, I'm going to keep it.

Buying a car, especially a nice car like this and then just give it away? It just doesn't make sense. Did he take your car?"

"No. He said he didn't want it."

"Well, if I were you, I'd hang on to it, at least long enough to be sure somebody's not going to come take this one away from you."

Buddy said, "That's not going to happen."

The whole time he and Buddy were talking, Kathy and Sally Jo were inside the car, going over everything.

Two Months Later

Signal Yarn and Thread was now two months old, and in that short time, it had already become very successful. Joe, capitalizing on his years of experience in the cotton and yarn business, was successful in opening several large hosiery accounts, including Shepherd Hosiery. He had become one of the leaders in yarn sales, both in Fort Payne Alabama and Hickory, North Carolina, as well as in nearly all the cities and towns in the south where hosiery mills were located.

Buddy was selling both thread and yarn, but he was concentrating mostly on thread. He had opened some nice accounts, including Shepherd Apparel, and he was traveling quite a bit in his new Suburban.

They still didn't have very much furniture in their apartment. They made sure to get a bed, first, and a TV, second. Every spare penny they had was going for something they needed for the town house. Even though furniture was kinda sparse at the apartment, they thought they had enough to start housekeeping after they were married.

His and Sally Jo's wedding was quickly approaching, and both families were as busy as bees, trying to get everything ready. Two of Sally Jo's friends had given showers for her, and Sylvia Neville gave her a bachelorette party, which was fun. Billy Neville gave Buddy a Bachelor party, which was probably the most sober bachelor party ever, because

Billy and Buddy neither one drank, and Billy invited Buddy's friends who he knew didn't drink or didn't drink much. They had a great time, anyway.

The wedding was not going to be large, as some weddings are. Sally Jo was only having three attendants, and Buddy the same amount. Sally Jo would be wearing a beautiful white wedding gown, and her attendants were going to be dressed in aqua color dresses.

Instead of tuxedos, the men were going to be wearing very nice navy-blue suits, white shirts, maroon ties and black shoes.

Joe and Buddy were going to work through Thursday and take off Friday, except for a meeting between the two on Friday morning. Buddy was going to be gone the following week on his honeymoon, and he and Joe wanted to be sure that while he was gone, his customers would be taken care of. He had anticipated the honeymoon week and had notified all his accounts that he would be gone and wrote backup orders for some of them, just in case they ran out. He thought he had everything taken care of, but in business, one never knows for sure.

Joe and Kathy had reserved a room at Ryan's restaurant for the rehearsal dinner, after the rehearsal at Sally Jo's Church, and everyone was getting excited. Joe had gone all out for his little girl's rehearsal dinner. The menu consisted of beef wellington appetizers and for the main course, the guests had a choice of filets with baked potatoes and garlic asparagus spears or chicken divan with green beans and garlic asparagus spears. They were planning for thirty guests, and all thirty came. Sally Jo's Pastor asked God's blessing on the food, and everyone dug in. The food was delicious, and a good time was had by all.

Sally Jo gave each of her bridesmaids a pair of beautiful earrings, and Buddy gave each of his groomsmen a very nice money clip.

The day of the wedding was a beautiful, sunny, warm Autumn Day, and Buddy was so nervous, he didn't appreciate the beauty of the day. Sally Jo was scared to death. Buddy was just nervous about the fact that he was going to get married, and both of them were virgins and nervous about going to bed together: Sally Jo more so than Buddy. Both were looking forward to going to bed, but still, they were a little scared.

As soon as he thought the car wash was open, he took the Suburban to get cleaned up. He took it to one that cleaned the inside as well as the exterior. He got back home around ten and checked his suitcase to be sure he had everything he needed for a week away from home.

About eleven o'clock, Billy picked Buddy up and took him to the Krystal for lunch. He was trying to occupy Buddy's mind until that night. After lunch, they rode out to the recreation area where they used to go all the time at Lake Tanisi, but things were different. A new, younger crowd was there, and neither guy knew anybody, so they left and went to Buddy's house. While they were sitting on the porch, Billy asked, "What time do we have to be at the Church?"

"I think they told the girls to be there by five thirty, so I'm guessing we have to be there at the same time. The ceremony is at seven. I don't know why we have to be there so early, but that's what the woman in charge said."

"Are you ready to get married, Buddy?"

"Yeah, I'm ready. I'm getting a good woman, and I've got a good job, and I'm still going to be surrounded by my lifelong friends that I love, and I hope love me, so yeah, I'm ready."

"Atta boy. Look, I've gotta go get ready if I'm going to get to the Church in time to get you married. Calm down, Bro. Once you see Sally Jo in all her finery, you'll be alright."

"Okay, Pal. You're a good friend. I'll see you later."

When Billy left, it was after three o'clock, so he took a shower, shaved, and laid out his clothes. Then, he took a nap. At four thirty, Helen woke him up, and he jumped up and got ready.

All the guys dressed before they came, but the girls brought their dresses with them and changed at the Church. Buddy understood then why they had to be there so early, but he still didn't know why the guys had to be there at that time.

He and the guys killed time in a lounge area until

time for the ceremony to begin, and then they took their places.

The Church was beautiful in its own right, but with the flowers placed the way they were, it was outstanding. Sally Jo didn't want an extravagant show, and the decorations were very tastefully done. Just the way she would want them.

Exactly at seven o'clock, the music started. Before Buddy and Henry went into the sanctuary, Henry told Buddy, "Son, have you got the ring?"

Buddy said, "Yes sir. Here it is," and then they went in and stood before the preacher. In a few seconds, the groomsmen walked down the aisle, and then after them, the bridesmaids came down, and finally, Sally Jo appeared, escorted by Joe, who looked like a million dollars, and Buddy smiled with a huge smile until she got down front.

She had on a Princess style, sparkling lace wedding dress. It had luxury beaded long sleeves and was ideal for a Fairy Tale Wedding.

Before the preacher said anything, D.W. stood up to sing in his Italian shoes and thousand-dollar suit. He sang 'I Can Only Imagine', and those who hadn't heard him sing were totally surprised at his beautiful voice. Joe was extremely impressed. Many of the women in the crowd cried during the song, and several men were using their handkerchief to wipe their eyes. It was a beautiful rendition of a beautiful song.

The ceremony was just a traditional ceremony;

nothing more and nothing less. When the vows were finished, D.W. sang *'The Lord's Prayer.'* Afterwards, the preacher pronounced Sally Jo and Buddy husband and wife, and told Buddy he could kiss his bride, which he did. The reception was going to be in the Family Life Center at the Church, and after the pictures, everyone who wanted to, went to the celebration, where it was very festive.

The wedding planner set up a receiving line, so the newlyweds could receive their friends and relatives. The line started with Buddy, then Sally Jo, then Kathy and Joe, and finally, Helen and Henry. It seemed as if just about everybody who had gone to the wedding was at the reception, because it took a really long time for the line to end. Then, the couple went over to a table where the wedding cake was, and as was customary, they cut the cake, and each fed the other a bite, not caring if they got cake all over the other's face.

Most people stayed just long enough to get refreshments, and then they left. When they crowd dwindled down to just a few, Buddy and Sally Jo gathered both sets of parents around them and told them how much they loved them, and how much they appreciated the very nice wedding and reception. They made sure they knew where they would be the next week, and then they went into the proper locations and changed into their street clothes.

When they got dressed, they came out and hugged and kissed their parents one more time. Buddy kissed his mother on the cheek, and then hugged his daddy, and as he was pulling away from his daddy, his daddy slipped two one-hundred-dollar bills into his hand. He lip synced 'thank you' and then turned to Kathy and Joe. He kissed Kathy on the cheek, the way he did his mother and then turned to Joe. He shook Joe's hand and Joe handed him a credit card.

He told Buddy, "Use this card to pay for your hotel and anything else you might need it for. I'm glad to have you for my son-in-law. Take good care of my little girl, and I'll see you when you get back.

"Thank you, Joe, and I'm glad to be your son-in-law. I love y'all."

They left their parents and went outside to where they were parked. They got in the Suburban and left for Jekyll Island. It was Buddy's intention to stop on the way and go on to Jekyll Island the next day. He didn't know what time they would be leaving Belmont, so he didn't make a reservation anywhere. He felt that they could find a motel on the way, and he wanted to get at least as far as Birmingham and preferably to somewhere on Interstate twenty, east of Birmingham.

Luckily, they found a Quality Inn, just as soon as they got on Interstate Twenty, and it had a vacancy. Buddy pulled in under the canopy and got out and went in the lobby. He asked for a king-size room, and they had one left. He agreed to take it, and after he registered, he went to the car and got Sally Jo and the bag they had packed for just one night. She seemed very happy and was joking and playful until the elevator got to their floor. Then, her attitude changed from jovial to one of apprehension. Buddy kind of felt the same way, but he didn't want Sally Jo to see it. He kept up the act of a newlywed husband until they got to their room, and just as soon as they got in and closed the door, they locked lips for probably thirty seconds or more.

"Well, here we are, Mrs. Russo," Buddy said.

"I know, Mr. Russo," she answered. "What do we do now?"

"Guess." He grabbed her and gave her a kiss and asked, "Nervous?"

She said, "A little. You know, I've never been in a hotel with a man before."

"I know, but you've never been married before," and joking, he asked, "Have you?"

She smiled and said, "No, I haven't, and for my first time, I'm thankful, it's with you."

"Me, too. You want to change first?"

"If you want me too."

"Why don't you, then I'll change."

She opened the suitcase, and after going through some things, she took out a couple of items and went into the bathroom and closed the door. Her mood must have changed because he could hear her in the bathroom, humming, as she changed into her sleepwear. In a few minutes, the door opened and there stood the most beautiful sight Buddy had ever seen. She came into the room and said, "Your turn."

Buddy said, "I won't be but a minute," and that's about all it took; a minute.

He came out and went over to her and they kissed. After the first kiss, she slipped her peignoir off, and they continued to hug and kiss as Buddy came out of his t-shirt. They held each other as they laid across the bed and stared into each other's eyes, and in a minute, Buddy asked, "Are you ready to get under the covers?"

She said, "If you are," and they both removed what they had on.

Lying under the covers, naked, and up close against each other, was the most indescribable, wonderful feeling that either had ever had. They remained there, loving, and letting nature take over, and finally, drifting off to sleep, they slept 'til morning.

Buddy was the first up, and he fixed some coffee in the little two cup coffeemaker in the room, and the noise woke Sally Jo. She got up and went to the bathroom and then sat down with Buddy and had some coffee. The little coffeemaker only made one cup for each of them, so Buddy went downstairs and got each one of them another cup. When he got back to the room, he told Sally Jo, "They've got a pretty good-looking breakfast downstairs, and we can eat down there if you want to, or we can get ready and leave and eat somewhere on down the road. What would you like to do?"

She said, "I'm really not hungry right now. Why

don't we grab a bite somewhere in about an hour or so?"

"Sounds good to me. Wanna mess around a little before we go?"

"That's awfully tempting, but after last night, I think I should probably wait at least until tonight. Is that alright with you?"

"Sweetheart, anything you want or don't want is alright with me. Let's get ready and head to Jekyll Island. I'm anxious to hit the beach. It's about four hundred and fifty miles from here, and it will probably take us about seven hours."

"Okay, I'll try to hurry."

"Take your time. We have all week."

She didn't. She hurriedly got ready, and they took off. They drove until I-20 crossed over into Georgia, and they stopped at the little town of Bremen to eat breakfast.

From Bremen, they stayed on I-20 until they got to Atlanta and picked up I-75 South. From there, they got on I-16 in Macon and drove until I-16 ran into I-95 in Savannah and then to Brunswick, close to where Jekyll Island is located.

They checked in the Residence Inn when they got to Jekyll Island, and they had a beautiful room overlooking the beach. It was close to suppertime when they got there, and someone told them that Sonny's Bar B Q over in Brunswick was good, so after resting for a little while, they went to Sonny's. They hadn't stopped for lunch, so they were both hungry, and the bar b q was outstanding.

It was dark when they finished eating, so they went back to the hotel and sat around the pool. Buddy was dying to get upstairs and take his bride to bed, and Sally Jo might have felt the same way, but she didn't show it. She could have just wanted her new husband to be the leader and make the decisions, and she would follow.

It wasn't too long before her wish came true. Buddy said, "Baby, why don't we go upstairs and see what we can find to do?"

"Okay, honey. I'm with you," so they got up and went to their room.

When they got inside, they didn't even take time to put on their bedclothes. They quickly locked up, and laid across the bed, undressing as they moved around, and in a minute, they were turned around and under the covers. Sally Jo was much more comfortable that time than she was when they were in the motel, their first night, and Buddy could easily tell the difference. They loved each other until they were both worn out, and they went to sleep, and slept all night without ever getting up to get dressed.

On Monday morning, Buddy was up first, as usual, and when Sally Jo woke up, she asked, "Good morning, Darling. What are you doing?"

"I'm just looking at a list of things to do. There's a lot going on down here, so we shouldn't have any trouble staying busy. Look at this, and I'll pour you a cup of coffee." After they had a cup, she got dressed, and they went downstairs and had breakfast.

Over breakfast, they decided that they would stay at the hotel and play tennis. After tennis, they would go to the beach and get some sun. On the list that Buddy had, it showed that there were horses to rent for horseback riding, bicycles to rent, a boat tour that shows the area from water, and on the tour, it goes to an area where there is a lot of dolphins that pretty much put on a natural show.

Buddy asked, "If you would like to, we could do one of these every day, and that would take us through Thursday, and then we can decide what we want to do on Friday. I think we ought to go home Saturday, so we can have Sunday to rest before we have to go back to work. What do you think?"

"I think you're right. We're probably going to be worn out by the time we get home and will need a day to rest up. We can even leave Friday, if you want to."

"Aren't you having a good time?"

"Oh yes. I'm having a wonderful time. I was just thinking of you, if you have to travel next week. If you do, then you don't need to be so tired."

"I'm not going to be tired. If I get to rest Sunday, I'll be in great shape, and I might not have to travel next week, anyway. I did extra for my customers before we left, and they may all still be in good shape when we get back, so we'll do whatever you want to do. It doesn't matter to me. Let's do some of the things in the brochure and see how we feel Thursday evening, okay?"

"Okay, let's do that."

They were busy as all get out, doing all the things they read about in the brochure and by the time Thursday night came, they were ready to go home, so they got up Friday morning, had breakfast, and loaded the car, and headed toward Belmont. It was nearly an eight hour drive, and they took their time because they didn't have to be in any hurry. They stopped at an outlet mall, where Sally Jo was in shoppers' heaven, and they stopped to sightsee in another place, and when it got dark, they were still more than a hundred miles from Belmont, so they decided to stop in Birmingham to spend the night.

Traffic in Birmingham is always like rush hour, even on Saturday mornings, so they took their time and waited until it cleared a little before they left at ten o'clock. It was only a couple of hours to Belmont, and Buddy figured they would be home around noon.

Arriving in Belmont at twelve thirty, they stopped at Micki-Dees before they went to their apartment. After they got all their stuff unloaded, they couldn't wait to sit down and rest. Their week at Jekyll Island was supposed to have been restful, but it was just the opposite. They were both thankful that they had a half day, Saturday and all day, Sunday to just do nothing.

They did go see Helen and Henry, late Saturday afternoon, and they went to Church with Joe and Kathy, Sunday morning, but other than that, they did nothing 'til Monday morning, when they went to work.

The first thing Buddy did when he got to the office was check his emails and phone messages, and he nearly shouted with joy when he saw that he had received messages from two large thread buyers, wanting to see him; one in North Carolina and one in Mississippi, but before he called them back, he got with Joe, to get any advice that he might have.

Joe said, "You know, both of those guys are tough nuts to crack, and if they called you, you must be doing something right. I suggest you do just what you've been doing; whatever that is because it seems to be working. When are you going to call them?"

"Just as soon as you and I get through talking."

Chapter Nine

Three Months Later

Coco Cochran was surprised to hear her phone ring, because it never rang, unless it was D.W., and she knew that it wasn't him because he had to go out of town. She answered, "Hello."

"Is this Mrs. Cochran?"

"Yes, it is. Who's calling?"

"Mrs. Cochran, this is Jerry Nelson with Northwest Bank. How are you, this morning?"

"I'm okay."

"That's good. Mrs. Cochran, auditors just finished a complete audit at our bank, and it has brought to our attention some irregularities in some of your accounts. Would it be possible for you to come down here to discuss what the auditors found?"

"I'm afraid not. You see, I don't drive anymore, and the person who looks after my affairs is not here."

"That's fine. Actually, you're the one we need to talk to. Could we send a car for you?"

"I guess. When will you send it?"

"We can have it there right after lunch, today, or first thing in the morning. Would either one of those suit you?"

She was puzzled about what he said, and she wanted to get to the bottom of what was going on, so she said, "After lunch, today will be alright."

"Great. Will one o'clock work for you?"

"Yes sir. One o'clock will be fine."

"Thank you, Mrs. Cochran. I'll look forward to seeing you."

She was ready when the bank car arrived at one o'clock, and the driver got out and went to the door to get her and then helped her get in the back seat, when they got to the car. He tried talking to her on the way to the bank, but couldn't get any response from her, so he stopped trying. He pulled up front when they reached the bank, and he got out, came around, and helped her out of the car, and then escorted her into the bank and back to Jerry Nelson' office.

Jerry stood up and welcomed her in, He said, "Hello, Mrs. Cochran. I'm Jerry Nelson. I don't think we have met before, and I'm very glad to meet you."

She just nodded and didn't acknowledge anything he said.

He said, "Mrs. Cochran, if you don't mind, John Easter, who is our Vice President will be in here with us during our conversation." He picked up his phone, punched in a couple of numbers and then said, "Mrs. Cochran is here," and hung up.

In about two seconds, a tall, stately looking man came in the office and said, Mrs. Cochran, I'm John Easter. I'm happy to meet you. I knew your husband, and I thought he was a fine man."

She didn't acknowledge anything he said, either. Instead, she asked, "What is this all about?"

"Mrs. Cochran, did you say you have someone

looking after your affairs?"

"Yes."

"Is this person authorized to withdraw funds from your accounts?"

"Well, yes. He has my Power of Attorney. Again, what is this all about?"

"Mrs. Cochran, we know you live alone and don't have family to spend your money on. Are you aware that almost two million dollars has disappeared from your holdings over the last year?"

"Two million dollars has disappeared?"

"Yes ma'am. Were you aware of that?"

"I certainly was not. Where did it go?"

"This is what we're trying to find out. There have been sales of stocks and large withdrawals from your money market, and you say you didn't do any of this. Can you fully trust the person who has your Power of Attorney?"

"I thought I could, but now, I'm not so sure. Why? Do you think he took it?"

"We think maybe he did. Since there are only two people that can deposit and withdraw and buy and sell from your accounts, and you say you didn't do it, what else can we think?"

"Are you going to talk to him about it?"

"No ma'am. You'll have to do that, or maybe you can get your attorney to talk to him for you. We'll give you the list of questionable transactions, and you or your attorney can go over each item with him. Who is your attorney?"

"Andrew Cagle."

"Would you like for us to call him?"

"No. I'll handle this myself. Can you take me home now?"

"Yes ma'am, we can take you home."

She went in the house and immediately brewed herself a cup of tea and sat in her chair and stewed about D.W. taking her money. She was furious with him, and at the same time, she was deeply hurt. She wished her husband was still there, so he could comfort her, but she had no friends or relatives and had to handle this on her own.

Later that week, D.W. got back, and the next day, after he returned, he went to see Coco. He rang her doorbell, and after a couple of minutes, she came to the door. As she opened the door, she glared at him, and he said in his charismatic way, "Hi, Coco. I'm glad to see you. Have you been okay while I've been gone?"

She didn't answer and turned and went into the living room and sat down in her chair. She looked at him and said, "Sit down, D.W."

He sensed that something was wrong, and in a second, she asked, "D.W., why have you been stealing from me? I've given you everything you wanted, and you didn't have to steal from me."

His heart was up in his throat, and he said, "I don't know what you mean. I haven't stolen from you. What do you mean?"

"Yes, you do. A man from the bank called and

sent a car for me and took me down there, the other day. I met with him and the vice president of the bank, and they showed me where some of my stocks have been sold and the money put in my checking account, and then withdrawn. The men also said some very large withdrawals have been made from my checking and money market accounts. I knew I didn't do it, and you're the only other person authorized to do it. Why did you do that, D.W.? I think I have been awfully good to you. If you had needed money, you could have asked me for it, and I probably would have given it to you. I'm deeply hurt by this and would just like to know why you did this to me. I'm going to call Andrew Cagle next week and have him cancel the Power of Attorney that you have, and the reason I didn't do it this week is because I wanted to talk to you and see what your reasons are as to why you did it, so tell me why, if you can."

D.W. tried his best to be convincing, and he said, "Coco, I haven't been stealing from you. You're right, I have been withdrawing funds, but I thought you wanted me to. Some of my friends have had some really bad luck, and you told me more than once to help them, and rather than bother you, I just took it upon myself to help them out. I didn't realize it amounted to so much, but I truly thought it was alright because of what you had told me. I'm sorry if I did wrong. I wouldn't intentionally hurt you for the world."

Coco said, "I don't recall telling you to help out

all those people, but if you say I did, then I guess I did."

He asked, "Am I forgiven," and she didn't answer, and then he asked, "Is there anything you want me to do while I'm here?"

She answered, curtly, "No, I don't need for you to do anything."

Then, he said, "You said you are going to Andrew Cagle's office next week. I'll check with you when you get an appointment, and I'll take you."

That time, she didn't say anything, and then he said, "Okay, Coco, I'm going to take off. I'm tired from traveling. I'll talk to you tomorrow or the next day. See ya," and he left.

He was upset, driving back to his apartment because he had had a good thing going, and now, unless he could somehow convince Coco that he didn't take her money, his golden goose was going to fly away. He had to think of something, and he had to do it before she went to Andrew Cagle's and had his Power of Attorney canceled.

The next day, Buddy was in town, and he went to the Steak & Shake for lunch. Like so many times before, he ran into D.W., and D.W. asked, "How's the Suburban running?"

"Like a dream," Buddy said. "I just got back from North Carolina, and it was such a pleasure to drive."

"That's great," and he didn't say anything else, and if Buddy said anything or asked a question, he would just answer with a one-word answer if he could. That was not like D.W., and Buddy noticed it. He asked, "D.W., are you alright?"

"Yeah, thank you for asking. I've just got a lot on my mind right now."

Buddy didn't want to pry, so he didn't say anything else, and when he got his food, he sat down, and when D.W. got his, he went to another table, instead of to Buddy's.

Buddy had never seen him that way. When he finished his lunch, he got up to leave, and D.W. was still sitting where he was. He caught D.W.'s eye and threw up his hand to wave goodbye, and D.W. didn't respond. After another ten to fifteen minutes, he got up and went back to the funeral home.

The funeral home business is most of the time, feast or famine. Several people may pass on at about the same time, and they are really busy, while days later, there are no deaths. That happened to be one of those times, and D.W. didn't have anything to do. He had some things on his mind, and he asked Bobby if he could leave early to take care of some personal business, and Bobby said he could.

When he got to his apartment, it was three in the afternoon, and after drinking a beer, he laid down and took a long nap, which was unheard of for him, but he was planning something for that night, and he needed to be very alert, thus the nap.

He knew Coco was going to take the Power of Attorney away from him, and he hoped he could do something to keep her from doing it. He came up with an idea and thought he would go to her house that night to see if he could convince her not to do it.

When he got to her house, all the lights were out, and he knew she had gone to bed, so he let himself in with the key she had given him. It was dark inside, but he knew every nook and cranny in the house, and he could do what he came to do in the dark. After a while, he was finished, and he let himself out and locked the door behind him.

D.W. checked in with Bobby the next morning, and asked him, "Bobby, do you have any new bodies in this morning?

Bobby said, "No, not yet. But there will probably be one or two come in today."

D.W. told him, I still have a few things to do this morning, and if we don't have anything new, this will be a good time to do them, don't you think?"

"Yeah, it will. What time do you think you will be in?"

"I should be there right after lunch. Is that alright?"

"Yeah, I'll see you then."

As soon as he got off the phone, he got in his car and headed for Coco's. He was convinced that he could get everything worked out, if he could just spend a couple of hours out there with her. She had some bills that were due, and he wrote checks for them while he was there. All in all, when he left, he felt good about what he had accomplished. Coco was not going to take the Power of Attorney away from him, now, and he was going to pick up where he left off before he went out of town.

He got back to work right after lunch, just as he had promised Bobby, and everything seemed to be the way it had always been. Two new bodies came in that morning, and D.W. was his old self, serving the families.

Buddy was out of town the first three days of the following week and got back on Thursday afternoon. He went to lunch at the Steak & Shake on Friday, and as what was getting to be a usual thing, he ran into D.W. Not knowing how to approach him because of the way he acted the last time he saw him, Buddy just said a simple, "Hi, D.W.," and surprisingly, D.W. said, "Buddy, I'm glad to see you. I want to apologize to you for the way I acted the last time I saw you, and I'd like to buy your lunch. I'll come back there and we'll order together, okay?"

Buddy said, "You don't have to do that. I should be buying your lunch."

"No, no. I want to," and he came back and stood with him, so they could order together. When they got their food, they sat together, and Buddy couldn't tell that there had ever been anything wrong with him.

On Tuesday, the following week, D.W. got a phone call at work. When he answered, the voice on the other end said, "Mr. Handy, this is Jerry Nelson, with Northwest Bank. How are you this morning?"

"I'm fine, thank you," his heart beating about a

hundred miles an hour.

"Mr. Handy, I'm trying to get in touch with Mrs. Coco Cochran, but I'm not having any luck reaching her by phone. I understand that you help her out with her business, and I thought you might be able to help me reach her. Can you help me?"

"No sir. I'm afraid I can't. She's out of town, and I don't have any idea how to reach her."

"Do you think she'll be calling you?"

"I doubt it, but if she does, I'll tell her you want to talk to her."

"Do you know where she is?" Jerry asked.

"No sir. All I know is that she said something about going to see an old friend in upstate New York."

"Do you know when she will be back?"

"No sir, I don't."

"I guess she flew, didn't she?"

"I think so. This old friend was going to send a plane to get her." Trying to be a little laid back, he said, "You know, these wealthy people hardly ever fly commercial."

"Well, thank you, Mr. Handy. I'll keep trying."

"I'm sorry I couldn't help," D.W. said. "If she gets back, and you still haven't talked to her, I'll ask her to call you."

Jerry didn't try to reach Coco anymore that week because he wanted to give her plenty of time with her friend in New York, but the week after that, he began trying to call her again. After two days, trying, he called D.W. again. "Mr. Handy, Jerry Nelson here. Have you heard from your friend, Coco, yet?"

"No sir, not a word."

"Okay, thank you."

When he didn't get anything from D.W., he went to John Easter. He said, "John, I don't know what's going on with the Coco Cochran thing. I've been trying for two or three weeks now, and I haven't been able to get hold of her. I've talked to D.W. Handy twice, and he says he doesn't know where she is or when she will be back. It doesn't make sense to me for someone that looks after someone else's business not to know where they are or when they will be where they can get in touch with them. From what I can find out, this Handy fellow is the one who has Mrs. Cochran's Power of Attorney."

John said, "It doesn't make sense, does it? Tell you what. Let's give it another week or so, and if she hasn't surfaced by then, we'll get the authorities involved."

Buddy hadn't talked to Billy in a good while, so he decided to call him one night to see what he was doing. When Billy answered, Buddy asked, "Whatta ya say, stranger? I haven't seen you in forever. You doing alright?"

"Yeah, I'm fine. I've been real busy. How are you doing?"

"Good. You knew that I went in with Sally Jo's daddy, didn't you?"

"Yeah, you told me at your wedding. How's that working out?"

"It's really good, and I'm doing exactly what I've always wanted to do. Are you and your dad building a lot?"

"We're covered up. I've been trying to do something on my own, but mine and Daddy's business is so good, I'm having a hard time doing anything on my own, plus, I did something that I may or may not regret."

"What's that?"

"Do you know where Rising Fawn is?"

"Yeah."

"Well, I bought a mountain in Rising Fawn, and I'm going to build Sylvia and me a house up there. I don't know if Sally Jo told you or not, but Sylvia's pregnant, and I'd like to have it finished by the time the baby is born."

"So you're gonna be a daddy."

"Yep, and I can't hardly wait. It's due in September, and I'm going to have to really bust my butt to get everything ready in time."

"Well, let me ask you this: Do you think you guys can find a night when we can go out and eat together?"

"I bet we can. When do you want to go?"

"How about Friday or Saturday night?"

"Saturday sounds good. I'll tell Sylvia to talk to Sally Jo about it at work, and we'll just plan on it."

"Okay, good," and they talked for a few more minutes before they hung up.

D.W. and Buddy ran into each other at lunch the

next day, and D.W. was complaining about how busy Coco was keeping him. Buddy said, "Maybe you should choose between working for her and the funeral home."

"I know, but you know what, Buddy? Coco is almost eighty years old, and of course, nobody knows how long they're going to live, but it just stands to reason thar she's not going to live as long as I am, and if she should die, then I'd be out of a job, and I have to work. Listen, would you and Sally Jo like to go out and eat with Jolene and I this weekend?"

"Sounds nice, but I'm afraid we can't. Billy wants us to eat out with him and Sylvia, and we're going Saturday. Sally Jo can't do it Friday because she has something she has to do, but can we have a raincheck?"

"Yeah, okay. We'll do it another time."

Sally Jo told Sylvia how much they enjoyed the Lighthouse Restaurant, so that's where they decided to go when they went out Saturday night.

Billy and Sylvia arrived at the restaurant before Buddy and Sally Jo, and they waited outside for them. When Buddy drove up in that big, beautiful Suburban, Billy was blown away. "When did you get that," Billy asked. "You must be selling thread by the ton."

"Do you like it," Buddy asked.

"Are you kidding? I love it. When did you get it?"

Buddy said, "A while back. Let's get a table and sit down, and I'll tell you all about it. You're not going to believe what I'm going to tell you."

"I can't wait to hear it."

Sylvia and Billy hadn't been there before, so it took them a couple of minutes to decide on what they wanted, and finally they were ready to order. After the waitress took their order, Sally Jo told Sylvia that they had been there a couple of times with D.W. and Jolene, and how much they liked the food and said some other things about D.W. and Jolene, and in a minute, Billy said, "Okay, Buddy, tell me what you were going to tell me that I'm not going to believe."

"Okay but hold on to your hat. I don't know if I told you, when I first decided to go in business with Sally Jo's daddy, that I felt like I needed a better car to travel in, since mine had so many miles on it. I looked everywhere but couldn't find what I wanted. The dealers either didn't have anything, or if they did have something, I couldn't afford it. I looked for a long time, but I never did find anything. Then, one night, Sally Jo and I met D.W. and Jolene out here, and when we were leaving to go home, D.W. said, "Come over here with me. I want to show you something," and when we got to where he was parked, the Suburban is what he had driven, and he said, "This is for you," and he handed me the keys and all the paperwork."

Billy said, "I can't believe what I'm hearing."

"I told you, you wouldn't believe it, but that's what happened."

"Had you and D.W. become best friends or something?"

"No, and that's the strange part of it. We see each other, maybe once a week at the Steak & Shake at lunch, and sometimes we sit together, and sometimes we don't, and that's the extent of my relationship with him, except for the two times the four of us have been out to eat. I've had it now, for four or five months, and the police haven't come to get it. I have the title showing me as the owner with nothing owed on it, so I guess Mr. D.W. gave me a wonderful gift. He says that Mrs. Cochran encourages him to do things for his friends, and I'm glad he counts me as one of them. Now, tell me about that mountain you bought. Is it a big mountain?"

"It's not a big mountain, like Lookout Mountain. It's really just a big hill, but they call it a mountain. It has two hundred and fifty acres, and about half of it is cleared. The other half is still in timber.

On the cleared part, there is a section of about thirty-five acres that overlooks a beautiful stream, and we're going to build a house on it. We're also going to build a small barn with two or three stalls and buy a couple or three horses. You know, Sylvia has had horses her whole life, so that won't be anything new to her. We're excited about it, and we can't wait to get started."

Buddy asked, "How big a house are you going to build?"

"Our plans say it will be thirty-eight hundred square feet. That's a big house, but if we have a handful of kids, it won't seem too big when they get here."

The food was delicious, as usual, and Billy and Sylvia really enjoyed it. They sat and talked for a long time after they finished eating, and finally, they got up to leave. Sylvia said, "We have really enjoyed this, and I hope we can do it again before long. We'd love for you to come see us, and Billy can take you to see our mountain."

Sally Jo responded, "We'd love to, and weren't those scallops the best you ever had?"

Billy and Buddy shook hands and hugged each other. They grew up as best friends, and the evening just reinforced those feelings. They hated to leave each other, but all good things must come to an end, and they finally said goodbye again and went to their cars.

On the way home, both couples talked about how much they enjoyed the evening and promised they would do it again soon.

It looked as if the following week was going to be an easy one for Joe and Buddy because they had really 'turned it on' the previous week, and their accounts were all booked up for the foreseeable future. Buddy was so aggressive that he felt guilty if he wasn't trying to open new accounts every spare minute, and he was trying to decide where he could go and who he could see that week, until Joe suggested that maybe he shouldn't travel that week and just do some work in the office. He suggested that maybe they could even take a couple of afternoons off.

Things weren't going to be like that for D.W. Handy. He had a funeral on Monday afternoon, and as part of his job, he had to look after the family until after the meal at the Church and other details. At last, he got away around five o'clock, and he went straight to Coco's. He wrote a couple of checks and paid some things online, and then, when he was through, he checked things in the house, including the kitchen and utility room. He left Coco's around six thirty and went home. When he got in bed, he remembered that he had forgotten something at Coco's and would have to go back out there the next morning.

Pearson's had another funeral the next afternoon, but he wasn't required to be there until about eleven o'clock, and he decided to go back to Coco's before he went to work the next morning.

He was going through some papers when the doorbell rang. Puzzled, he asked himself *I wonder who that is. Nobody knows I'm here.* He went to the door and a man in uniform said, "Good morning. I'd like to see Mrs. George Cochran. Is she here? I'm Deputy Tom Turner."

D.W. answered and said, "Nice to meet you. I'm D.W. Handy. No, Coco's not here. She's out of town, and I don't know when she'll be back. She has been gone for about three weeks now, so I don't think she'll be gone much longer."

The Deputy asked, "Do you know how she can be reached?"

D.W. said, "Northwest Bank must have sent you.

They've called a couple of times, and I've told them all I know. She's somewhere in upstate New York, and I have no idea where she is, other than she's at a friend's. Her friend's family sent their plane to pick her up, and that's all I know. If she calls or comes home, I'll be sure to have her call you."

"What are you doing here, Mr. Handy?"

"I'm paying bills and doing other paperwork."

"Do you normally do that when Mrs. Cochran is not at home?"

"Yes. Yes, I do. You see, I have her Power of Attorney, and she depends on me for just about everything having to do with her estate."

Very well. I won't disturb you any longer. If you see or hear from Mrs. Cochran, please be sure to have her get in touch with Mr. John Easter at Northwest Bank, but I've got to tell you: The bank is getting impatient, and Mr. Easter will press this matter as far as it will go, and we, at the Sheriff's Department will have no choice but to do what they say."

"Will do."

Deputy Turner's visit unnerved D.W., and he finished up what he was doing and headed for work at the funeral home. On the way, a million thoughts ran through his mind, and he didn't know exactly what to do. When he arrived at Pearson's, his demeanor did a hundred-and-eighty-degree turnaround, and he became the D.W. that everyone knew.

He wasn't bothered by the bank or the Sheriff's

Department for the rest of the week and into the first of the following week. Then, on Wednesday of the following week, he got a phone call from Deputy Turner. The Deputy said, "Good morning, Mr. Handy. Tom Turner here. Look, we have a search warrant for Mrs. Cochran's home, and we hate to damage it in any way, so would you be kind enough to meet us out there and let us in, so we won't have to break down the door?"

D.W. asked, "What do you have a search warrant for? There's nothing in her house that's out of order."

"I'm sure there's not, but the folks at Northwest Bank are very upset, and they insist on a search warrant."

"When do you want to meet me?"

"We're leaving the Sheriff's office now and will meet you when you get there, and oh yeah, be sure and bring the keys to the house."

D.W. was beside himself, and his hands were shaking so, that he could hardly get the keys in the ignition. Finally, he was on his way, and all the way out to Coco's, he wondered what they would be looking for. When he got to Coco's, there were three police cars parked out front. Deputy Turner greeted him and introduced him to his Sergeant, Jack Ramsey. They shook hands and Sergeant Ramsey said, "Mr. Handy, if you don't mind, unlock the door for us, and we'll get this over with."

There were six officers, and they divided up into pairs; one pair per room, and before they got started good, one of the officers asked, "Sergeant, what are we looking for?"

He answered, "I can't tell you exactly, but you'll know it when you find it," and they began to look at everything. They opened closets, dresser drawers, kitchen cabinets, and everything they came within sight of. Nothing suspicious was found, and then, as an afterthought, one of the officers opened the chest type freezer in the utility room. Everything looked normal, and then he began moving things around. All at once, when he moved a package of spinach, there was a face staring up at him.

He yelled for his Sergeant, and when the Sergeant got into the room where he was, he asked, "What is it?"

The officer said, "Look," and he called D.W. into the room. When D.W. got in there, he asked him, "Mr. Handy, do you know anything about this?"

D.W. looked at the face and said, "Oh my gosh. No sir, I don't know anything about this. I've been looking after her business as usual, and there have not been any unusual happenings. I thought she had been gone a long time, but I had no idea anything like this had happened. Oh my gosh," he said again.

Sergeant Ramsey called his office and told them what they found, and it wasn't long until two detectives came, and they called the coroner's office and asked someone from their department to come out there. They instructed a couple of deputies to unload the freezer while they waited on the coroner to get there. At last he got there along with a vehicle that looked like an ambulance, and he went straight into the utility room where Coco's corpse was lying on the floor in a puddle of thawed ice.

When the coroner left, and while the fingerprint people and forensic people were doing their work, Sergeant Ramsey told D.W. that he would have to go down to the Sheriff's office and answer some questions. D.W. couldn't stand to look at her any longer, so he went into another room, where a couple of deputies had also gone.

The coroner's office sent some forensic specialists along with a couple or three fingerprint specialists, and with all the experts doing their work, the house was pretty full. After the coroner had taken no telling how many pictures, his people loaded the corpse onto the vehicle they had brought and took her off. Soon, after they left with the body, Sergeant Ramsey came in to D.W. and asked," Are you ready to go to our office with us, Mr. Handy?"

"I'm ready," D.W. answered. Then he asked, "Can't you ask your questions here, so I can get to work when we finish?"

"No sir. We have to go to our office. You can go to work from there, if all goes well. We'll need to get your fingerprints when we get there, if you don't mind."

D.W. said, "I don't mind, and I'll tell you now; you're going to find my prints all over the place, along with Mrs. Cochran's because I have been working in here for months.

"Since you're voluntarily coming in, you can drive your car and just follow us. Hopefully, you won't be there too long.

At the Sheriff's office, everything went surprisingly well. The questions were pretty bland, and D.W. answered them all freely and without hesitation. He gave them his fingerprints, and then they let him leave, knowing that he would be called back after more investigating was done.

He felt pretty good when he left and was surprisingly upbeat, considering what had happened that morning; in fact, he called Jolene to see if she wanted to go out and eat with him that night.

The next day, still, no more contact with the Sheriff's Department, and D.W. felt a sense of relief. He went to the Steak & Shake for lunch, and as happened many times before, he ran into Buddy Russo. They sat together, and Buddy made sure to not ask any questions or make any comments about Coco Cochran. He would let D.W. initiate anything on that subject, and finally, he told him, "Buddy, I don't know if you've heard anything about Coco or not, but she's dead. Someone killed her, and I think the police think I did it. I spent all day, yesterday with them, and they said they'll more than likely call me back in at some point. They haven't accused me of anything yet, but I'm afraid they're going to.

His hunch was right on. Shortly, after he got back to the funeral home, he got a call from Sergeant

Ramsey. "Mr. Handy, do you own any firearms?"

"No sir, I don't."

"Okay. Thank you."

"You're welcome."

That afternoon, one of the investigators at Coco's house was moving the washer and dryer in the utility room in order to check the dirt and trash under them, and he found a 9mm shell casing. He carefully picked it up with a ballpoint pen and put it in a small plastic bag and marked it as evidence. Later, that afternoon, a latent print examiner went over the shell casing and found a partial print on it. They compared the print with those that D.W. had given, earlier, and they matched.

They contacted Judge Frank Reynolds, and he issued an arrest warrant for D.W. Two detectives went to the funeral home, but he had already left for the day. Then, they went to his apartment, and he wasn't there either, so they went back to the Sheriff's office and decided to wait until the next morning to arrest him.

Chapter Ten

Within just a few minutes after the got back to the office, it seemed as if every light and phone and all the electronic instruments lit up and went off. One of the machines indicated that Hans Von Steen was found dead at his home.

Detective Rutledge asked Detective Hill, "Do you know who that is?"

"Yeah, he was the new General Manager of Southern Mills. It looks like this is a city problem instead of the county."

"I thought Charles Nichols was the G.M. at Southern."

"He was for years, but he retired, and this Von Steen or Von Stein, or whatever his name replaced him."

Detective Hill said, "Unbelievable. How long has it been since we've had a homicide in Belmont County, and now, we've had two, right together. I'm glad the City police will have to handle this one instead of us, although I think the Cochran case will wind up pretty soon, since we have a fingerprint and know who's it is."

"I think you're right." answered Detective Rutledge. "I'm happy that this new one belongs to the city."

Joe had an appointment with Jordan Acker, the

cotton buyer at Southern, that morning, but before he left to go, he received a phone call from Peggy Shipley, Jordan's assistant, and she said, "Joe, Jordan asked me to call and tell you that he can't see you this morning. Mr. Von Steen was murdered, and everything around here is pure pandemonium. He said he will call you when he can."

"Hans was murdered? Before you hang up, Peggy, what happened?"

"I'm not really sure, but I heard that someone beat him with a baseball bat and stabbed him. The police are everywhere, and they are questioning several people."

"Peggy, if you find out anything, will you call me?"

"I will. I'm sure they're not going to tell me anything, but there will be a lot of talk going around. I'll let you know if I hear anything, Joe."

"Thanks, Peg. Talk to you later."

"Bye Joe."

Buddy was on the road, and Joe called him. "Buddy, I just got off the phone with Peggy Shipley, Jordan Acker's assistant, and she said somebody killed Hans Von Steen."

"What? When did that happen?"

"I'm not sure. She didn't say, but I guess over the weekend or this morning. She doesn't know anything other than he was killed, and she said she would call me whenever she finds out something."

"Man, that's a shocker. I didn't know him well,

but he seemed like a nice man. You had an appointment over there this morning, didn't you?"

"Yeah, that's why Peggy called. It'll probably be a few days before things get back to any kind of normal."

About two hours after Peggy first called Joe, she called him again. "Joe, hi. I still don't know anything, but I thought you'd like to know that the Police are going to hold a press conference at three o'clock this afternoon. Jordan's going to be there, and I thought you might want to come. Word is that Mr. Von Steen was beaten with a baseball bat and then butchered."

"Do they have any suspects, Peg?"

"I don't think so, but rumor has it that it might be one of his stepsons. You know, you can hear everything, but I don't think anybody knows at this point. The press conference might shed some information; I don't know."

"Where's it going to be, Peg?"

"Right outside Southern's main entrance. Do you think you'll be there? If you are, I may see you and can let you know about anymore rumors floating around."

"I'll try to be there. I'll look for you and Jordan."

"Okay. See ya, Joe."

Joe left early enough to get to Southern in plenty of time before the press conference. There were several people standing outside, and the group consisted of both press reporters and regular citizens. As time drew near for the conference, the speakers began filing in, and it was turning out to be a much bigger deal than Joe had originally thought. Not only was the Chief of Police of the City of Belmont and the Sheriff of Madison County there, but the mayor of the city of Belmont and the president of Southern Mills were also there.

President Wolfe opened the conference with a few words about Mr. Von Steen and what a tragedy his murder was, and then he turned the meeting over to Chief Shelton, the Chief of Police.

Chief Shelton began by saying, "This is truly a sad day for Belmont and Madison County. Last evening 911 received a call from someone identifying herself as Martha Von Steen, saying she and her husband, Hans Von Steen, were attacked in their home by an unknown assailant. She said she was injured, and she thought her husband was dead. Police and EMS were immediately dispatched to the Von Steen home where they found Mr. Hans Von Steen deceased and Mrs. Martha Von Steen wounded and bleeding. It appeared that Mr. Von Steen had been assaulted with a baseball bat and a knife with maybe a ten inch blade. Mrs. Von Steen had been attacked with the knife and was rushed to the hospital with critical injuries. No one has been arrested at this time and there are no suspects."

One of the reporters asked, "Chief Shelton, what time did this happen?"

"The 911 call was recorded at one forty-seven a.m. this morning."

Another reporter asked, "Were any other family members injured?"

"No. Mr. and Mrs. Von Steen were the only ones at home."

Another asked, "Do you know where the children were?"

Chief Shelton said, "They're hardly children anymore. The daughter and both sons are in college. As far as we know now, all three were at school when the attack occurred."

The same reporter asked, "Chief, there have been rumors that the younger son was a problem for his dad. Do you know anything about that?"

The Chief said, "I have no comment about anything at this time. This is an open investigation, and we're not going to comment on rumors. That's all I have to say right now, and we'll keep you updated from time to time as we make progress in the investigation."

He turned and began walking off the stage while two or three reporters asked questions that went ignored by the Chief.

When he returned to headquarters, he immediately called a meeting with the personnel that would be involved in the investigation of the attack on the Von Steens. He assigned Detectives Carl Mathis and Foy Luffman to be the lead detectives with Detective Mathis to be the head.

The group immediately began to gather and put together information and facts that they had, which was not much. Based on the comments and question that the reporter at the news conference had, Detective Mathis thought checking out that son would be a good place to start. One thing stood out: all three children's last name was Frye, meaning they must have been Han's stepchildren. It was late in the day, and their plans to investigate were made, so they called it a day and everybody went home.

The first thing Detectives Mathis and Luffman did the next morning was go to the hospital to see if Martha Von Steen was able to talk and possibly answer some questions. The hospital personnel didn't want to let them in to see her because of the seriousness of her injuries, but Detective Mathis insisted and asked to speak to her doctor. He impressed on him the importance of the investigation and finally was able to go in to see her.

She was awake when they went in, and Detective Mathis introduced himself as Carl and told her how sorry he was about her husband's death and her injuries and promised to be brief.

The first thing he did before asking any questions about the attack was to try to put her at ease. He asked, "Mrs. Von Steen, I see your name is Martha. May I call you that?"

She nodded, indicating that it was alright, and then he said, I hope you'll call me Carl. Detective sounds too formal. Will you do that?"

Again, she nodded yes.

Martha, did you recognize your attacker at all?"

She said, "No, I didn't."

"Was there anything that stood out about him, such as a tattoo or scar or anything else that could help him be identified. Was he wearing a hat or cap?"

She said no about the tattoos and scars, but she said yes, he was wearing a cap."

"Did his cap have any markings on it?"

"Yes, it had an Auburn logo on it."

"Do you remember what color his hair was?"

"Brown," she said.

"Okay, Martha. We won't bother you any more today. I hope you have as good a day as possible, and I also hope you have a speedy recovery. I'm going to leave my card on the table, here, and ask that you call me if you should think of anything else. Thank you for talking to us."

When they got outside the hospital, Carl said to Foy, "I think we need to talk to the children next. I feel sure they've been notified, don't you?"

"Surely somebody called them."

"Do you have any idea where they will be staying? I doubt they'll be at home since home is a crime scene."

Foy said, "I don't have the answer to any of that. Maybe we need to go back to the office and see if anybody knows."

"Good idea. Let's do that."

Not really knowing who to ask when they got back, they went to Deputy Chief Virgil Gaines. Carl asked, "Chief, I guess the Von Steen kids have been notified about their parents, haven't they?"

"Yeah, Chaplain Stone called them."

"Do you know where they are staying?"

"I think they're staying with Charles Nichols. You know, he had Von Steen's job before he retired, and I think he got kind of close to their kids before he quit working."

Carl asked Foy, "Do we know anything about those kids?"

"Only that they're all in college. Two are supposed to be good kids, but it's rumored that one of the boys caused major problems for his mother and daddy."

"Let's go talk to 'em."

They looked up Charles Nichols' address and drove over there. When they got there, all three of the Von Steen's children were there. They wanted to talk to each of them, separately, so Carl asked Mary if she would mind if he asked her some questions on the front porch. She agreed, and they went out and sat down.

He began by saying, "Miss Von Steen…"

She interrupted him and said, "Detective, my name is Frye; not Von Steen."

"I'm very sorry. Now, Miss Frye, you go to Jacksonville State, don't you?"

"Yes sir."

"Are things going well for you? Do you have any problems?"

"Yes sir, things are going very well, and I don't

have any problems, other than missing my mother."

"Are you two very close?"

"Yes sir, very close."

"Have you ever had any problems with your stepfather?"

"No sir. He became my father the minute my mother married him, and I loved him dearly. I never had any problems with him."

"Okay, Mary. That will do for today. I'm very sorry about the loss of your father."

As she was going in the house, Carl said, "Mary, would you please ask David to come out?"

In a minute, David came out on the porch, and he held out his hand to shake hands with Carl and Foy. That was a pleasant surprise to the detectives, and Carl asked him to sit down.

He said to David, "You're at the University of Alabama, aren't you, David?"

"Yes sir, I am."

"What are you studying for?"

"Civil Engineering. I'm in graduate school now, and I hope to graduate with a master's degree in the spring."

"Good boy. David, I'm very sorry about your stepfather's death. Were you close?"

"Very close. Hans supported me in everything I tried to do. I was little when my mother and daddy divorced, and I still remember how cruel and mean my daddy was. He abused my mother and as the oldest, I took whippings for everything, even though most of the time I hadn't done anything. Sometimes he would hit me with his fist, and I remember one time, I went to school with a blackeye, and all the other kids teased me. It was awful, Detective Mathis, and I remember how relieved I was when my mother finally left him. Then, a few years later, when she met Hans, and they got married, my sister and brother and I were so happy. Hans treated us as if we were his own children, and we had never been treated that way. He encouraged us to be the best we could be, and my sister and I thrived on his praise. We tried to be as perfect as we could because we didn't want to disappoint him."

"You said your sister and you. How about your brother?"

"Freddy never gave him a chance to be his father. From the gitgo, he rebelled at everything, no matter how hard Hans tried to please him, and he made it hard on our mother."

"Did he pay your tuition to college, or did your real father do that?"

"Hans did. Mother wanted to try and make our daddy do it, but Hans insisted that he do it. He said if he was going to be our father, he wanted to be like a real father. He told mother that he loved us and wanted to be the one to send us to college."

"David, did you ever have any problems with Hans?"

"No sir. Never. He could not have been a more loving father, and I'm going to miss him terribly. I sure hope you catch the monster that killed him."

Carl said, "We will. It may take a little while, but we'll get him. Thanks for talking to us, David. Now, would you ask your brother to come out and talk to us?"

Freddy came out and Carl held out his hand to him, and said, "I'm Detective Mathis, and this is Detective Luffman."

Freddy ignored the gesture and sat down in one of the porch chairs. He rubbed Carl the wrong way from the beginning, but he didn't let on. He said, "You're at Auburn, aren't you, Freddy?"

Trying to be funny, he said, "Yeah, I'm a regular War Eagle."

"A War Eagle, hunh? Are you pretty much involved with a lot of school activities?"

"Nah, just about everything down there is made up with a bunch of nerds, and I don't like nerds."

"I guess that means you're not in a fraternity or any clubs, doesn't it?"

"Yeah, there's a group of us that get together and just do our thing."

"What kind of thing?"

"Oh nothing. You wouldn't understand if I told you."

Carl said, "Try me. I'm smarter than I look. Tell me what kind of things you and your friends do. Do they involve any kind of drugs?"

"No."

"Alcohol?"

"No."

"What then?"

"Nothing. Absolutely nothing."

Carl then said, "Okay, then. Let's go to something else. Freddy, what kind of relationship did you have with your stepfather?"

"We didn't really have what you call a relationship. I did my thing, and he did his."

"Didn't he pay for your education at Auburn? I'd call that a relationship, wouldn't you?"

"I'd call it an obligation. He was obligated to send me to college because he was married to my mother. That's all. He didn't care anything about me."

"Did you care about him?"

"Not really."

"We talked to your brother and sister, and they both said they loved him a lot and felt like he was their real daddy and truly loved him. You don't feel that way?"

"No. All he did was find fault with everything I did. How can you love somebody like that?"

"Okay, Freddy. That will be all for right now. Be sure and leave your contact numbers because we will more than likely want to talk to you some more. Have a good day."

Freddy said, "Thanks. It's already a good day," and he walked back into the house.

Carl asked Foy, "Can you believe there are people like that in the world?"

Foy answered, "I guess it takes all kinds."

Carl said, "When I was in college, we had what was called Faculty Advisors, who sort of kept track of the students assigned to them. Do you think Auburn would have Faculty Advisors? I think I'll see because I would like to talk to him or her. He took out his cell phone and called Police headquarters. When someone answered on the other end, he said, "Elizabeth, hi. This is Carl. I'd like for you to do something for me. How about calling Auburn University and find out if they have Faculty Advisors. If they do, then find out who the advisor is for a Fred or Freddy Frye. If you're successful, ask to talk to him and set up an appointment for Foy and I to come see him ASAP. If he asks why, tell him it has to do with a homicide investigation in Belmont. We can go down there as soon as tomorrow, if he will talk to us. Call me back and let me know the details, okay? Thanks, Sweetie. Talk to you later."

It was almost lunch time, and they decided to go to the Sandwich Shack to get one of their famous treats. Carl ordered a Reuben while Foy ordered a spicy chicken all the way.

Sitting at one of the small tables, they discussed their interviews with the Frye children that morning, and Carl said, "You know, Foy, I had a good feeling about Mary and David and their love for their stepdad, but red flags began waving when we got to Freddy. What did you think?"

"I felt the same way. I don't know if he actually did the deed, but I won't be at all surprised if we find out that he was involved in some way.

After lunch, they were kind of at loose ends. They had already talked to Mrs. Von Steen, one of the victims, and her two sons and daughter, and it looked as if the next step was to talk to Freddy Frye's Faculty Advisor at Auburn University, and there was no appointment for that as yet, so they went back to their office.

When they walked in the office, Elizabeth Farmer, the one Carl had asked to find out about the Faculty Advisor, saw them come in and called out to Carl. He turned and said, "Elizabeth, you're just the one I want to see. Were you able to find out about a Faculty Advisor for Freddy Frye at Auburn?"

"I was and his name is Brad Lambert. He said to call him, and he would be glad to talk to you and would be happy to have you come to his office. Here's his private number and address."

"Elizabeth, what would we do without you? Thanks for this. I'll call Mr. Lambert right now."

He called the number Elizabeth gave him, and Brad Lambert answered. "Mr. Lambert, this is Detective Carl Mathis with the Belmont Police Department. How are you today?"

"I'm fine, Detective. What can I do for you?"

"Mr. Lambert, we're investigating a homicide here in Belmont, and one of your students is a person of interest to us. If my partner and I come to Auburn, would you be open to see and talk to us?"

"Detective, do you mind telling me the student's name?"

"It's Fred Frye. You know him, don't you?"

"Oh yes. I know Fred. Why am I not surprised that the police are interested in him? When do you want to come, Detective?"

"When would be good for you? We can come down as soon as tomorrow or whenever you prefer."

"Tomorrow will be fine. What time?"

"Well, I looked on the computer, and it shows that you're a little over two hundred miles and about three and a half hours from here. We could be there shortly after noon, if that would work for you."

"That would be perfect. Tell you what. If you can get here around one o'clock, I'll take you and your partner to lunch at the Faculty Club, here at the University."

"That sounds great. Can you give me directions after we get into the town of Auburn?"

"I can," and he gave him detailed directions on how to find his office.

"Thanks a million, Mr. Lambert. We'll see you around one tomorrow and my name is Carl. My partner is Foy. We'll see you then."

"Great, and my name is Brad. I hope you'll call me that. See ya tomorrow."

Carl and Foy met the next morning at eight o'clock at the Police station for their drive to Auburn. They knew it wouldn't take five hours, but they wanted to have plenty of time to take a leisurely coffee break and maybe take a tour of the campus when they got there.

Their plans worked out perfectly, and at twelve forty-five they found themselves in front of Brad Lambert's building. They went in and when they got to Brad's office, he was waiting on them, and they left immediately for the Faculty Club for lunch.

The Faculty Club was a very rich-looking place, with dark paneling and expensive looking furniture. They were shown to a table and given menus. Carl asked Brad for suggestions, and when the waiter came back, they all ordered. Brad knew why the Detectives had driven down, as did the Detectives, of course, but Fred Frye and the investigation were not even mentioned during lunch. Instead, the conversation was almost exclusively about War Eagle football and how they were going to put it to the Alabama Crimson Tide in their upcoming game.

Finally, when Brad was sure he had convinced the Detectives that Auburn was going to beat Alabama, he said, "Well gentlemen, this has been very nice, but I know you didn't drive four hours to hear me talk about Auburn football, so if you're ready, we'll go to my office and talk about why you really came down today.

After each of them had used the restroom, they sat down to talk. Brad started the conversation by saying, "You said you are conducting a homicide investigation, and you want to talk to me about Fred Frye. What does one have to do with the other, Carl?"

"I don't know if you've heard or not, but Fred's stepfather, Hans Von Steen, was murdered three days ago. We don't have any suspect as yet, but we have interviewed the family, and when we got to Fred or Freddy as he goes by, he was very hostile. His brother and sister loved their stepfather deeply, but there was a marked contrast when we talked to Freddy. His attitude raised a red flag with us, and we thought we needed to find out some more about this guy, and we hope you can shed some light on his life here at school."

"I had not heard about his stepfather, but knowing how Fred is, I can understand why you would want to investigate him. It's kind of funny that you would call me about him because I had his file in front of me when you called. We have had some serious questions about him and his activities for some time, and he has been on the verge of flunking out. We think because of his friends and their way of life here at Auburn."

"What kind of activities, Brad?"

"Drinking and Drugs for starters, and then there's Demons and Dragons. Those are the three things that take up most of his time. I talked to Mr. Von Steen recently, and he told me he had had a conversation with Fred and had threatened to cut him off without a penny if he flunked out and didn't get his act together. As I mentioned, he is on the verge of flunking out of school."

Carl said, "You mentioned Dungeons and Dragons. What is that? It doesn't sound like something very nice."

"I really don't know much about it. From what I hear, the creators of the game intended for it to be fun, but it has developed into something sinister and in some cases evil. I think each player has to decide on the character he or she wants to be and what race, and I don't know what all. I hear the instruction book costs about seventy-five dollars, and then deciding what character you want to be is complicated. It's my understanding that there are books on selecting characters that run twenty-five to about fifty dollars and some over a hundred, so you see, if somebody wants to really get into the game, they can drop several hundred dollars. I think most people, such as Fred Frye, decide to be wizards or witches or evil beings, and evil activities go along with their characters."

Foy asked, "Do you know who some of the others in the group are?"

"I know who three are, definitely, and I'm pretty sure about a few more, but I don't know who the others are for sure."

Carl asked, "Brad, could we get the names of the ones you know, and any others outside Dungeons and Dragons that may be connected to Fred?"

"Let me give you the names of the ones I know for sure that are friends of Fred, but I hate to give you any other names because I don't know for sure that they are connected to him. Could I do thar?"

"Yes sir. Give us the names you know for sure, but we may have to come back for others later if these don't work out."

"Okay. There are three, plus Fred, that I think you should be interested in. Their names are Nick Webster, and Nick lives in Huntsville. Bookie Adams, and he lives in Florence, and finally, there's Luke Sanders, and he lives in Belmont. Between those four, you've got a dark group of people. I wouldn't be surprised at anything they do."

Carl said, "Okay, Brad. Thank you. We'll be in touch, and thanks for lunch. It was delicious."

Brad said, "It was nice meeting you gentlemen. If I can do anything else for you, please let me know. Have a safe trip back to Belmont."

On the way back, they talked about what Brad had told them, and Carl said, "Foy, the more Brad talked, the surer I was that Freddy had something to do with his dad's death."

"I feel the same way. I don't know what you're thinking, but I think we should talk to Mary and David Frye again to see if they can shed some light on Freddy's friends."

"We'll try to see them either before or after the funeral."

"Yeah, we definitely need to see them before they go back to school."

The next morning, when they got to the office, they sat down with the Chief of Detectives and went over everything they talked about at Auburn the day before.

Carl said, "Chief, since two of the boys live out of town, how can we require them to meet with us so we can talk to them?"

"Well, you might have to go back to Auburn and talk to them while they're at school. You said one of them lives here, so you can call him in here whenever you need to, but if he's at school, and you go to Auburn to talk to the others, you can talk to him down there when you see the other two. What are your plans now?"

Foy said, "We want to see the Von Steen children again before they leave to go back to school, to see if we can get some information about their brother's friends. By the way, Chief, what do you know about the Dungeons and Dragons game?"

"Dungeons and Dragons? I don't know anything except I think it's full of witches, wizards, and goblins. Why?"

"Because Freddy and his friends are deep into it."

When their meeting with the Chief was over, Carl called David Frye and told him he and Foy would like to come by and talk to him and Mary again. David said, "Detective, we will be glad to meet with you, but we can't this morning; we're going to town to buy something to wear to the funeral."

"Is Freddy going with y'all?"

"No sir. Freddy just does his own thing."

"David, are y'all going to Beltown Mall?"

"Yes sir, among other places."

"Well, what if we meet you at the food court in the mall at whatever time you say?"

"That will be good. We're planning to eat lunch there, anyway."

"Do you know where?"

"Probably at Chick Fil A. Will that be alright?"

"That will be perfect. We don't want to interrupt your lunch, so give me a time, and we'll be there."

How about if you come at one o'clock?"

"Again, that will be perfect. We'll see you at one."

Carl said, "Foy, we have plenty of time before we have to meet the Frye kids, so I think I would like to make a courtesy call on their mother. You want to go?"

"No, I don't think so. I think I'll go get a haircut. My wife says I look like something animal control will pick up."

"You don't look that bad."

"Maybe not, but I don't want to take a chance. You want to meet back here at, say twelve forty-five?"

"That will be good. I'll see you then."

He went to the hospital and took the elevator up to the fourth floor where Mrs. Von Steen was a patient. She was surprised when he walked in and acted as though she was truly glad to see him.

"Good morning, Mrs. Von Steen. How are you this morning?"

"Good morning, Detective. It's good to see you. I'm really sore, but I think I feel a lot better. Have you caught the person who attacked Hans and me?"

"No ma'am, not yet, but we're working hard to find him or them. Don't worry. We'll get him. Have the doctors said how long you will be in here?"

"Not for sure, but they hinted that I might be here for at least another week. I can hardly wait to get home and sleep in my own bed again and get something good to eat."

Kidding, Carl said, "Surely you'd rather stay here and eat this good hospital food. You'll have to have someone stay with you when you get home, won't you?"

"They say I will. I guess I'll have to get a home healthcare nurse to come in and take care of me, at least in the beginning."

Carl stayed for another twenty or twenty-five minutes, and they talked about several things, finally, he said, "Well, Mrs. Von Steen, I need to go. I have to meet my partner, and then we have to see some people this afternoon. It was great seeing you, and I'm really glad that you're doing better. I'll try to stop in again."

"Thank you, Detective. I appreciate you coming to see me."

"I was happy to do it, and will you please call me Carl? Detective sounds so formal."

"I'll call you Carl if you'll call me Martha. I don't like to be called Mrs. Von Steen."

"Okay, Martha. It's a deal. I'll see you again soon."

"I hope so. Goodbye."

Both Carl and Martha were glad he made the visit. He told himself that he would do it again within the next few days, and Martha told herself that she hoped he would come back real soon.

He got back to the police station at twelve thirty, and Foy wasn't there yet, so he went to some of the different desks and visited with various detectives and others.

When Foy got there, they left immediately for Beltown Mall. They didn't want to be late because David and Mary could leave if they weren't there because it was going to be such an informal meeting.

Since they were in an official car, they could park pretty much anywhere they wanted, so they pulled up to a place that was reserved for police vehicles. It was right at twelve forty-five when they got there, so they hurried to the food court to meet David and Mary.

They were just finishing eating when Carl and Foy got there, and after the greetings, the detectives sat down.

Carl led off by saying, "I went by to see your mother before I came to meet you, and she seems to be doing better. She said she's real sore."

David said, "I'm sure she is. You'd have to be sore if you got cut the way she did."

Carl said, "I'm sure of that. Look, Guys, we just wanted to talk to you again to see if you might have recollected anything you may have missed when we talked to you before."

David said, "I can't think if anything," and Mary said, "Me neither."

"Well, let me ask you this. Are you familiar with any of these?" And he read out the names, "Nick

Webster, Bookie Adams, and Luke Sanders."

Mary said, "Those are friends of Freddy's."

"Do you know them?"

"Not really. I've only seen them once; when they came by the house to pick up something for Freddy."

"When was that? Do you remember?"

"Yes sir. It was last weekend."

"Last weekend? Were you home?"

"Yes sir. I go to Jacksonville State, so I'm not too far, and I come home most weekends."

"When they came to your house, did they all come?"

"Yes sir."

"Did they all come in?"

"No sir, just Luke Sanders."

"What did they pick up?"

"Some sort of video machine."

"Do either of you know any of those guys?"

They both said they did not.

Carl asked, "Can you describe what they looked like?"

Mary said, "Two of them stayed in the car, and the one who came to our door was unbelievably weird looking. He was skinny as a rail and had long hair. There were earrings everywhere, including his cheek, and he was nearly a hundred percent tattooed. He had on a black t-shirt, and tattoos protruded through the neck up into his neck. I don't know how his parents could permit all that."

"Do you happen to know where they live?"

"No sir, but the one who came to our house, the one named Luke, lives here in Belmont. I know because my mother asked him where he lived."

"Let me ask you this. Do either of you have a hunch or a feeling of who could have killed you dad and injured your mother?"

David said, "No sir. I don't, and I don't believe Mary has any idea, but the people you're asking us about could certainly have done it. Our brother, Freddy, and his friends were of the mindset that would let any of them do such a thing. I wish we could help you, but we weren't there and don't know what we can do. I would sure hate to think our brother could do such a thing, but I just don't know."

"Well, thank you both for talking with us, and we assure you, we're not going to stop until we find your dad's killer."

David and Mary both thanked the Detectives and continued on their shopping trip.

Carl said, "Foy, I think we need to go back to Auburn and talk to all four of those guys. Let's go to the station and call Brad and ask him to help us get them in for questioning."

They still had no proof, but they felt strongly that one or more of Freddy's friends did the attack on Freddy's dad and mother, and while the distance between them and their suspects was very inconvenient, it wasn't going to stop them from pursuing their investigation. As soon as they returned to their office, Carl grabbed the phone and called Brad Lambert.

When Brad answered, Carl said, "Brad, Carl Mathis. How ya doing?"

"I'm fine Carl. What can I do for you today?"

"I need to ask another favor if I may."

"Sure. What do you need?"

Well, if you remember, when we were down there the other day, you told us about some friends that Fred Frye has, and how they're into drugs, Dungeons and Dragons, and no telling what else. Well, at this point, we can't pin the attack on Fred's parents on any of them, but we do have reason to want to talk to each of them, and we're wondering if you would be willing to let us talk to them in your little conference room. We can do it at the Police Dept. if you'd rather not, but we thought it would be better if we could do it while they're at school. I thought that if you could call them in, one at a time, we could talk to them, and if possible get each of their permission to search their car. We can get a warrant, if necessary, but we'd rather just get their permission. I know this is an imposition on you, but the Von Steens didn't deserve what was done to them, and hopefully, this will really help. Are you willing to do this?"

"Absolutely. What do I need to do first?"

"We think it will take forty five minutes to an hour to talk to each of them, so if you could check their schedules and let us know when you think would be the best time for us to come, we'll appreciate it. You might not need to include Fred in it because he may still be at home, and if he is, we'll see him up here, but if he's back at Auburn, we'll want to talk to him."

"Carl, of course you can question the boys down here, but can you give me 'til tomorrow to set up times?"

"Yeah, that'll be fine. Just let me know. If we could do it the following day, it would be good, and if we have to stay overnight, we can do that, too. Just let me know."

"Okay, Friend. I'll be in touch."

"Thanks a million, Brad. See ya."

Chapter Eleven

The next day, Brad called Carl and said, "Good morning. I've gone over the class schedules for the four guys, and it looks as if Friday will be the best time for you to come down. That way, they'll all have classes, and I can call each one of them out as I need to. That way, none of them will know that I've called any of the others out, at least they won't know why I've called the others. I'm sure even if they do know, it won't be a surprise because they have all been called in here before. Sorry I can't have lunch with you, but I have an eleven o'clock meeting that will run into lunch, but I should be back in my office by one o'clock, so why don't you guys get here around one or one thirty?"

"Great. We'll see you Friday and thanks."

The two detectives did almost exactly the way they did on their first trip to Auburn, only on the second trip, they allowed for time to eat lunch before they got to Brad's office. Their timing was good, and they arrived at Brad's around one fifteen. When Brad came in, he and the detectives talked for a few minutes, and then he called for Luke Sanders to come to his office.

When Luke got to Brad's office, the detectives were shocked at his appearance. They didn't know why they were shocked because Mary Frye had told them how he looked, but to see him in person was something else.

Brad introduced him to Carl and Foy, and both detectives offered their hands, but Luke ignored the gesture and said, "What's up man?"

Carl began the questioning by saying, "Luke, Freddy Frye's father was murdered last weekend, and his mother was stabbed and cut real bad. Did you know about that?"

"Yeah, man. I heard about it."

"Weren't you in Belmont last weekend?"

"Yeah, man. I was there."

Carl said, "Luke, my name is not man, so I would appreciate it if you would call me Detective, Mr. Mathis, or Carl but not man. Got that?"

"Got it, man."

Carl gave him a look that would melt an iceberg and then asked, "Where were you last Sunday night?"

"I was with my buddies, man. We went to a club and drank beer 'til they closed on us."

"Who was with you?"

"Freddy, Nick, and Bookie."

"Didn't you go by Freddy's house Sunday night?"

"No, man. We were at a club, drinking beer."

"Was Freddy with you when you went to his house?"

"I told you, man, we didn't go by there."

"We were told that you went by to pick up something for Freddy. Is that not right? Freddy's sister said you came by. Which one of you is lying?"

"You said Sunday night?"

"Yes."

"I forgot. Maybe we did go by there."

"Luke, did you have any part in the attacks on Freddy's parents?

"No, man. I didn't have no part in that."

"Luke, is your car parked close by?"

"Yeah, it's pretty close. Why?"

"We'd like to look in it."

"No. man. Ain't nobody going through my ride."

Carl grinned and said, "Well, man. If you won't let us, we'll call the police and get a warrant. It'll be easier if you just give us permission, so which is it, man? You give us permission or we ger a warrant?"

"Alright, you can look in it."

"You're smart. Now, show us where it is," and the three of them walked about a block to a car that was not much better looking than Luke was. Carl looked in the front, and Foy looked in the back, and in addition to a lot of trash, they didn't find anything incriminating. They walked back to Brad's office, and Carl said, "Thanks, man. You can go back to class now. We'll call you if we need you again. Okay man?"

Next, they had Brad call Nick Webster. Nick was a fairly nice-looking young man, and he was dressed just like all the other students they saw. One thing the detectives noticed were his manners. He seemed to have some. Carl asked him basically the same questions he asked Luke, and he got pretty much the same answers, except in a more civilized way. He readily agreed to let them search his car, and overall, their experience with him was very pleasant. When they got back to Brad's office, and they told him he was free to go, he shook both their hands before he left them.

Finally, Brad called Bookie Adams, and Bookie was a little like a cross between Luke and Nick. Like Nick, he exhibited good manners, but he also used profanity when he answered their questions. Carl said, "Bookie, Fred Frye's parents were attacked last weekend, and his dad was killed, and his mother seriously injured. Did you know that?"

"Yes sir. I heard about it."

"Did you have anything to do with the attack, Bookie?"

"No, I didn't even know about it 'til later."

"What did you do Sunday night?"

"We went to a club or you might call it a beer joint and drank beer 'til they closed."

"Who's we?"

"My friends, Luke, and Nick."

"Did Freddy go with you?"

"No."

"Why didn't he go with you?"

"Well, at first we were going to Freddy's to pick up a video machine that he wanted, and then he decided he didn't want to go because he knew his dad would be there, and he didn't want to see him."

"He didn't want to see his dad?"

"No sir. He said he didn't want to go see that son-of-a-bitch. His words. He said his dad didn't like him, and they didn't get along. He got upset when he thought we were going, and he put up a fuss. Finally, we decided that we would go somewhere and drink beer, and he said he didn't want to go, so we dropped him off at Luke's, since we were pretty close to his place.'"

"Where was Freddy's car?"

"At Auburn. We all came up here in Bookie's car."

"Did you do any drugs that night?"

Bookie paused and didn't say anything for a minute, then said, "We might have smoked a few joints."

"Any other kinds of drugs?"

"No sir."

"Did all of you smoke weed?"

"Yes sir."

"Where else did you go?"

"Nowhere."

"Are you sure you didn't go out to Freddy's?"

"I'm sure."

"Did Freddy ever go out there that weekend?"

"I don't think so."

"Bookie, did you drive to the club?"

"Yeah, I drove."

"Listen, we need to see your car. Are you parked pretty close?"

"Yeah, down in the next block."

"Will you walk us down there?"

"Why do you need to see my car? It's my private property."

"We're not going to do anything to it. We just need to see it and go through it."

"What if I don't want you to go through it?"

"You can either give us permission or we can go get a warrant. Either way, you don't have a choice. It'll be a lot easier if you just walk us to it and let us look at it. Now, which is it going to be?"

"Okay. I'll show you the car." They walked to almost where Nick was parked, and Bookie gave them the keys. As before, Carl went through the front seat, and Foy went through the back. This time, when Carl opened the glove compartment, lying on top of some other papers was a hand drawn map. He said, "Foy, look here," and he showed him the map. They both looked at it carefully, and Foy said in a low voice, "Carl, this is a map showing how to get to the Von Steen's house," and before they put it in a bag, they asked Bookie, "Bookie, what's this map of?"

"It's a map of how to get to this girl's house that I was going to see."

"I know you don't live in Belmont. Who drew the map for you?"

"A friend of mine."

"Was it Freddy? It looks like a map to his house."

"No, it's to a girl's house named Joan, and I don't remember who drew it."

"Okay, we'll let that go for now."

Then they opened the trunk, and the first thing they saw was a baseball bat. Examining the bat carefully, they noticed some dark reddish-brown stains on it, and they immediately laid it back down. Continuing on through the trunk, they picked up some clothes that were lying on the right-hand side, and when they picked them up, a large GVDV hunting knife fell out. The detectives looked at each other, and Carl told Foy, "We had better call the Auburn Police and have them come out here."

He told Bookie to stay right there, and he told Foy to watch him. He told his cell phone to call the Auburn Police Dept., and when someone answered, he identified himself and asked to speak to a detective. In a minute, a voice said, "This is Detective Hill. May I help you?"

Carl said, "Detective Hill, this is Detective Carl Mathis with the Belmont Police Department. My partner and I are here in Auburn, questioning some suspects in a homicide that happened last weekend in Belmont. We think we might have found the murder weapons, and we wanted to notify your department, and ask that you send someone out here. We have one of the suspects here with us, and we know where the others are." He gave Detective Hill the information where he was and asked, "Can we expect someone shortly?"

Detective Hill said, "Yes sir. I'll relay this to our Chief of Detectives, and someone should be out there in just a few minutes."

It only took about five minutes for the Auburn police to get there. Two officers were in the car; Detective Hill and Officer Cox. Carl told them what happened to the Von Steens the week before, and then he showed them what he and Foy had found. It was very convincing, and Detective Hill asked Carl what they were going to do.

Carl said, "What we would like to do is arrest this man here and take him back to Belmont with us. We talked to the other two suspects a little while ago, and if they haven't left school yet, we'll arrest them and ask that you keep them in your jail until we can get someone down here to pick them up. Will that work for you?"

"It sure will. If you would like, if the other two have left school and gone somewhere else, we can help you find them."

"That would be wonderful," Foy said.

Carl said, "If they're still at school, we can arrest them in just a few minutes. Could you guys stay here for a little bit 'til we can get back up to the Faculty Advisors office and have him call them to come to his office? On second thought, it might be best if we had a couple of uniformed officers there when we arrest them, just in case they try to get cute."

"Yes sir. I'll call for some uniforms and we'll wait here with this guy until you get the other two."

He radioed his dept and told them he needed backup at the university, and he gave them the pinpoint address. It wasn't but four to five minutes before two officers arrived and went into Brad's office with Carl, Foy, and Detective Hill.

When they got inside the office, Carl asked Brad to call Luke and Nick into his office. They were shocked when they walked into the office and saw the police, and Carl told them, "You're both under arrest. You have the right to remain silent. Anything you say can and will be used against you in a court of law. You have the right to an attorney, and if you can't afford one, one will be appointed for you. Do either of you have any questions?"

Nick asked, as he was being handcuffed, "What are we being arrested for?"

Carl said, "For the murder to Hans Von Steen and the attempted murder of Martha Von Steen."

Nick said, "I didn't murder anybody. I don't even know the Von Steens. You're making a huge mistake."

Luke didn't say anything, and Carl, being a little sarcastic asked him, "Do you have any questions, man?"

He still didn't say anything."

Brad was about as shocked as Nick and Luke were, and he was so stunned, he didn't say anything. Carl told him, "Brad, sorry to completely disrupt your day, but this had to be done. Let us get these guys on their way to jail, and Foy and I will come back and talk to you, if you're going to be here for a little while longer."

Brad said, "Go ahead. I'll be here for quite a while."

The officers and detectives took the guys down to meet Bookie and the other policeman, and then they handcuffed him, told him he was under arrest, and read him his rights. Carl asked Foy, "What would you think if we keep all three of these guys together instead of taking Bookie back to Belmont with us?"

"I think that would be good. That way, we won't have to worry with him. Let's do that."

Detective Hill called for a vehicle to take the three to jail.

Carl and Foy worked out a plan for the Belmont Police to come down and get the three prisoners, and then they went back up to Brad's office to thank him for his help and to explain everything to him."

Walking into his office, he was looking at notes he had made about previous encounters he had had with the three suspects. He looked up when they came in and asked, "Did you get those three in jail?"

Carl said, "They're in jail, and I'd say for a long, long time. Brad, we want to thank you again for your help. You made this job much easier for us."

Brad asked, "What happens now?"

Carl asked, "Before I answer you, is Fred Frye back in school yet?"

Brad checked with Freddy's professor and was told that he hadn't come back yet.

"Okay," Carl said. "Now to answer your question, the suspects are going to be taken back to Belmont, where they'll be in jail until their arraignment. At the arraignment, the charges against them will be presented. The judge will read the charges against each man, and a plea will be asked for. Their lawyer or a lawyer appointed by the court should be there to represent them. The defense lawyer will confer with the prosecutor to determine if bail will be allowed, and that's the time for plea negotiations to take place. If there is no plea deal or bail, then the suspects will remain in jail until their trial."

"Will they be tried together?" Brad asked.

"I doubt it. Each of the four could, in my opinion, face different charges. I'm guessing that each one will be tried separately, but you never know what the courts are going to do."

"Should I call their parents?" Brad asked.

"Not unless you want to," Carl said. "They can make a phone call from jail, and I feel sure each one will call their parents, but if you would feel better calling them, I have no objection. I'll tell you, Brad, this whole situation stinks, and while I don't think Freddy Frye had much to do with his father's actual murder, I think his father would still be alive if it weren't for him. What do you think, Foy?"

"I totally agree."

"Well, Foy, I guess we had better head back north, don't you? It's going to be late when we get home, and we're going to have to try and find Freddy Frye tomorrow. I dread that, don't you? He has such a sweet mother and sister, and I'm crazy about his brother, David. I'm sure it will alienate all of them when we arrest Freddy, but it can't be helped. I just hate it. Brad, thanks again, Pal, and we'll stay in touch."

Brad said, "Carl, Foy, it has been a genuine pleasure meeting you both, and if you ever come this way again, I hope you'll come by to see me. Have a safe trip."

Carl and Foy went to their car and headed north to Belmont. They figured if they stopped for dinner, they should be home by eleven o'clock or midnight.

Foy had left his car at the police station, as did Carl, but Carl was going to drive the detective car home, but he took Foy by to get his. They said they would see each other the next morning, and they both headed home.

The next morning, they met at the station and took time to brief Virgil Gaines, the Deputy Chief of Police and have a couple of cups of coffee before they went out. Virgil was going to send a nine-passenger van to Auburn, along with three officers, to pick up the suspects that Carl and Foy arrested the day before.

They talked it over and decided to go straight to the Von Steen house and hopefully surprise Freddy Frye before he had a chance to leave. Knowing that young people didn't get out of bed at daylight, they waited until about ten o'clock to ring the Von Steen doorbell. After ringing the bell twice and waiting a pretty long time, the front door finally opened. It was David in a t-shirt and a pair of lounge pants. The detectives could tell by his eyes that they woke him up, but he was very nice about it. Carl said, "David, we're here to see Freddy. Is he here?"

"Hang on a minute and let me check his room." In a minute, he came back in the room and said, "No sir. He's not here. From the looks of his room, he must not have come home last night."

"Do you have any idea where he might be?"

"Unless he's at his friend, Luke's, I don't know.

Carl said, "No, he's not at Luke's. Do you know of any other place where he might be? We really need to see him."

By that time, Mary had come into the room in her bathrobe and asked, "What's going on"

David said, "The detectives are looking for Freddy. It doesn't look like he came home last night. Do you know where he might be?"

"No. He never tells me anything."

David said, "Detective Mathis, you seem to be really anxious to find our brother. Can you tell us why?"

"Why don't you both sit down?"

After they were seated, Carl began to talk. He said, "I'm afraid I have some bad news for you. We have found out that Freddy was involved with three of his friends in the attacks on your mother and stepfather. We have the other three in custody, and as soon as we find Freddy, we'll have to arrest him, too. I really hated to have to tell you this because I think a lot of you both, as well as your mother, and I really dread telling her. Probably none of you will ever speak to me again, but arresting Freddy is something

I have to do. I'm not going to ask you to turn him in because he's your brother, but if he comes in voluntarily, it may go easier on him, and you can tell him that. Any questions?"

Mary said, "Yes, I have one. What's going to happen to Freddy if you catch him?"

"Honey, I can't answer that. After his arrest, everything will then be up to the court system. Do your parents have a lawyer?"

David said, "Yes sir, they do."

Carl asked, "David, would you rather tell your mother about this instead of me?"

"Yes sir, I would. It might not be so hard on her if Mary and I tell her."

"Okay. I'll let you tell her, and after you tell her, I suggest y'all call your lawyer."

"Foy and I are going to go now, and we hope Freddy will turn himself in. If you should talk to him, tell him that if he'll call me and turned himself into me, I'll help him all I can through the arrest and booking process. Good luck telling your mother. See ya later."

When they got almost to the car, David yelled, "Detective, wait a minute." He ran out to see Carl and said, "Detective Mathis, I've been thinking ever since you got here about telling Mother, and I'm wondering if you would consider going with Mary and me to tell her. She seems to think a lot of you, and I think you could explain everything to her better than we can. Will you go with us?"

"Of course, I will. Can you get ready now?"

"Thank you so much. Yes sir, we can be ready in just a few minutes."

He went back into the house, followed by Carl and Foy, and he told Mary, "They said they would go with us, so hurry and get ready, and we'll go now."

All four of them went to the hospital in two cars: David and Mary in David's, and the two detectives in theirs. When they had parked, they all walked in together, and they were all dreading what was ahead. David said, "Detective Mathis, do you think you could tell her? I don't know if I can or not, and I know Mary can't."

Carl said, "Yeah, I'll do my best not to destroy her. I'm sure she'll never speak to me again, and I truly hate that."

Mary said, "Detective Mathis, I'll bet you anything that Mother won't hold that against you. She knows you didn't have anything to do with all this, and she knows that you're just doing your job. She's a very understanding lady."

"I sure hope so. Thank you , Honey," he said.

When they got to her room, Martha was sitting up in a chair. She was thrilled to see all of them, including Carl. "I'm glad to see y'all. What did you do, run into each other downstairs?"

David said, "No ma'am. Detective Mathis came out here with us. He wants to tell you something." When he told her that, he stood by her chair and held her hand.

That was Carl's que, and he said, "Martha, you know I told you that when we found the person or people that did this to you, I would come tell you. Well, we have found who attacked you and Hans, and three of them are in jail, however, there is one more that we haven't caught yet. It seems that the three we have in custody are friends of Freddy."

Martha said, "You said there is one more that you haven't caught yet. Do you know who that is?"

"Yes, we know who it is."

"You said the three are Freddy's friends. Is the fourth one someone I know?"

"Yes ma'am, you know him. I hate like the dickens to have to tell you this, but the fourth one involved in the attack is Freddy."

She screamed in a loud whisper, "WHAT?"

David then took her hand in both of his, and Mary went over and put her arms around her mother's shoulder, and David said, "Mother, the detectives came to the house this morning to arrest Freddy, but he didn't come home last night, and we don't know where he is. Detective Mathis then told Mary and me, and I asked them if they would come with us to tell you. I hope you're not mad at the detectives. They're only doing their job."

Martha said, "No, I'm not mad at them. I'm mad at your brother. Why would he do such a thing?"

After a few more minutes, Carl told Martha, "Martha, Foy and I are going to leave now and get out of your hair. I'm so sorry that things are working out the way they are, but you have two rocks here to help give you the strength you need. You'll be going home in a couple of days, and if you can find it in your heart to let me, I'd like to come by and see you."

"Carl, you're always welcome anytime you want to come see me. Are you going to try and find Freddy now?"

"Yes, I have to."

"Well, when you catch him, will you give him a message from me?"

"Yes, of course. What is it?"

"Tell him I don't know why he did these terrible things, but I still love him, and I forgive him, and I hope he can get some help."

"I'll tell him. Okay, we're going to go now, and I'm glad to see you feeling better. I guess the next time I see you will be at your house, Bye now."

"Bye, Carl, and thank you for being so sensitive. I won't forget you."

As they were leaving, Carl turned and said, "Bye Mary, Bye David. If you guys need me, give me a call."

"Okay, thanks. Bye Detective."

After they were in the car and on their way, Carl said, "Well, Foy, I think I made it through that without everybody hating me."

Foy said, "I think you were great, the way you handled things. Maybe you should have been a psychologist."

"Yeah, right. Alright, let's go find Freddy. Any idea where?"

"No, not really, but I've been thinking. You know, when we questioned his buddies, they said they went to a beer joint and drank beer 'til the place closed. There shouldn't be that many beer joints in Belmont, so maybe we could check out some of them at night and see if he's there. Right now, that's the only thing I can think of. Do you have any ideas?"

"No, but yours is a good one. Why don't we ask around and get the names of some places where young people hang out. With NAU being located here in Belmont, there should be some favorite hangouts that the students use. Let's see what we can find."

Chapter Twelve

In the meantime, while the Belmont City Police were looking for Freddy Frye, the County Sheriff's Office was determined to find D.W. Handy and charge him with the murder of Coco Cochran, but D.W. was slicker than anyone thought.

The previous Saturday, he went to the local Ford dealer and sold his 1967 Shelby Mustang. It was a high-priced car, but he was in a hurry to sell it, and he sold it for a ridiculously low price. He then, took a cab to the local airport and rented a car to take one way to Atlanta. At three o'clock, Sunday morning, he left where he was staying and drove to the Delta Airlines section at the Atlanta airport. There, he bought a one way business class ticket to Tokyo, Japan. He paid cash for the ticket and used his real name. His flight wasn't scheduled to take off until ten forty, and he didn't want to get on the plane too early, so he went into a small food service place at the airport and had a biscuit and cup of coffee. Nearer time to board, he went to the assigned gate and boarded a huge 747 for his trip. Wheels were up almost exactly at ten forty, and he was on his way on the little over fourteen-hour trip.

He breathed a sigh of relief when they took off because he felt that, although he still had a long way to go and several things to do, he might have made a successful escape from arrest. There was little sleep the night before, because he had gotten to bed late, and then he got up at two o'clock that morning, so he was tired. On business class, the seats lay back to make a fairly comfortable bed, and he took advantage of that. After they reached altitude, he laid his seat back, not all the way, but back far enough to make it easy to nap, and he immediately went to sleep. About an hour later, even though he was in a mild sleep, he felt that someone was staring at him, and when he opened his eyes, a flight attendant was standing by him, and she asked, "Mr. Handy, would you like some lunch?"

He immediately asked, "How did you know my name?"

She said, "Oh, we have a list of our passengers and their seat numbers. I'm sorry if I startled you. Would you like some lunch?"

"Oh, that's okay. Yeah, I'd love to have some lunch."

"Good. I'll be right back,"

Sha was true to her word. It wasn't but three or four minutes until she returned with his lunch. It consisted of a chicken sandwich, a bag of chips, a Coke and a small dish of peach cobbler. He ate as if he hadn't eaten in a long time, and when he was through the attendant picked up his tray, and he settled down for a long flight.

He found a couple of magazines, and he wasn't interested in them, but he went through the motions of reading them for a few minutes, and then he put them down. The 747 was a wonder, and he wanted to explore some, so he got out of his seat and walked around. He went to the restroom first, and then he walked from the back to the front of the plane, and then he went upstairs. He was surprised to find a cute, circular bar on the upper deck and told himself he would come back up there a little later.

Around three or three thirty, he decided to go back upstairs and have a drink. When he got there, there were three or four men sitting there, and one very attractive young lady. He slid into the seat next to the lady and spoke. She also spoke, and D.W. said, "I'm J.C. Who are you?"

That was the first time he had used his new alias.

She replied, "I'm Sandy. Sandy Moore."

D.W. ordered a Margarita and Sandy was finishing a Whiskey Sour. When D.W. ordered his Margarita, she ordered another Whiskey Sour, and they began talking as if they had known each other for a long time. She gave him an earful about her life, and he was very careful not to share anything about his.

The more she drank, the more she talked. She told him that she had just left her husband, and from the way she described his professional life, D.W. decided that he was a really successful stockbroker, and he was loaded. From some of the things she said, it was easy to see that she was loaded as well, and as friendly as she was becoming to D.W., he didn't want to mess up.

He asked her, "Are you going to Tokyo only?"

"What do you mean?"

"Are you going anywhere besides Tokyo?"

"I don't know. I haven't thought that far ahead. Who knows? I might just wind up on some South Sea Island."

"Are you going anywhere else," she asked.

"I'm not sure. Maybe."

"Where is maybe?"

"I don't know. I may wind up on the same South Sea Island that you do."

She said, in her slightly tipsy voice, "Darling, that would be wonderful."

He said, "Wouldn't it, though?"

She realized that she had had enough to drink, and she said, "Darling, I'm getting drunk, so I'm gonna go back to my seat. I'll see you later. I loved meeting you."

He responded, "I loved it too. Bye."

He finished his third Margarita and decided that he should probably go back to his seat, too. He certainly didn't want to run his mouth too much, especially with all he had at stake. The Margaritas relaxed him so much, he took another nap after he sat down, and that time, the same flight attendant woke him up and asked if he would like some dinner.

He perked up and said, "I guess you think I sleep all the time. You had to wake me up for lunch, and now, you're waking me up for dinner." Joking, he said, "I promise I haven't been asleep all afternoon.

I've been upstairs having a drink with a beautiful woman. Do you believe that?"

"I believe anything you say. Now, do you want some dinner?"

"I absolutely do."

After dinner, he decided to look for Sandy, but after walking the entire length of the plane, he didn't see her, and the only thing he could figure was that she was in first class, and regular people were not allowed up there, so he went back to his seat and began watching a movie. About half-way through the movie, a lovely voice said, "Hi, J.C."

He looked up, and there stood Sandy. He said, "I just got back to my seat. I've been looking for you."

"I'm in first class." She sat down on the edge of his seat and said, "I just wanted to see you in case I missed you when we land tomorrow. Will you be staying in Tokyo overnight?"

"Yes, probably."

She smiled and said, "Well, if you decide to probably stay, I'll be at the Shinegawa Prince Hotel. Stop by, and I'll buy you a drink."

"You twisted my arm. I'll try to get by there and see you, and in case you forgot, I drink Margaritas."

"I remember. Do you remember my drink of choice?"

"I do, unless you changed from a Whiskey Sour."

The plane landed at the Tokyo International Airport a little after midnight. D.W., or J.C. as he was being called now, went to the Japan Airline ticket counter and booked a one-way flight to Bali, on a flight leaving at eleven twenty, the next morning. Again, he paid cash for his ticket.

Then, he caught a shuttle bus to the Shinegawa Prince Hotel for a ten-minute ride. Fortunately, they had a vacancy, and he checked in. As soon as he got in his room, he picked up the phone and told the operator to please connect him with Ms. Sandy Moore. She answered on the third ring, and he asked, "Is it too late for that drink?"

"Hi. No, it's not too late."

"Good. Meet me downstairs in the bar in ten minutes."

"I'll be there."

J.C. started to pay for their drinks, and Sandy said, "No, no. I invited you, remember?" and she paid for the first round, and then she paid for the second one. By then, it was almost three A.M., and J.C. said, "Honey, this has been nice, but I'm tuckered out, and I think I'll go to my room and go to bed."

"I didn't think you were a party pooper. It's still early. Let's have one more."

He said, "No. I'm dead on my feet. I'm going to bed. Good night."

Sandy said, "You can go to bed in my room, if you want to. Would you like that?"

"Normally I would, but not tonight. Thanks, anyway."

"Well, how about tomorrow? Maybe you'll be rested by then."

"I feel sure I will. I'll call you in the morning. Good night."

"Okay, last chance, Spoil Sport."

"Good night, Sandy."

He was sorely tempted, and he wasn't that tired, but his main goal was in the forefront of his mind, and he had to focus on that. He had to get to Bali ASAP where there was no extradition treaty with the United States and passing up what promised to be an experience of a lifetime was just one of the prices he had to pay.

He left a wakeup call at the desk for seven o'clock because he wanted to get to the airport early, just in case he had overlooked doing something, and someone would be looking for him. Just as he was leaving, his phone rang, and he didn't answer. He figured it was Sandy because he didn't know who else would be calling him in Tokyo, Japan. He skipped breakfast at the hotel and took the shuttle to the airport where he found a little restaurant, and he ordered an American breakfast of sausage and eggs and toast there. It was still almost three hours before his plane took off, so he spent some extra time in the restaurant, and then he went to a news stand and thumbed through some books and papers. When he tired of doing that, he went to a gate that wasn't the one he would leave from and sat down to wait until time to go to his gate shortly before boarding his plane.

Finally, it was time to board, and the plane took

off right on time, and as soon as they were airborne, he felt an unbelievable sense of relief. The flight was almost seven and a half hours, and he had plenty of time to think before they landed in Bali. His feelings were a mixed bag of emotions. First, he was going to miss his parents in Pulaski, Tennessee, even though he didn't see them very much, and he was going to miss Jolene. He had thought that if things worked out with them, he would ask her to marry him. He thought about all the people he was friendly with in Belmont, and he was going to miss all of them, and finally, he wondered if he had really pursued Sandy, from the plane and hotel, would she have moved with him to Bali. He bet in his own mind that she would have. Then, he thought that she was probably used to having everything, and to be with a man on the run and not having those things would definitely conflict with her lifestyle, so he was glad he didn't push for a relationship with her.

The plane landed in Denpasar at six forty-five, Bali time, and the first thing he had to do was to present his Passport to customs. Then, after getting his luggage, the first thing he did was to look at brochures on hotels. He chose the Grand Hyatt Bali after looking at his choices, and they had an airport limousine, which he took. Afraid they would be full; he was relieved when he found they had several vacancies. He registered as J.C. Hodges of Tampa, Florida and thought he would stay there until he could find a place to live, permanently.

He needed a counterfeiter but had no idea how to find one. The only thing he could think of was to frequent some of the bars in the lower end of town and maybe get acquainted with some questionable characters who may or may not know someone that could make him a new social security card, and other forms of identification. In the states, it wouldn't be a problem, but he didn't know how it would be in Indonesia. He had seen people on TV who had been put in prison in other countries for violating that country's laws, and he knew full well how strict some foreign laws were, and he didn't want to take any chances. So far, his plan was working, and he wanted to make sure it would continue to work, even if he didn't have any identification. As far as he knew, he was the only one in the world that knew he was D.W. Handy, and he wanted D.W. Handy to disappear completely.

He was a newcomer to Bali, and he wanted very much to fit in, even though Indonesia was primarily Muslim, and he felt like he was smart enough to do that. It might take a while, but if he was patient, he thought things would work out for him. Still, when he thought about home and the people he left there, especially Jolene, he was a little sad, but he fussed at himself and knew he couldn't get bogged down in depression, so for the next two or three days, he went with a couple of realtors to look at houses, and that made him feel better. On the third day, he found a great little bungalow on the beach in Seminyak and began moving the few things he had brought with him, the next day. He had to buy some furniture, but other than a bed, he didn't have to hurry. He actually bought a full bedroom suite and had it delivered and set up the same day he moved his clothes. Then, he wished he had bought a TV. He made a list of things he needed, such as silverware and dishes and two or three pans, a TV, and some other furniture. He didn't realize that he needed all that until he moved in his bungalow and only had a bed. He just took for granted that all those things would already be there because they were, where he lived before.

*****

Buddy had just returned from a trip to North Carolina and had gone by the office to give his orders to Penny, so she could process them.

While he was still there, Joe came in from a call he had made at Southern. "Hey, Buddy."

"Hi, Joe. Have a good day?"

"Yeah, it was good. I've been at Southern most of the day, and someone said they captured three of the guys that killed Hans Von Steen, and they're looking for another one. They know who it is, and you'll never believe who they're looking for. They're looking for one of Hans' sons."

"You're kidding. Which one?"

"Freddy."

"That makes sense. He's a real jerk."

"You know him?"

"Not really. I met him one time out at the lake, and I didn't like him. Like I said. He's a real jerk."

"What about his sister and brother? Did you meet them too?"

"Yeah. They seemed nice. His sister seemed very shy, but his brother was outgoing, and from what little I saw of them, he had a good personality. I think he goes to Alabama. Are they sure Freddy was mixed up in the killing?"

"From what I heard today, they're positive he was. I guess we'll know if and when they catch him."

"Mrs. Von Steen was hurt in the attack, wasn't she?"

"Yeah, she was hurt bad; in fact, she was in critical condition for a while, but I heard that she's doing a lot better."

Buddy said, "Boy, that would be rough, having a son that killed your husband and tried to kill you, wouldn't it?"

"I'd say so. Did you sell any thread on your trip?"

"Yeah, it was a good trip. I went by to see Hanes, and they want us to send them some samples. I'm going to put a packet together tomorrow. I feel like we're going to open them. They aren't as big as Shepherds, but they're huge. How about saying a prayer that we get them."

"I will. You do the same."

"I already have been. Look, I'm pretty tired, and I think I'll go home. This has been a rough week. I'll see you in the morning, okay?"

"Okay. Kiss Sally Jo for me, will you?"

"I'll do it."

That evening, when Sally Jo and Buddy were having dinner, Buddy's phone rang. He answered and after he had said hello, a voice on the other end said, "Buddy, hi. This is Jolene."

He looked at Sally Jo and said, "Jolene, how ya doin?"

She said, "I'm fine, but I'm worried about D.W. Have you seen him lately?"

"No, I haven't. I've been out of town since Monday. Why? Can't you find him?"

"I haven't seen him or talked to him all week, and he usually calls every day. I saw him last Friday night, and he acted kind of strange, and at the time, I didn't really pay much attention to it, but now that I've had time to think, I realize something is wrong. I'm calling his friends to see if anybody has seen or heard from him, but nobody has, and I'm worried sick about him."

Buddy said, "You said he acted funny when you were with him last Friday. What did he do that was different?"

"Well, first of all, he said he was tired of living up here, and he was thinking about moving down to the Caribbean, and wondered if I would go with him. He said it in sort of a kidding way, but now that I think about it, I think he might have been serious."

"What did you tell him when he asked you to go with him?"

"I told him it sounded really nice, but I reminded him that my mother is sick, and I can't leave her."

"What did he say when you told him that?"

"Nothing, really. He just started talking about something else, and I didn't think any more about it. There's another thing, Buddy. He said that they were redoing the floors in his apartment, and he was staying at the Quality Inn until they finished, and not until after he left, did I realize that his apartment has carpet, so why would they redo the floors. Another thing, Buddy, I called the funeral home two or three times, and they said he wasn't there, and then this morning, I called down there again, and this time, I talked to Bobby Pearson, and he said D.W. hadn't showed up for work all week, and he didn't know what to think or where he was. Finally, I went to his apartment after I talked to Bobby, and the police were there. It looked as if they were going all through his apartment. I tried to keep them from noticing me, and I think I was successful, but this whole thing has got me stumped."

"Deep down, where do you think he is?"

"Buddy, I don't know, but thinking back to last Friday, I'm wondering if he might have left for the Caribbean or somewhere. I thought he was kidding, but he must have been serious, and if he did, why did he do it, especially this way, and why were the police at his place?"

"Jolene, I wish I could help you, but I'm just as stumped as you are. If you find him, how about letting me know, and I'll do the same. Try not to worry. There's probably some simple explanation."

"Okay, Buddy. Thanks, anyway."

When he hung up, Sally Jo asked, "What was that all about?"

"That was Jolene, and she's worried about D.W. She said he's disappeared."

"Disappeared? What does that mean?"

"She saw him last Friday, and she said he acted strange. He said he was tired of living up here and wanted to maybe move down to the Caribbean. He wanted to know if she would move with him. She thought he was just kidding, and she told him she couldn't. She said he always calls her every day, but she hasn't heard from him all week; not since she saw him last Friday. She said she went by his apartment this morning, and the police were there, going through his apartment. I'd like to know what's going on."

Neither of them knew what was going on with D.W., of course, but they talked about it almost until bedtime. They went to bed, thinking about D.W., and he was still on their mind when they woke up the next morning.

Sally Jo left for work before Buddy, and as she was leaving, she said, "If you hear anything about D.W. today, call me."

"Okay, Sweetie, I will."

Sally Jo left, and Buddy sat down and had another cup of coffee before he got ready. He had been out of town all week, and he was looking forward to a fairly easy day, and since it was Friday, he might decide to take off at noon, if Joe was agreeable to it.

Joe was agreeable, and he was going to take off early as well, so before they left, they sat down in Joe's office and made plans for the next week. Before they went home, Joe told Buddy, "Kathy wanted me to tell you she wants y'all to come over for dinner, tonight."

"Okay, as far as I know, we can come. See ya then."

Buddy stopped at the Krystal on the way home, and picked up a sack full of hamburgers, and went out on the patio and ate them. He finished his burgers and then decided to wash the Suburban. When he got through and put all his stuff up, he went inside and thought he would take a nap. Just as he was about to doze off, his phone rang, and it was Jolene.

"Hi Jolene. What's up? Did you find D.W.?"

"No, I didn't, but I found out some other things. The police called me this morning and wanted to talk to me, so I left work and came home at noon to meet them. Buddy, they're looking for D.W., too, and when they find him, they're going to charge him with the murder of Mrs. Cochran. I was floored when they told me that."

"They're going to charge D.W. for that? How did they find you, Jolene?"

"They said they had D.W.'s phone records, and there were a lot of calls to me and from me, so they wanted to find out what our connection was."

"What did you tell them?"

"I told them there was really no connection other than our going out to eat together, and an occasional movie and stuff like that."

"Did that satisfy them?"

"I don't know. They asked me all kinds of questions about what D.W. did for Mrs. Cochran, and did he ever give me any large amounts of money. I told them I didn't know what he did for Mrs. Cochran, and no, he never gave me any money. Why do you think they ask me that, Buddy?"

"I don't know."

"I hope they don't talk to me again. Do you think they will?"

"I don't know, but if they do, just answer their questions the best you can. When y'all were together last Friday, and he talked about going to the Caribbean, did he mention any specific country?"

"No, and I've been thinking about that. Buddy, if he killed Mrs. Cochran, he had to know the police would be looking for him, and if he knew he was going to run away, he didn't want me to know where he was going because he knew they would be questioning me, and if I knew where he was, I would have to tell them. I know one thing, Buddy, and that's that D.W. is smart. He probably didn't even go to the Caribbean. He just knew I'd tell them that if they questioned me. I do wish I knew where he is."

"Has he ever mentioned going anywhere else in

the times you all have been together?"

"None that I remember. You know, he could be in Germany or Italy or somewhere in Europe as far as I know."

"I know. Well, Jolene, D.W. has been awfully good to me. You can tell that by the beautiful vehicle that I drive. I guess I hope he gets away, but on the other hand, if he killed Mrs. Cochran, he needs to pay for it. Don't you agree?"

"I guess I do, but Buddy, I love him, and how can I think he should go to jail?"

"Getting away from the subject of D.W. for a minute, you know the Fryes don't you? Mary, David, and Freddy?"

"I've met them, but I can't say I know them. Why?"

"We've been talking about D.W. being hunted for murder. Well, the police are looking for Freddy Frye for murdering his daddy and seriously injuring his mother. That's two people we both know that are being hunted for murder right now. Can you believe that?"

"I hadn't heard about Freddy Frye. When did that happen?"

"About a week ago."

"You never know about people, do you? Well, Buddy, I won't keep you any longer. I guess I'll just have to wait and see what happens next. I know I've already bothered you too much, but do you mind if I call you from time to time? You're the only one I feel like I can talk to."

"Call me any time, Jolene. I always enjoy talking to you."

"Thank you, Buddy."

It has been more than a week now, since Hans Von Steen and his wife were attacked, and Detectives Mathis and Luffman's efforts to find Freddy Frye have turned up nothing. They had searched everywhere they knew to look in the Belmont area, and then Carl had the idea that he may have gone back to the Auburn area and holed up with one of his Dungeons and Dragons cronies.

First, he called Brad Lambert, just to see if Freddy would have been dumb enough to go back to school, but Brad told him as far as he knew, he hadn't showed up down there.

Carl said, "Brad, when Foy and I were down at your place the first time, you gave us the names of three of Freddy Frye's companions and said you knew for sure that they were close to him, and you were right; we arrested them. You told us then that you thought you knew some others, but you weren't sure about them, but now, I'm hoping you'll give us some more names because Freddy has completely disappeared, and we need to find him."

Brad gave him some names, but he didn't think they were guys who were with Freddy when they attacked the Von Steens, so Carl thought it would be better if he talked to the police about them, rather than he and Foy messing with something that was not in his jurisdiction. He was still pretty sure that that was where Freddy was, so he and Foy went to the Auburn Police and talked to Detective Charles Hill, the one who assisted them when they caught the other three.

He told him, "We hope you can help us. We've turned over every rock in our whole county trying to find this guy, and we firmly believe that he has returned to this area because this is where his friends are. We have the names of some of his friends, and we don't think they are involved in the attack on the Von Steens, other than possibly helping him hide from us."

He gave him a picture and personal details of Fred, such as date of birth and physical description. Detective Hill looked at the addresses of two or three of the people whose names Carl gave him and said, "You know what, Carl? It has been a long time since we did this, but I think it's time we did a driver's license check on a couple of these streets. Who knows what might turn up?"

"Carl said, "You're a sly dude, Charley. Let me know if you find anything."

"I'll do it. I'll see if Traffic can set something up for next week."

"That'll be great. See ya."

Foy and Carl went back to Belmont, hoping that the Auburn Police would turn up something with their driver's license checks.

On Tuesday morning, Carl's phone rang, and when he answered, it was Charles Hill of the Auburn Police Dept. Charles said, "Guess what?"

Carl said, "I don't know. What?"

Charles said, "We got him. We got your man."

"Bless your heart," Carl said. How did you do it?"

"Remember me telling you it was time for some driver's license checks?"

"Yeah, is that how you did it?"

"It is. We set up a check point on South Jackson Street this morning, and when the cars were lined up, one of our officers noticed that one car turned around and went the other way to keep from going through the check. The officer chased him down, and when he checked his license and looked at the picture you gave us, he knew he had caught a bad guy. He radioed it in and we sent a car and another officer to get him, and we now have him in one of our hospitality suites waiting on somebody from Belmont to come pick him up."

"Foy and I will be there in the morning. Take good care of him, and we'll bring him up here, where he belongs." Joking, he said, "Charley, promise me you won't spoil him by pampering him too much because our D.A. won't like it."

"I promise," Charley said.

The detectives were getting used to the route to Auburn, and they were looking forward to that last one. When they arrived at the Auburn Police Department the next afternoon, Detective Hill took them back into the jail to verify that the one they caught was Fred Frye. Getting arrested and put in jail did nothing to calm Freddy's obnoxious arrogance.

Charley said, "Fred, there are a couple of people here who want to see you."

Carl and Foy stepped up from behind Charley and Freddy said, "Well, well. If it isn't Frick and Frack. What are you two doing down here? Are you lost or something?"

"Yeah, we're here for something. We're going to take your little butt back to where you're going to stand trial for killing your stepdaddy and hurting your mother. I hate to contaminate our nice jail with the likes of you, but these good people down here don't want you contaminating theirs either. We'll go in here and do the paperwork and be back to get you in a few minutes for our ride to Belmont."

When they got to Belmont, they delivered Freddy straight to the Belmont City Jail. They went through the booking process of photographing him, taking all his fingerprints, getting a DNA sample, and whatever else they had to do in order to make him a bona fide prisoner. After finishing all the routine, a jailer was called to escort Freddy to a cell, and on the walk to his cell, he passed by cells holding Nick, Bookie, and Luke, his accomplices in the crime against his parents. Each of them spoke to him as he went by, but he didn't say anything to any of them.

The next morning, Thursday, Andrew Collins, the District Attorney, went to the jail and said he wanted to see all four of the suspects in the Von Steen case in the conference room in an hour.

All four were escorted to the conference room by

three guards, and when they got in the room, each one was handcuffed to a chair. The guards stayed in there with them, and in a few minutes, Mr. Collins came in. He looked at the four, and Freddy, Luke, and Bookie were smiling, at which time he said, "Fellas, I'm certainly glad to see that you're so happy, but I'm afraid things are going to change drastically. Word got to me that you college boys are not taking this situation seriously, and I'm here to tell you that for your own good, you had better take it very seriously. You guys are accused of murder, and that means if you're convicted, you'll be spending most of your lives, if not all you're lives, in prison. Now prison is really a social venue, and when you get there, there will more than likely be some big bucks, who will want to take you as their wives. Now, if that doesn't get to you, maybe we need to just go ahead and send you to the Alabama Hospital for the Insane.

"Now, enough of that. The reason I wanted to see you all today is to tell you that your arraignments will be next Monday. Do each of you have an attorney? How about you, Nick Webster?

"Yes sir."

"Bookie Adams?"

"Yes sir."

"Luke Sanders?"

"Yeah."

"Fred Frye?"

"Nope."

"Mr. Frye, you don't have an attorney?"

"Nope."

Mr. Collins asked, "Why?"

"I can't afford one."

"Don't you have anyone to furnish you with a lawyer?"

"Nope."

"How about your parents?"

"Look, Ace, my daddy's dead, and my mother is in the hospital. The reason I'm here is because you characters are saying I killed daddy and hurt mother. Do you seriously think I can get money from them? If you can figure out how I can do that, then let me know, and I'll call my mother."

"Mr. Frye, we'll get you a court appointed attorney. I'll contact the judge, and ask that he appoint you one, and he or she will be with you Monday at your arraignment."

Nick and Bookie tried to ask him a question, and he told them, "Fellas, you don't want to ask me any questions. I'm the one who will be prosecuting you. You need to ask your attorneys any questions you might have."

Nick said, "Well, Mr. Collins, answer this, if you will. Should we wait until our arraignment to talk to our lawyers? I'd like to find out some things."

Bookie said, "I would, too."

Mr. Collins said, "You don't have to wait for your arraignment. You can ask them to come in tomorrow, if you want to."

Nick said, "Thank you, sir."

At nine o'clock. Monday morning, all four defendants were delivered to what Alabama calls High Court for their arraignments. Nick Webster's parents were there, as was Bookie Adams'. Luke Sanders mother was there for Luke, and Mary and David Frye were there for Freddy.

Nick Webster was held out, and the other three were put in a holding cell in the courthouse, and a guard took Nick to Courtroom A to face Judge Bradford Oliver.

Judge Oliver spoke to Benjamin Price, Nick's attorney, and then he made some preliminary remarks before he said, "Good morning, Mr. Webster. You are here this morning because you are accused of the first degree murder of Hans Von Steen and the attempted first degree murder of Martha Von Steen. How do you plead?"

Benjamin nudged Nick, and Nick said, "Not guilty, Your Honor."

Then Judge Oliver said, "In a murder case in Alabama, there can be no bond, so we'll schedule you for trial one month from today. Does that work for you Mr. Price?"

"Yes, Your Honor."

The guard then took Nick down to the holding cell and took Bookie Adams out and to the Courtroom.

Bookie was next, after Nick, and it went almost exactly the way it did for Nick, except the Judge told Bookie and his attorney that their trial would be the day after Nick's trial was over.

Third, was Luke Sanders, and Luke's appearance was much better than anyone expected. There was nothing he could do for all his tattoos, but he did remove all of his many earrings, and he had on some clean clothes. Mark Williams, his attorney had successfully managed to clean him up, but his arrogant language was still there. When the Judge asked him how did he plead, he said, "Not guilty, Man."

His lawyer just looked down at the floor and shook his head. Judge Oliver told him his trial would follow Bookie's, and he said, "Whatever."

Finally, it was Freddy's turn. Mary had taken him some clean clothes and some toiletries, so he looked fairly nice. The court had appointed him an attorney named Denise Johnson, and she seemed pretty sharp. As with the others, the Judge said his trial would follow Luke's, and at that point, the guard tool Freddy back to the holding cell, and rather than putting him in it, he took the others out, and all four were taken back to jail to await their trials.

Chapter Thirteen

Detective Carl Mathis was concerned about Martha Von Steen, and he went to see her again at the hospital. When he walked in, she was surprisingly bright eyed and perky. Carl asked how she was feeling, and she said, "They told me this morning that I can go home tomorrow.

"That's great, Carl said. You must be feeling better."

"I am," she said, "and you're being here is helping me all the more. Thank you for coming. Carl, have you seen Freddy?"

"No, not since I brought him back from Auburn."

"Carl, do you mind if I ask you a personal question?"

"Not at all. Ask me whatever you want to."

"I've just been wondering what your wife is like. Does she like for you to have such a dangerous job?"

"Martha, thank you for asking, but my wife passed away a little over a year ago."

"Oh, I'm so sorry. Can you tell me what caused her death?"

"She had Ovarian cancer. She died two weeks after they diagnosed it."

"My word. That's fast."

"It sure was."

"I didn't mean to pry, Carl. I was just interested,

like I'm interested in you."

He didn't say anything. He just looked at her and smiled.

Then she asked, "Do you have children?"

"I have a son. His name is Donald Lee, and he's the apple of my eye."

"Where is he? Does he live here?"

"He lives here and in Huntsville. After he got his Masters in Aeronautical Science, he took a job with the Marshall Space Flight Center, and he's doing very well, so far. He stays in Huntsville Monday through Thursday, and then he's here Friday through Sunday."

"Is he married?"

"Not yet."

Carl asked, "Now that you know all about me, can I ask you some questions?"

"You can ask me anything."

"Well how about you and Hans? Did you have a good marriage?"

She paused a little and then said, "Well, yes. I guess you could say it was a good marriage. There was not a great deal of love in it, at least not on Hans' part, but he was a good man, and he took our marriage seriously, and he loved my children."

"How could you stay in a marriage where there was no love?"

"Well, I kind of loved him. He never mistreated me. He sent all three of my children to college, and I never wanted for a thing, materially. He was an excellent provider, and that's kind of hard to find nowadays. He showed that he cared, although he was not affectionate. I would have done anything for him."

He almost asked her about her children, but with Freddy up for murder, he decided to leave that alone. He said, "Lady, I guess I had better go before your nurses run me off. When you get home, would you care if I come see you?"

"I'll be really mad if you don't."

He took her hand, and before he walked away, he leaned over and gave her a kiss on the cheek. He asked, "Was I wrong to do that?"

"No, you were right."

"I'll see you when you get home."

"You had better. Bye."

The lawyers for the four defendants were working hard on their cases, and even Denise Johnson was giving it her best even though she was not getting paid a big fee like her normal cases paid. After she waded through Freddy's arrogance, she was convinced that he didn't have an active part in the attack on his parents.

She felt that getting the prosecutor to accept Freddy's plea to Accessory Before the Fact would be his best chance at a lower sentence because based on the evidence that she knew they had on the four would likely make him spend most of his life in prison.

On their first meeting, she presented her idea to

him, and he adamantly denied having any part in the attack. Then she asked, "Fred, did you not draw the map to your parent's house that they found?"

"Yeah, but that didn't have anything to do with the attack."

"Yes, it did. Even though you weren't with them when they attacked your parents, your map enabled them to get there. That's the only way I can see for you to get a minimum sentence. Otherwise, if the jury finds you guilty, you will spend many years in prison; possibly even your entire life."

"You're kidding. Life?"

"It's entirely possible. Now, what do you say?"

"If I plead guilty to Accessory, how much time do you think I will get?"

"It will be up to the prosecutor, but I think it will probably mean less than ten years; maybe as little as two or three."

"But you think that no matter what I do, I'll have to go to prison?"

"I hate to tell you that, but my experience tells me you will, so we need to do everything we can to make it as short a time as possible."

"Can I think about it?"

"You can think all you want, but it won't change things. The sooner you let me talk to the prosecutor, the better it will be for you."

"Okay, go ahead and talk to him."

"Smart boy. I'll set it up," and she assured him again that he made the right decision and left.

In the meantime, in another interrogation room at the jail, Nick Webster and his attorney, Benjamin Price were discussing his case and the strategy for defending him. When it looked as if there was no way out for him, with the evidence they had against him and the others, he asked his lawyer, "What if I told what happened that night? Would it help me?"

Mr. Price answered, "Nick, I'd say it would. It depends on what you have to tell. First, do you swear to me that you didn't have anything to do with the attack on the Von Steens?"

"Yes sir. I was there, but I swear that I didn't have anything to do with the attack."

"Well, Nick, what can you tell that might help you get some kind of deal with the District Attorney?"

Nick said, "I can tell what actually happened."

"Why don't you tell me, and we'll decide whether or not to tell the prosecution."

"Okay. Well, the four of us came to Belmont from school on Saturday morning, and we all rode in Bookie Adams car. We stayed at Luke's house, because his mother is so liberal, we didn't have to worry about what we did. We went to a club Saturday night, and we were all tired after our trip from Auburn, so we went back to Luke's house and turned in fairly early. On Sunday, we just hung out until about mid-afternoon, and then we decided to go out and try to find something to do. Freddy hadn't been home, and Bookie asked him if he wanted to go see his parents. At first, he said he did, and Bookie asked him to draw a map of how to get there in case he couldn't find the house when he came back to get him. Freddy started talking about his stepdad, and he got so worked up talking about him, he decided he didn't want to go, and he didn't want to go with us, so Bookie took him back to Luke's. At one point, while he was ranting about his stepdad, Luke asked him if his stepdad kept much money at home, and I don't remember what he said. After we dropped Freddy off, we went to a club and drank beer until they closed. Luke said, "Let's go out to Freddy's and see if we can get some of his stepdad's money. I asked him how he planned to do that, and he said he didn't know. He would have to figure that out when he got there."

Mr. Price asked Nick, "What time was that?"

"It was probably around one thirty or two o'clock."

Mr. Price then asked him, "What did you do then?"

"We found their house and Bookie stopped down the street from it, and Luke got out. He told Bookie to pop the trunk, and he looked in it and found a knife and a baseball bat. He left us and went down the street to Freddy's, and after a long time, he came back, and he had blood all over him. He put the knife and bat back in the trunk, and then he got in the car and said, "I can't believe I did that." Nobody said a word, and Bookie started the car, and we went to Luke's. We got up on Monday morning and returned to Auburn, and nothing was ever mentioned about what Luke did to Freddy's parents. As Mr. Paul Harvey used to say, Now, you know the rest of the story."

Nick's lawyer asked, "Nick, will you tell that story to the District Attorney?"

"It depends."

"Depends on what?"

"It depends on how much good it does for me. If it cuts my sentence down from life to twenty or thirty years, I won't tell him, but if it cuts it down to probation or something like that, I'll tell him. What do you think?"

"I think probation is out of the question, but let me throw this out to you. What if I can get him to agree to a change of plea to Accessory After the Fact, which carries a term of from two to eight years. Mr. Collins is a friend of mine, and I think I can get him to agree to a term of something under five years."

"See if you can get it down to two years or less, and if you can, then I'll tell him the whole story. That's only right because I didn't have anything to do with the attack. I just happened to be there."

"Okay. Let me see what I can do."

Bookie and Luke spent quite a bit of time with their attorneys, and neither one had anything to bargain with, and the future looked grim for both of them. They would just have to hope for the best at trial.

Since the murder of Hans Von Steen, there was no one to take over as General Manager of the Belmont

Southern Mills plant until Monty Shelton was transferred in from their plant in Burlington, North Carolina.

Monty was married to Sarah Shelton, and he had two beautiful daughters named Jean and June. Jean was twenty-three years old and single, and June was twenty two. They had just graduated from North Carolina State University and were considering going back for their Masters. Having scouted the entire town of Belmont, they moved into the same neighborhood as where the Von Steens lived, and the way most southern towns do, they were welcomed by a host of locals. Fearing that somebody else would ring their doorbell, they were afraid to get ready for bed too early every night. Among those welcoming them was Detective Carl Mathis and his son, Donald Lee. Ever since Carl's wife, Chelsea died, Donald Lee spent quite a bit of time with his dad to try and help with the loneliness. Donald Lee was still single, and he was keeping his eyes open for the right mate and was blown away when he met the Shelton sisters, especially Jean.

The Shelton girls and Donald Lee were the youngest in the group that night, and they kind of kept to themselves, rather than be in the mix of older adults. Sitting in a corner of the living room, Donald Lee was trying desperately to score points with Jean, but she was a little standoffish. He wasn't used to that because all his life, he had been the recognized leader of the pack. At one point, he asked the girls if they would like to exchange numbers, just in case they needed to get in touch with each other sometime. He took out one of his business cards, and June eagerly took it and wrote down her number, but Jean didn't take it until Donald Lee asked her if she would give him her number. She reluctantly took the card and wrote down her number and handed it back. He gave them another card with his numbers, and in a few minutes, his dad was ready to go, so he had to say goodbye, but before he left, he asked Jean if she would like to go out for a cup of coffee or maybe lunch on Saturday, but she said, "I don't think so, but thank you for asking."

He couldn't believe he was turned down, and he left their house with his tail between his legs. For the rest of the week, all he could think about was how Jean Shelton turned him down for lunch, and what he could do to get her to change her mind, and things were possibly going to change.

He was at the mall Friday night, and he ran into Buddy and Sally Jo. They talked for a while and wondered why it had been so long since they saw each other. Buddy said, "Donald Lee, Sally Jo and I are going to Coach's to eat tomorrow night. Why don't you go with us?"

"Are just the two of you going?"

"Yeah, but you know what? Why don't I call Billy Neville and see if he and Sylvia would like to go? We could have a reunion."

"That sounds great. Listen, there's a girl I'm

interested in, and we haven't been out together yet. She's new in town, and would you mind if I ask her?"

"No, we would like that. Call her and ask her."

"Okay, I will, and I'll let you know tomorrow. If she doesn't go, will it be alright if I go by myself?

"Absolutely."

"Okay. I'll see you guys tomorrow night. What time?"

"Why don't we meet at Coach's at seven thirty?"

"Sounds like a winner. I'll see you guys. I'm gonna go and call this girl right now, and hopefully, since there's going to be two couples besides me, she'll agree to go. See ya."

Donald Lee didn't wait until he got home to call Jean. He went straight from Buddy and Sally Jo to his car in the mall parking lot, and as soon as he got in his car, he called her. As soon as she answered, he said, "Jean, this is Don Mathis. Remember me?"

"Yes, I remember you. How are you?"

"I'm fine, thank you. Listen, the reason I'm calling is that I just ran into some friends of mine in the mall, and while we were talking, they said they are going to go to Coach's tomorrow night and asked me to go with them, along with another couple, and they said they would love it if you would go, too, so I'm asking, will you go with me and four of my best friends to eat tomorrow night? Their names are Buddy and Sally Jo Russo and Billy and Sylvia Neville. I know your daddy is the new head man at Southern Mills, and Buddy and his father-in-law do a lot of business with Southern. You can ask your daddy about them if you want to get a reference, but anyway, I'd like for you to go with us. Will you?"

She said, "So, if I go, there will be three couples of us, right?"

"That's right. Three couples. Will you go?"

"I guess so. Where did you say you're going?"

"To Coach's. It's a very nice restaurant, and it's owned by two of my old high school football coaches. Have you been there yet?"

"No, I haven't really been anywhere. We've only been in Belmont for a little over two weeks."

"Jean, I'm excited that you said you'll go with us. I think you'll like my friends, and I know they'll like you. Sally Jo and Buddy said we'd meet at the restaurant at seven thirty. Is that alright with you?"

"Yes, that's fine. What time will you pick me up?"

"How about I get you at ten after?"

"Fine, I'll look forward to it. Thanks, Don."

"Me too. Thank you, Jean."

He picked her up at ten after seven the next night, and she looked like a million dollars. He couldn't believe a woman that beautiful would actually go out with him. They got to Coach's the same time Buddy and Sally Jo did, and Donald Lee introduced them to Jean. While they were walking to the entrance, Billy and Sylvia drove up, and he introduced them to Jean as well. When they got inside, they told the hostess who they were and that they had reservations, and they were promptly seated.

The six of them spent a very enjoyable evening, and the food was delicious. Jean fit in as if she was an old friend, and Sylvia and Sally Jo liked her a lot, and at one point, Sylvia told her that she hoped she would continue to see Donald Lee because he was the real thing. Eventually, they finished their evening together, and each couple told the others how much they enjoyed the meal and the evening and left to go home.

As Donald Lee and Jean were driving to her house, she asked, "Don, can I ask you a question?"

He said, "Sure. Ask me anything."

"Well, when you called me, you said you were Don, and your business card says your name is Don, but your friends called you Donald Lee. Which do you prefer; Don or Donald Lee?"

"It doesn't really matter. I guess I prefer Don. When I was younger, everybody called me Donald Lee; even my parents, but when I grew up and went to college, most people called me Don, and I guess I thought Don sounded more mature, so now I go by that everywhere except with my family and friends. I guess I'll always be Donald Lee to them, and you can call me anything you want to call me. Now can I ask you something?"

"Yes. What do you want to know?"

"Actually, there is more than one question. The first is did you enjoy tonight?"

"I had the best time I've had in a very long time. What's the next question?"

"Do you think you would like to go out with me again?"

"Don, I would very much like to go out with you again."

"Fantastic. Maybe we can go out next week. I'll call you."

Surprisingly, she asked, "What about tomorrow? You don't have to work, do you?"

"No, I don't have to work. Tomorrow would be great. Have you ever been to the Steak & Shake?"

"No, but I'd like to. When do you want to go?

"You mentioned tomorrow. Do you want to go tomorrow? I've got a better idea. Why don't we spend the whole afternoon together, tomorrow? I can show you Belmont, the lake where we all hung out and other things. Then we can go to the Steak & Shake and have the best burger and shake you've ever had. You wanna do that?"

"I'd love to. What time?"

"Well, I usually go to Church with my dad, and we have lunch together. Would you be ready to go about one thirty or two o'clock?"

"That sounds just about perfect. Let's do that."

They got to her house, and he walked her to the door. She didn't invite him in, so they stood on the front porch and talked for a few minutes. While they were talking, he kept inching toward her, and in a couple of minutes, he was standing almost against her. Then, he said, "Well, I guess I had better be going. I'll look toward to tomorrow." He leaned over and gave her a short kiss on the cheek, and she didn't resist. He turned to leave and said, "I'll see you tomorrow."

She said, "I can't wait."

Donald Lee got to her house about one forty-five the next day, and they had a wonderful time together. That was what looked to be the beginning of a serious romance, and for the next month, they were together every time Donald Lee was off from work or got home early enough in the evenings to go out. Monty and Sarah, Jean's parents just loved Donald Lee, and from all appearances, they would welcome him into their family, if the romance advanced to that stage.

Chapter Fourteen

The four defendants in the Von Steen trial were a collective bundle of nerves, even Freddy Frye, who was considered the cool one of the four. Their trials were to begin the following Monday morning, with Nick Websters leading off.

Nick had given a sworn statement to his lawyer, Benjamin Price, and then to the District Attorney, Andrew Collins, in return for being charged with a lesser crime. In Nick's case, the D.A. agreed to reduce the charge from First Degree Murder to Accessory After the Fact, which carries a penalty of between two years to eight years in prison. Nick's lawyer was a friend of the D.A., and he hoped he could maybe call on that friendship to give Nick only two years. Two years doesn't sound like a lot to the average person, but when a person is more than likely going to have to go to jail for that length of time, it sounds a whole lot longer.

At nine o'clock, Monday morning, the Bailiff called the courtroom to order, and Judge Oliver said, "Good morning, Mr. Price. Am I to understand that your client wishes to change his plea?"

"Good morning, Your Honor. Yes, Your Honor. My client wants to change his pleas from Not Guilty to Accessory After the Fact."

Judge Oliver looked at Nick and asked, "Young

man, is that what you want to do?"

Nick replied, "Yes, Your Honor."

Then Judge Oliver asked the District Attorney, "Mr. Collins, is that your understanding also?"

"Yes, Your Honor."

Then the judge asked Mr. Price, "Counsel, have you and the Prosecutor worked out any kind of deal?"

"Yes sir. My client has given a sworn statement in which he voluntarily told everything that happened the night of the attack on Mr. and Mrs. Von Steen, and Mr. Collins has agreed to a term of two years or less, if it pleases the court."

"Mr. Collins, is that your agreement?"

"Yes sir."

"Very well. Mr. Collins, as you know when we have a trial where a bargain had been made, the prosecution still has to question the defendant, even though there is no jury present. Are you prepared to question the defendant now?"

"Yes, Your Honor."

"Okay, then. Mr. Webster, will you please take the stand?"

Nick went up to the witness stand, and the Bailiff swore him in. The District Attorney then began to ask him questions about the night in question. Every question and answer was on the statement that Nick had already given, but according to the law, it had to be brought out in court.

When the D.A. finished, he sat down, and Nick left the witness stand and went back to his chair and sat down. Then, the judge asked Mr. Price, the defense attorney, if he had anything to say, and he said no.

Then the judge told Nick, "Nick Webster, you have been tried in the High Court of Alabama and have been found guilty of the crime of Accessory After the Fact in the murder of Hans Von Steen and the attempted murder of Martha Von Steen. You have pled Guilty to these charges, and it's now my duty to declare sentence.

"Mr. Webster, I hereby sentence you to two years in the Alabama Department of Corrections in Decatur, Alabama."

After the judge pronounced the sentence, two guards went over to Nick and handcuffed him. On the way out of the courtroom, they stopped long enough to let Nick's parents and sister hug him. Then, they took him to a room downstairs in the Courthouse, where his Attorney would be allowed to talk to him before they took him to Decatur.

In just a few minutes, Benjamin Price went in the room where Nick was, to talk about how he should act when he gets to prison and several other things. One thing that made Nick feel better was when Mr. Price told him that if he behaved and stayed out of trouble, he could likely get out after serving half his sentence. He had already spent a month in jail, and that would count as part of his sentence, so he could probably count on getting out in eleven months.

No more trials were scheduled for that day

because there had been the entire day set aside for Nick's, and the judge didn't want to begin Bookie's and only have a half day, because there would have to be a jury picked, and that might take a long time. He set Bookie's trial to start the next day, which was Tuesday, and he didn't schedule Luke's until the following week. Jury trials, especially murder trial could take some time, and nobody knew just how long they would take.

The next morning, Tuesday, sharply at nine o'clock, the courtroom was called to order. There were several potential jurors seated in the rear of the courtroom, waiting on twelve to be selected. The first thing that happened was the leading in of Bookie Adams. The guard seated him next to his attorney, Brian Park. Then Judge Oliver came in, and the Bailiff said, "All rise," and everybody stood up until the Judge said, "Be seated."

The first order of business was that of selecting a jury. Each jury candidate had been given a sticker to put on their shirt with a number on it. When their number was called, they got up and went to the witness stand to be questioned by both attorneys. If their answers were accepted by the attorneys and Bookie, they were instructed to be seated in another area until a total of twelve was selected.

If a candidate gave an answer to a question that neither lawyer liked of if they thought the person might be prejudiced against Bookie for some reason, they were rejected. All in all, sixteen people were called, and four were rejected. By then it was almost noon, so Judge Oliver said they would take a break for lunch, and he ordered everybody connected to the trial to be back before one o'clock. He said opening statements by the attorneys would start at one.

Everybody filed back into Courtroom A at one o'clock, and Judge Oliver asked Andrew Collins, the District Attorney if he was ready to begin. "Yes, Your Honor," he said.

"Mr. Park, are you ready?"

"Yes sir."

"Very well. Mr. Collins, why don't you start things off? You can make your opening statement."

The District Attorney thanked the Judge and addressed the jury. He told them that Mr. and Mrs. Hans Von Steen were viciously attacked, killing Mr. Von Steen and critically injuring Mrs. Martha Von Steen, and the prosecution would prove that the defendant was one of the four that did the deed. He went on and told them several more things that the prosecution would prove and he would expect them to find the defendant guilty of first degree murder.

When he finished his statement, he turned and walked toward his seat and table, and Judge Oliver said, "Mr. Park, you may address the jury. Brian Park thanked the judge and took his turn addressing the jury. He told them about the attack on the Von Steens, but he assured them that his client, Bookie Adams, could not have been the attacker. He then went to his seat, and Judge Oliver told Mr. Collins to call his first witness.

Since the attack took place late at night, and there were no witnesses other than the three in Bookie's car, Mr. Collins called Nick Webster. Nick took the stand dressed in his orange jumpsuit provided by the Belmont City Jail. He would wear different kind of clothes when he was transferred to the prison to begin serving his sentence.

Mr. Collins began by asking questions based on the confession statement that Nick had previously furnished. Of course, Mr. Collins knew the answers to his questions, but the jury did not. He continued to question Nick until he finished around three thirty.

The District Attorney's questions were so strong, and Nick's answers were so damaging, that the defense attorney looked defeated when he began questioning Nick. It was hard to imagine Bookie's feelings while Nick was pretty much driving nails in his coffin with every question. The only good thing that Nick said was that Bookie stayed in the car while Luke went into the Von Steen's house and didn't have a part in the actual attack.

As a last, desperate point, Mr. Park went to the part of Nick's testimony where he said that Bookie didn't have any part of the attack on the Von Steens, and that he stayed in the car while Luke went in, and he asked Bookie to verify it, which he did. The two things that hurt Bookie's case the most was the fact that he drove his car to the Von Steens for the attack, and that he owned the murder weapons. There was no doubt about either, and Bookie's lawyer had no defense against it. Mr. Park turned and said, "Your Honor, that's all I have."

"Very well. Call your next witness."

Mr. Park said, "The defense has no more witnesses. We rest."

Judge Oliver asked, "Mr. Collins, do you have any more witnesses?"

"No, Your Honor. The prosecution rests."

By the time Judge Oliver finished charging the jury. He gave them the option of deciding on a first-degree murder charge or a second degree murder charge. It was after three o'clock, and most people in the courtroom felt that they wouldn't have enough time to deliberate very much. Many felt that the judge should have waited until the next morning to send the jury out. When the judge sent the jury out, nearly everyone got up and left because they were sure it would be at least sometime the next day before any verdict would be reached. A few people milled around in the hall outside the courtroom, just in case.

All at once, at four thirty, the announcement was made that the jury had reached a verdict. By the time they got everybody back and got Bookie back from the holding cell, it was almost five o'clock.

The Judge said, "Madam Forelady, would you please read your verdict?"

The lady stood and read the verdict. "We, the jury find the defendant, Bookie R. Adams guilty of Murder in the Second Degree. On the charge of Attempted murder, we find the defendant Bookie R.

Adams guilty of Attempted Murder in the Second Degree."

Judge Oliver asked, "Have you decided on a recommended sentence for the defendant?"

"Yes, Your Honor, we the jury feel that the sentence should be from five to fifteen years on each count. We recommend the sentences be served concurrently."

The judge said, "Mr. Adams, please stand," and when Bookie stood up, Judge Oliver said, "Bookie R. Adams, you have been found guilty of Second Degree murder and Second Degree Attempted murder by a jury of your peers, and it's my duty to sentence you to from five years to fifteen years in the Alabama State Department of Corrections in Huntsville, Alabama.

Bookie's parents didn't scream, but they cried loudly, and Bookie turned while the guard was handcuffing him, with tears in his eyes, and he mouthed the words I love you to them.

There weren't any trials scheduled for the next day. Luke's was next, but the judge thought Bookie's would take longer than it did, so rather than move Luke's up a day, he decided to just keep it set for Thursday as planned.

On Wednesday, Mark Williams, Luke's attorney, called Andrew Collins, the District Attorney, and told him that Luke wanted to change his plea from Not Guilty to Guilty and not have a trial.

"Why does he want to change," the D.A. asked.

"Because he's afraid that if he's found guilty by a jury, they'll give him the death penalty, and he knows he's guilty. Can you take care of this for us?"

"Yeah, I'll call the judge, but you and your client will still have to come to court Thursday. The judge will sentence him when he gets there."

On Thursday morning, Mark Williams, Luke Sanders, two guards, the bailiff, Judge Oliver, and Luke's mother were the only ones in the courtroom. Judge Oliver asked Luke, "Son, your attorney has informed the court that you wish to change your pleas from Not Guilty to Guilty. Do you, in fact, wish to change it?"

"Yes sir."

"Are you fully aware of the sentence for a guilty plea to murder?"

"Yes sir."

"And you still want to change it?"

"Yes sir."

"Very well. Luke B. Sanders, in response to your plea of Guilty in the murder of Hans Von Steen and the attempted murder of Martha Von Steen, it is my duty to pass sentence. Therefore, Luke Sanders, I sentence you to spend the rest of your natural life in Holman Correctional Facility in Atmore, Alabama."

Luke looked stunned, even though he knew what was coming, but he didn't cry. His mother was there, and she just bawled. She was pitiful because she was alone and had nobody to help comfort her.

Mark Williams saw her, and he asked the Judge if

Luke and his mother could have just a couple of minutes together before they took Luke away, and Judge Oliver granted his request.

Now, the only one remaining of the four accused was Freddy Frye, and he was scheduled to go before the judge on the following Monday. Freddy had agreed to his attorney's suggestion to plead Guilty to Accessory Before the Fact, so there would not be a jury trial. It would be similar to Nick Webster's.

Carl Mathis had been keeping up with the trials of the four, and he knew that Freddy's was coming up, and he couldn't help but think about Martha, Freddy's mother. He wrestled with the thought of going to see her, in his mind, and Saturday morning, he called to see if she would mind if he went out to her house to pay her a visit.

She acted thrilled to hear from him, and she told him to come out as soon as he could because she wanted to see him. He felt good when he hung up because he wasn't sure she felt the same way he did. When he got there he rang the doorbell, and Mary let him in. She had come home from Jacksonville State for the weekend. She led him into the den, and when Martha saw him, she stood up and held out both hands, inviting him to come closer to her. When he took her hands, she pulled him to her and gave him a kiss on the cheek and said, "Carl, I'm so glad to see you. I was wondering if you were ever going to come see me again. Sit down here, in this chair beside me, and let's talk.

Carl sat down and the first thing Martha said was, "I guess you know Freddy's trial is Monday, don't you?"

"Yeah, I know. Do you know what you're going to do about going?"

"I've had the hardest time trying to decide what to do. What would you do, Carl?"

"I really don't know. I've been thinking a lot about that, and as a father, if the same thing happened to me that happened to you, I'd probably wind up going, but thankfully, I don't have to make that decision because I might not go."

"That would be my reason for going. If I go, it will be because I'm his mother, and regardless of what he did, he's still my son, and I shouldn't, but I love him."

"Tell me how you've been doing, Martha."

"I've been doing okay. I'm still sore, but the doctor says I'm healing well, and it shouldn't be much longer until I'm back to normal."

"Mary, how have you been doing?"

"Fine, I'm ready for school to get out, but I'm doing good."

"How's David?"

"David's doing well," Martha said. "It looks like he's going to graduate with honors, and I'm so proud of him. He's going to come to work at Southern when he gets out."

"That's great," Carl said."

Martha and Carl talked for a long time about nothing important, and when it came the time when

Martha thought he was going to leave, she asked, "Carl, I hate to ask this, but if I decide for sure to go to Freddy's trial, Monday, do you think you could take me?"

He was shocked, but his life as a detective that was used to shocks, didn't bat an eye, and he said, "Of course, I'll take you. Just call me when you make up your mind for sure. Will you be here to go, Mary?"

"No sir. I'm going back to school, Sunday. I kind of got behind when I was home after the attack on Mother and Hans. I don't think Freddy cares whether I'm there or not, anyway."

Martha said, "Nonsense. Freddy loves you and you know it."

"The only one Freddy loves is Freddy," Mary said. "Maybe if he has to go to jail for a while, he'll grow up. Mother, I'm twice as mature as he is, and I'm four years younger."

Martha didn't respond to that, probably because she knew Mary was right.

Carl said, "Well ladies, I'm going to run, Martha, if you need me, give me a call. Mary, have a safe trip back to school."

She said, "Thank you."

He left and headed toward home, and for some unknown reason to him, he couldn't get Martha out of his mind. At the same time, at Martha Von Steen's house, Mary left for the mall right after Carl left, and all Martha could think about was Carl. She told herself, *I'm not supposed to have these thoughts. I'm supposed to still be in mourning. Come on, Martha, shape up.*

On Sunday night, she called Carl and said, "I've decided to go to court tomorrow. Are you still willing to go with me?"

"I am. Do you want me to pick you up, or do you want to meet me there?"

"If you don't mind, I'd appreciate it if you would pick me up. My doctor hasn't released me to drive yet. I hate to be such a bother, but I really feel that I should be there."

Carl said, "No bother at all. Court usually starts at nine o'clock, so how about I get you at eight thirty? That should give us plenty of time to get there without being late."

"Eight thirty will be fine. I'll be ready when you get here."

Court is pretty much the same every day with the exception of the people involved, and Monday morning was no exception. Martha and Carl arrived a few minutes before nine, and there was no one in the courtroom except Denise Johnson, Freddy's attorney.

She saw them come in, and she figured they were friends or relatives of Freddy's, and she went over to them and introduced herself. Carl responded with, I'm Carl Mathis, and this is Martha Von Steen. Martha is the mother of your client, Fred Frye."

She replied, "My goodness, it's sure nice to see you Mrs. Von Steen. I had no idea you are able to get out like this after your injury. I'm very glad to meet you. Mr. Mathis, your name is familiar. Do I know you?"

Martha spoke up. Mr. Mathis is the detective that arrested Freddy. He's not here as a detective; he's here as my friend."

"Well, I'm glad to meet you, detective. Mrs. Von Steen, I just want you to know that I'm terribly sorry for the attack on you and your husband. What do you hope happens to your son?"

Martha said, "Well, I hope the judge takes it easy on him. You see, He and his friends did a terrible thing, but he's my son, and I forgive him."

The lawyer said, "You forgive him? How can you forgive him, Mrs. Von Steen?"

Martha said, "Because my Jesus said I had to. He said if I don't forgive everybody else for what they've done, then God won't forgive me, and I have a lot to be forgiven for."

"Mrs. Von Steen, I don't know what to say. If something happened to me like happened to you, I don't think I could forgive the person, even if it was my son. I certainly admire you for that."

Just then the Bailiff came into the courtroom, and Denise said, "I had better go. It was nice meeting you both," and she went to the defense table and got ready for them to bring Freddy in. In a couple of minutes, a guard brought him into the courtroom, and Denise asked Martha if she would like to speak to him before the judge came in, and Martha said she would. Denise led her and Carl up to the defense table and told Freddy, "Look who's here to see you."

"Freddy, looking funny, said, "Hello Mother. What are you doing with this guy?"

She let the question pass, and she said, "Hi, Freddy. Are you alright?"

He said, "Yeah, I'm okay. I asked you, what are you doing here with this jerk?"

"Freddy, Carl is not a jerk. He's my friend and he has helped me as well as your sister and brother since you and your friends did what you did. While we have the chance, I just want you to know that I forgive you."

Just then, Judge Oliver entered, and The Bailiff said, "All rise." Martha and Carl stood up as well as Freddy and the two attorneys. When the judge got to his bench, he said, "Please be seated," and everyone sat down.

Judge Oliver began the proceedings by saying, "This trial is between the State of Alabama and Mr. Fred L. Frye. Mr. Frye is pleading Guilty to the charge of Accessory Before the Fact of the murder of Hans Von Steen and the attempted murder of Martha Von Steen."

He addressed Freddy and asked, "Mr. Frye, my understanding is that Mr. Von Steen was your stepfather and Mrs. Von Steen is your mother. Is that correct?"

Freddy mumbled, "Yeah."

"I didn't hear that, Mr. Frye. What did you say?"

That time, Freddy almost shouted the words, "I said, yeah, Ace, that's correct."

Then Judge Oliver stopped and addressed Freddy's lawyer. "Ms. Johnson, I suggest you explain to your client the proper way to address the court."

"I'm sorry, Your Honor. Give us a minute, please, and I'll explain that to him."

She told Freddy, "Fred, when the judge asks you something, you should say. Yes, Your Honor or No, Your Honor and not yeah. You need to remember that Judge Oliver can sentence you to up to ten years, if he wants to, so I suggest you give him some respect."

Then she said, "I'm sorry, Your Honor. I explained things to my client, and I hope it won't happen again."

"Thank you, Ms. Johnson. It looks as though your client could use some lessons in manners. Now, as I was about to say, even though the plea to the charge of Accessory Before the Fact is guilty, there will be no jury trial, however, as a formality the prosecutor must ask the questions that would be asked in a jury trial. Is that understood?"

Denise Johnson said, "Yes, Your Honor."

"Do you understand that, Mr. Frye?"

Freddy said, "Yeah."

The judge glowered at him when he answered that way, but he didn't say anything that time. Martha reached over and held Carl's hand tightly when Freddy said yeah the second time, and he put his other hand on top of hers.

"Are you ready to begin your questioning, Mr. Collins?"

"I am, Your Honor."

"Okay, you may begin."

The D.A. began by asking Freddy to state his name, and Freddy responded. He asked him where he went to college, what he majored in and several other questions that actually had nothing to do with the attack on his parents, and he answered all of them.

Then he started asking about his friends, Nick, Bookie, and Luke. He asked about their normal activities, and especially about their involvement in Dungeons and Dragons. That led up to their trip to Belmont on the weekend of the attack, and the D.A. asked him point blank, "Were you with your friends the night they attacked your parents?"

Freddy said, "No."

"Did you draw a map to show them how to get to your parents' home?"

"Yeah, but ….," Mr. Collins stopped him from saying anything else.

Freddy tried to say something else about the map, but he was stopped, and he yelled over the D.A.'s attempt to stop him, and the judge stopped him and told him to only answer what was asked him.

Freddy told the judge, "Look, Dude, I told this guy I drew the map, and I want to tell you why I drew it."

Judge Oliver stopped the process and said, "Ms. Johnson, would you approach the bench, please?"

She and the District Attorney both went up to the

bench, and Judge Oliver told Denise, "Obviously your client is not one to take directions. My name is not Ace or Dude. My name is Judge Oliver, Judge, or Your Honor. Anything else is unacceptable. If he forgets his manners one more time, I'm going to charge him with Contempt of Court and put him in the holding cell until this is finished. Ms. Johnson, I have the flexibility to decide on the length of your client's sentence, and the way he's behaving is not going to make it any shorter. Now, you go back and tell him that."

When she went back to Freddy, the judge gave her some time to tell him what he said before resuming the questioning, and then Judge Oliver said, "Okay, tell the court why you drew the map."

After Denise relayed the judge's remarks to Freddy, he said, "Okay, Judge, I didn't draw it so they could go to my house and attack my parents. Earlier that day they were going to take me home so I could see my parents, and I drew the map so they could find their way back when they came to pick me up. Later, before we got to my house, I decided that I didn't want to see my stepdad, and I had them take me back to Luke's house, where I stayed the rest of the day and night."

The judge said, "Thank you for that explanation of the map. Mr. District Attorney, do you have any more questions?"

"Yes sir, I have a few more," and he asked Freddy several more. When he was through, he said, "Your

Honor, that's all I have."

Judge Oliver asked Denise, "Ms. Johnson, do you have anything?"

"No, Your Honor."

Then, the judge said "Mr. Frye, please stand up," and he and Denise both stood. He said, Fred Frye, you have been found guilty of the charge of Accessory Before the Fact of the murder of Hans Von Steen and the attempted murder of Martha Von Steen. It's now my duty to pronounce sentence for the crimes. Fred Frye, I hereby sentence you to five years in the Alabama Department of Corrections in Huntsville, Alabama."

When he said five years, all the air went out of Freddy's sails, and Martha squeezed Carl's hand extra tight. She said in a low voice, "Lord, please help him."

While everyone was still in shock over the verdict, Judge Oliver said, "The verdict is to be suspended, and you will be under probation for five years. You will report to a probation officer once a month, and the prison system will be the ones to set everything up. Mr. Frye, I sincerely hope you will use this experience to do some soul searching and change your behavior to that of a respectable human being. I hope you will finish college and afterwards establish a good career. I must warn you that if you violate your probation in any way, you will be apprehended and taken to prison to serve your full five years. Any questions?"

That time, Freddy said, "No, Your Honor. Thank You."

After court was adjourned, Carl and Martha talked to Freddy and his lawyer, and Martha asked, "When will you be home?"

Freddy looked at Denise questioningly, and she said she didn't know exactly. She said he would have to get everything wound up at the jail and get things set up with the parole board. It might be the next day before everything could be handled.

Martha said, "That's okay; as long as he comes home."

Un-Freddy like, he gave his mother a hug, and what was a shock to everybody, he held out his hand to Carl. Carl, of course, shook hands with him, and Martha felt so good about that.

As they were getting ready to leave the courtroom, Carl said, "It's almost lunchtime. Do you want to go somewhere and get a bite?"

Martha said, "That would be nice."

"Anywhere special that you'd like to go to?"

"Have you ever been to Shirley's Tea Room?"

"No. That's a new one on me. Is it good?"

"Oh yes. They have the best chicken salad sandwiches that you've ever had, and their banana pudding is to die for."

"Sounds good. Tell me where it is, and we'll go."

She gave him the directions, and when they got to the car, that's where they headed.

Shirley's was upstairs over a popular women's

clothing boutique, and they had to wait about ten minutes before they could get a table. Carl was one of only three men in the Tea Room, and when he looked at the menu, he understood why. They had a few things for hearty appetites, but Shirley's catered mostly to women. Carl took Martha's recommendation and ordered the chicken salad sandwich with homemade chips and iced tea. They were delicious, and once again, he took Martha's recommendation and ordered the banana pudding. It reminded him of his mother's.

They talked while they waited and then while they ate, and they both seemed to enjoy each other's company. Carl asked, "Do you think Freddy will go back to school?"

She said, "I don't know. I hope so, but I don't think he'll go back to Auburn."

Carl said, "You know, Jacksonville State is a good school. Maybe he'd like to go over there with Mary."

"That's a thought, but I doubt if Mary would like that very much. I guess we'll just have to wait and see what he wants. With all that's happened, he may want to take off a year."

"Can he take off a year without working?"

"Oh no. He'll have to get a job somewhere."

They talked for a few minutes after they finished eating, then Carl asked, "Are you ready to go?"

"Yes, I'm ready."

Carl asked, "Do you need to go anywhere else before I take you home?"

"No, I don't need to go anywhere. Mary went to the store for me yesterday, so I have plenty of food until she comes home Friday, but thank you, anyway. Carl, can I ask you a question?"

"Sure, you can."

"Well, now that everybody's been tried and everything is over about the attack, are you going to desert me?"

"I can't believe you asked me that. Of course, I'm not going to desert you. You're someone I feel at home with, and I don't feel that with very many people. Why do you ask? Do you want me to leave you alone?"

"No. A hundred times no. It's awfully soon after Hans' death, and people may talk, but I need for you to be with me as much as possible."

"What are your kids going to say about it?"

"All Mary and David want is for me to be happy, and the fact that Freddy shook your hand at court today, may be a sign that he's going to start acting like a real human being. I want all three of them to give me their blessings, but if they don't, it's my life."

When they reached Martha's, Carl got out and went around and helped her out of the car and then walked her to the door. He said, "I'm glad everything turned out the way it did today. Maybe things can get back to normal now."

She asked, "Are you doing anything special tonight?"

"As a matter of fact, I am. Donald Lee has a new

girlfriend, and he wants me to go out with them so I can meet her. This is the first girl that he's acted the least bit serious over, and I'm anxious to meet her. Why do you ask?"

"Oh no reason. I just thought that if you didn't have anything to do, maybe I could cook dinner for you, but maybe we can do that later."

"I'm sure we can, and I'll look forward to it. Right now, I need to get to headquarters, since I've been gone all morning. I'll call you later to see how you're doing." He walked over to her, and she looked as if she wanted to put her arms around him, but he didn't respond to it. He did give her a kiss on the cheek, however, and said, "I'll see ya."

After the Von Steen case, there was not much for the detectives to do, so it didn't matter if Carl was not there all morning. When he finally did get there at two P.M., he and Foy pretty much killed the afternoon, rearranging some of their files and other things of no importance. He left at five and went home to get ready for his night out with Donald Lee and Jean. Soon after he showered and put on fresh clothes, Donald Lee came in from work, and said, "I'd better hurry. I didn't get away from work until late, and I don't want to be late getting Jean."

On their way to pick up Jean, Carl asked Donald Lee, "Where are we going tonight, Son?"

"I thought we would go to the Acropolis. It's a new place, and it's supposed to be really good. You do like Greek food, don't you, Dad?"

"Yeah. You know me. I like everything. If you can eat it, I like it."

On the way to pick up Jean, they had to go nearly all the way through her neighborhood, and when they passed one house, Carl said, "There's where my friend Martha lives," and nothing more was said about it.

When they got to the restaurant, they had a chance for Jean to get to know Carl, and he seemed to love her just as much as Donald Lee did. In fact, he hated to see the evening end. After they left the Acropolis, Donald Lee dropped him off at home, and he and Jean went somewhere else. Carl was glad that he got to meet Jean, and he was really glad that Donald Lee had found a nice girl. Who knows, maybe he'll marry her."

As soon as he got home, he called Martha. "Hi, Lady. What are you doing?"

"Just watching TV. What are you doing?"

"Nothing, yet. I just got home."

"Did you have a good time? Did you like Donald Lee's girlfriend?"

"I really did. I only met her tonight, but I wouldn't be disappointed if one day she became my daughter-in-law. Oh yeah, when we went to pick Jean up, we passed your house. She lives in your neighborhood."

"Really? What's her name?"

"Jean Shelton."

"Shelton? Would her daddy happen to be the new GM at Southern? I heard they moved out here."

Chapter Fifteen

Six Months Later

Donald Lee and Jean have missed very few days being together, and it looked as though wedding bells might be in their future. Carl and Martha Von Steen have been keeping steady company as well. Some people, close to each of them, thought they would have married already, but the word wedding had never been mentioned by either of them.

Freddy Frye took off one semester from school, and then he transferred to Walden University in Huntsville, where he could get a clean start. The trauma of his trial, and the attack on his parents made a lasting impression on him, and he changed so, one would think he wasn't even the same man. He, and his brother, David, and his sister, Mary were okay with their mother seeing Carl, and Donald Lee was okay with it, too. In fact, they all encouraged their parents because they felt they would be happy together.

Martha had had a tough life. Her first husband, and the father of her three children had severely abused her before she finally got up the courage to leave him, and then she and Hans were viciously attacked by a gang of drunken college students. She was tough, though. She managed to overcome all that and with God's help, she was living a comfortable life.

Carl hadn't had to go through as much as Martha had, but his wife Chelsea, suffered from ovarian cancer, and he took care of her the best he could, while being a wonderful father to Donald Lee. He never missed any of Donald Lee's ball games and was there for him whenever he needed to be.

Billy and Sylvia were very happy with their new baby, and Buddy and Sally Jo were expecting their first in three months.

Sally Jo was still working, and Buddy was traveling a lot, and one night, when he was home, the phone rang, and it was Jolene. Without saying all the usual preliminary talk, she immediately asked, "Buddy, do you happen to be watching PBS?"

"No, we're watching a movie."

"Well, I've been watching PBS, and they have a Travelogue kind of program that comes out of the UK, and they go all over the world, showing vacation spots that are supposed to be like heaven. Tonight, they were showing Bali, Indonesia, and at one point, they went into a very nice looking bar and restaurant and panned the inside and talked to some of the people in there. Buddy, I could swear D.W. was in there. They didn't talk to him, but I saw him, I'm sure. They panned over to where he was sitting, and then, when they did it a second time, he was not there. I was hoping you saw it."

"I wish I had. Are you sure it was D.W.?"

"Yeah, I'm almost positive. Buddy, I still miss him. I wonder if there's any way we could find out who the people were on that program."

"Did you say it was a UK program?"

"That's what it said on the screen."

"I don't know, Jolene. You could call PBS, and maybe they could tell you how you might be able to find out, but other than that, I couldn't even guess."

"I may try that. Thanks, Buddy. Are you and Sally Jo doing okay?"

"Yeah, we're fine. You knew that we're pregnant, didn't you?"

"No, I didn't. Well, congratulations. Tell Sally Jo to call ne sometime. I'll see you, Buddy."

"Bye, Jolene."

After he hung up, Sally Jo asked, "Who was that?"

"It was Jolene. She thinks she saw D.W. on TV a little while ago."

"Why in the world would he be on TV? Was it on a game show or something?"

"No, it was a Travelogue type program from Bali."

"Bali? Where's Bali, Honey?"

"I think it's in Indonesia."

"Wow. What would D.W. be doing in Bali?"

"My guess is he's hiding. Remember before he left Belmont, the police were looking for him? They thought he killed Coco Cochran. Maybe he is in Bali."

In the meantime, at the Forty Thieves Bar in Seminyak, D.W. or J.C. as he was now being called settled in for his first Margarita of the day. He kept his eyes on the exits because a few weeks ago, a camera crew from one of the British Broadcasting companies did one of their travelogue stories in Bali, and a part of the story was filmed and customers interviewed at Forty Thieves while he was there. He was afraid they got his picture without his knowing it, and as soon as he realized what was happening, he left the bar.

Now, on that particular day, they were showing reruns of that program while he was there, and he saw himself on television. It liked to have scared him to death. He thought, *they say you can run, but you can't hide. How true that is. Here I am, ten thousand miles from home with a new name, and somebody finds me. I pray this wasn't on in the states. I might need to go to another town to live, just in case. Maybe I need to go to another country.* He always had two margaritas, so he had one more after he finished the one he was drinking, then he got up and went home.

The next morning, he got some brochures of different places in Bali, and he decided to look for a place in Mount Agung. It was only a few miles away, so he got a cab and went to a realtor over there. When he got to Mount Agung, it was like a completely different place, even though it was just a short distance from Seminyak.

There weren't that many places in Mount Agung, and J.C. wasn't able to find anything on that trip, so he thought he might look at Komodo Island, the next day.

When he got to Komodo Island, he realized he had made a mistake when he saw some of the Komodo Dragons. Komodo Dragons are big lizards that grow up to ten feet long, and J.C. could picture one of them coming into his house while he was sleeping some night. He saw a couple of houses that he liked but the big lizards kept him from getting one, so he went back to Seminyak to re-assess his options.

At first, he thought he would contact a lawyer, but then he decided he didn't want to talk to anyone like that because he didn't know anyone he could trust. Then he thought he would go to the library, if they had one, so he asked around to see if they did, and glory bee, he found one. He got directions to it and took a cab. He searched the legal books for something; he didn't know exactly what, but after going through several books, he found one that had a section on admission to Indonesia, and while reading that section, he found what he was looking for. There is no extradition treaty between Indonesia and the United States, and he had a feeling of relief after he read that. He had already found out about that before he left Belmont, but when he saw himself on TV, it scared him, and he just wanted to reassure himself from the Indonesian side.

One Week Later

One day, when he went into the Forty Thieves Bar, where he had become fairly well known, and sat down at the bar. The bartender spoke to him and asked him if he wanted his regular, and J.C. told him he did. There was hardly anybody else at the bar, so he and the bartender were carrying on a conversation, and during the conversation, the bartender asked him, "You're an American. Do you happen to know anybody named D.W. Handy?" J.C.'s heart jumped up in his throat when he was asked that. "There was a fellow in here the other day asking if I knew him, and I told him I didn't. Do you know anybody with that name?"

"No, I've never heard of him. Who was the guy looking for him?"

"He said he was a P.I. out of Jakarta, and some woman from the states is looking for this D.W. guy, and she contacted him because she thought he might be in Bali."

J.C. asked, "Did he find the guy?"

"I don't know. I never saw him again."

He was unnerved to find out that someone was looking for him, and when the bartender walked away he did some serious thinking. After the initial shock, he came to the conclusion that it wasn't the authorities looking for him because he didn't think they would send a Private Investigator. After more thought, he came up with the idea that it must have been Jolene who hired the P.I., and she didn't know that he was no longer D.W. Handy. After further thought, he convinced himself that it must have definitely been Jolene, because she probably saw that British Travelogue program and saw his picture on it. He felt better after coming to that conclusion and told the bartender that he was ready for his second margarita. From that moment on, he paid close attention to anyone he saw come in to where he was that looked as if they might be a detective or somebody like that. He felt sure that since Bali was known as a tropical paradise, anyone in a business suit or uniform would not be on vacation. Anyone like that would be out of place, and he would be sure to see and avoid them.

Going to Forty Thieves every day had almost become a habit for him. He liked the people that frequented it, and he liked the bartender, who knew pretty much something about everybody that was considered a regular. It had been over a week since his scare about the TV program, and he was feeling more at ease every day. He had let his guard down and was not paying attention to the people that came in, and one day, while he was sitting at the bar, having a margarita, someone slipped up behind him, put their hands over his eyes and said, "Guess who."

At certain times, such as something serious happening, in less than a split second, one's life flashes before their eyes, and that was one of those times for J.C. In that split second, when those hands went over his eyes, he saw himself being arrested and taken back to Alabama, and nothing could describe his relief when the hands were removed, and he saw who it was. He turned and there stood Sandy Moore, the lady from the flight they both took to Tokyo. He didn't even stand up. He just grabbed her and hugged her as tight and as long as he dared. Finally, after his breath returned, he asked, "Sandy, how did you know I was here? I'm so glad to see you."

She said, "I saw you on TV. I wasn't sure it was you at first, and then after a few days, they showed a rerun, and when I saw it, I knew it had to be you. I've always wanted to come to Bali, and so I booked a flight to Denpasar, in hopes I could find you. I've been down here for two days already, and I must have been to twenty bars, looking for you with no luck until now."

He asked, "Have you been in Tokyo ever since I last saw you?"

"Yeah, I had thought I might just stay there, but now that I'm in Bali, I may change my mind. This place is fantastic, especially now that I've found you. Are you planning to stay here?"

"I'm not sure. I've already been here longer than I thought I would have been. I just don't want to make any permanent plans. Where are you staying?"

"I'm at the Grand Hyatt. Where are you?"

"I rent a little bungalow close to the beach here in Seminyak. You'll have to come see it while you're here. Have you been to the beach yet?"

"No. I haven't been anywhere except to about a hundred bars looking for you. Now that I've found you, I'm anxious to get to the beach. Is where you live nice?"

"My bungalow or the beach?"

"Both. Tell me about the beach first."

"Okay. At the risk of sounding like I'm the Chamber of Commerce, Seminyak Beach is considered the hippest beach in Bali. The beach is beautiful, and people say it has an infinite horizon. In the words of the Chamber, the sunsets are magical. I usually drink margaritas, but Seminyak Beach is known for its homemade Sangria. I would probably change, but Forty Thieves doesn't have that particular Sangria, and I like Forty Thieves' margaritas."

"You've sold me. Now tell me about your bungalow."

"It's nothing special: just a typical beach house. The main thing it has is what people say is important; location, location, location."

She said, "I'm dying to see them both."

"Let me finish my drink, and we'll go out there."

The whole time he was finishing his drink and listening to her talk, he had an uncomfortable feeling. He thought to himself, *I wonder what she's doing here. I've been so careful, and I've been able to spend several months, trouble free, and I sure don't want to mess things up because of a woman. She's sure good-looking, though. I'll just have to be extra careful.*

While he was thinking, she said, "Come on, J.C. let's go."

He said, "Okay, I'm ready."

She said, "Good. Do we pass any shops on the way where I can get a bathing suit. I didn't bring one."

"You mean you came to Bali and didn't bring a bathing suit?"

"You've got to remember that I've been in Tokyo, and you don't need a bathing suit there."

"Oh yeah, I forgot."

When they left Forty Thieves, they hailed a cab. J.C. had already told Sandy that he didn't know about any ladies' clothing stores, so when they got into the cab, she asked the cab driver if he knew of any nice ladies boutiques, and he said, "My girlfriend does a lot of shopping at a place called the Lizzy Gooch Shop, and she looks great."

"Okay, take us there, please."

J.C. thought she was going in to buy just a bathing suit, but before she left, she had bought two expensive bathing suits, two coverups, and a pair of flip flops, along with sunscreen and oil. He heard the clerk say, "That will be four hundred twenty-nine dollars and seventy four cents, U.S."

He was sitting in a chair when she came up and said, "Ready to go, Sweetie?"

"I'm ready."

They went outside and waved down another cab, and J.C. gave the driver the address.

When they got to J.C.'s, they went in, and Sandy said she was tired and plopped down on the sofa. In a few minutes, she asked J.C., "Are we going to the beach?"

He said, "You can go, but I think I'll pass this afternoon. Tell you what. Get your suit on, and I'll take a couple of chairs and go with you. It's going to be time for the sun to set before long, and you're going to like that. You've probably never seen a sunset like it before."

Sandy said, "You know, I don't think I'll dress for the beach today, it's so late. I think I'll just go down and sit with you and watch the sun set."

Each of them grabbed a chair and went down to the beach and found an empty spot that they liked and sat down. Sandy was very interested in what J.C. had been doing since she saw him in Tokyo, and she asked him a barrage of questions.

He tried to satisfy her with his answers, but he could tell by her expression, that he was being too vague about some things. He liked her a lot, but he was really careful not to drop his guard because there was just something about her that he didn't trust. When the question-and-answer session slowed down, the sun was beginning to set, and no words could describe it. They watched until the sun was completely gone, and then J.C. asked. "Are you hungry?"

"I'm starved. What are we going to do for dinner?"

"Well, I guess if you've been here for two days already, you've found out that most restaurants aren't what you are used to. Most of the better restaurants serve Indian food, but there are a few that serve American or Mediterranean, so the choices are limited. There are some fast food restaurants that serve burgers, if that's what you want, so it just depends on what you're hungry for. What would you like?"

"I'll leave it up to you. You've been down here long enough to have scouted out the best places. What do you suggest?"

"I suggest we go to the Boardwalk Restaurant. They serve American, and what I've had has been good."

"Good. Let's go to the Boardwalk."

"Do you need to go back to your hotel first?"

"No, I'm ready."

"Me too. Let's see if we can find a cab."

The food at the Boardwalk was just what they both wanted, and they had a great time, but J.C. was still a little uneasy. They talked about Sandy's divorce among other things after they finished eating, and J.C. was very careful with what he said.

Finally, they were ready to leave, and J.C. hailed a cab. When they were underway, he asked Sandy, "Are you going to take this cab back to your hotel, or do you want to stop by my house for a while?"

"I thought if you didn't care and wanted me to, I would stay with you tonight."

"Okay. Wow. I didn't know what you wanted to do."

She went back to J.C.'s with him and didn't leave. The first week or so was fun. A lot of people would say it was paradise, but J.C. was so paranoid about things, he couldn't relax enough to enjoy everything

Sandra offered. She kept talking about if they were married, or when they got married, or someday, after they were married for a long time, they would do this or that, and it was scaring him because he had no intention of getting married, especially to her. Another thing that bothered him was the fact that she had so much money, she wanted to do things that other rich people did, and he was certainly not rich.

Three Months Later

J.C. decided that he was going get away from Sandra, but he had to do it in such a way that she wouldn't know he was leaving. Every day, she spent most of the day lying on the beach and did nothing productive. Lying in the sun was her world.

He devised a plan and immediately started to set it up. He needed to figure out a way to get away from her during the day, sometimes, while she was at the beach, and he thought he had come up with the perfect plan.

One day he told her, "Honey, I met a couple of guys while I was at the store the other day, and they asked me to go fishing with them. They have a big boat, and they said they go out and catch big sailfish and marlin. They said they had another buddy that used to fish with them all the time, but he got sick and can't go out anymore, and they said they'd like for me to take his place, if I'd like to. I jumped at the chance because I've always wanted to do something like that. I'll just be gone two or three days a week, and I'll be here every night."

She said, "You're going to leave me here by myself two or three days a week? I don't know if I like that."

He said, "Well, you're at the beach all day, every day, and I'm not that big a beach person." He acted a little hurt and said, "But if you don't want me to do it, I don't guess I will."

She went over and put her arms around him and said, "Darling, if that's what you want to do, then do it. I don't mind."

The first day that he was going 'fishing', he went to the library. He wanted to see what other countries did not have extradition treaties with the United States besides Indonesia, and he was surprised by how many there were. He read about several of them, but he thought he would go to Nicaragua when he left Bali. His research showed that Nicaragua was about the same distance as Atlanta, meaning it's a long way. He went back home that evening, telling Sandy about all the fish they caught, and she was so happy for him.

He stayed at home with her the next day, and while she was sunbathing, he was working on his plans to leave. He thought that if he could put all the pieces together, he might be able to leave within a week.

Sometime, between then and the time when he first arrived at Bali, he had found a counterfeiter, and he had him make a new Passport, a Social Security card, a Tampa, Florida driver's license, and whatever kinds of other papers he thought he might need.

He stayed with Sandy one more day before he went 'fishing' again, and while he was supposedly 'fishing', he went to Prima Moda, a men's clothing store in Denpasar. He bought several items and had them hold them until he told them where to have them delivered.

From the clothing store, he went to the airport while he was in Denpasar, and he bought a one way ticket to Managua Nicaragua for the following Saturday . He wasn't sure if he could get away that day, but he thought he could, and he went ahead and bought the ticket. He could always cancel it if he couldn't use it that day. The flight was scheduled to leave Denpasar at seven thirty five, Saturday morning, and he would be flying business class to Managua on a Boeing 747, and then he would transfer to a regional airline from Managua to Bluefields, Nicaragua, a two hundred and fifty mile trip. He read that Nicaragua was split into three regions, and the region that included the city of Bluefields was largely English speaking, and that's where he wanted to go.

From the airport, he went to a pharmacy and bought a bottle of 10mg strength Melatonin, and then he went home. He and Sandy fixed a drink, and he told her about the three nice sailfish they caught that day.

Friday morning, he told Sandy that he was going to town, while she was at the beach, to buy some new t-shirts and pants and wouldn't be gone too long. He told her he would be back in time to go to the beach with her that afternoon, and they would go out for a nice dinner that evening. She was all for that, and when he got ready to leave for town, she gave him a kiss goodbye.

He hailed a cab and told the driver where to take him, and while he was in the cab, he asked the driver, "I'm going to need to get a cab to take me to the airport at four thirty in the morning. How should I make sure I can get one at that time?"

The driver said, "I can pick you up."

J.C. asked, "You're working today. Will you be working at that time in the morning?"

"Yes sir. I work nights on Friday, Saturday, and Sunday, so if you want me to, I can pick you up."

"Great. I'll want you to pick me up at four thirty and take me to the airport. Whatever you do, don't blow your horn when you come to pick me up. I'll be looking for you, so again, don't blow your horn. Is this going to be a problem for you?"

"Oh no. I'll get you at four thirty and take you to the airport, and I thank you."

"Good man. I can count on you, can't I?"

"You can count on me."

J.C. got out of the cab at Prima Moda and went in to talk to the salesclerk that sold him the clothes he bought before. He told the clerk, "I want you to please have my things delivered to the airport to the Qatar Airways ticket counter. I will be leaving on

Qatar tomorrow morning at seven thirty, and you can tell them to either hold my things, or you can go ahead and check them. I'll call and verify this just as soon as I get back home."

He gave the clerk some money in order to get him to handle all that for him, and he left. Unless something unforeseen came up, that was all he had to do to get ready to leave. He hated to leave, and wouldn't if it weren't for the fact that Sandy moved in on him, and he was afraid that his situation would one day be exposed because of her.

She was surprised that he got back so early, and he told her that he couldn't find anything he liked. He explained that the Melatonin he had in the sack was what he bought to help him sleep. She knew he hadn't been sleeping well, and his explanation of the sleep aid satisfied her. She was already dressed for the beach, and J.C. told her to go on down, and he would be there in a few minutes. They enjoyed the afternoon together, and in some ways, J.C. hated to see it end, but he knew he had to.

They had a sandwich for lunch at a Tiki hut on the beach, and about an hour later, Sandy said she had to go up to the house to use the bathroom. While she was in the bathroom, she looked over and J.C, had left his briefcase in there, and it was open. She saw something sticking out, and her curiosity got the best of her, and she looked at the folder. She was in shock when she saw what it was. It was J.C.'s United States Passport with the name D.W. Handy. There was also an Indonesian Passport with the name James Carleton Holmes.

She didn't know what to do or what to say, so she decided to say nothing for the time being. He seemed so excited about where he was taking her for dinner that night, that she didn't want to spoil it for him, and she decided to wait and confront him with the new information the next morning. They spent the rest of the afternoon at the beach, and then went up to the house to get ready for dinner. J.C. was planning to take her to the Apertif Restaurant; a high dollar restaurant where the prices ran from sixty to a hundred and fifty dollars per person. Normally, J.C. wouldn't splurge like that, but he thought on this occasion, it would be worth it.

Dinner was wonderful, and they had two or three drinks, each, before and after they ate. J.C. was careful not to get high, but Sandy was almost to the point of being intoxicated. After they were through, they took a cab home, and J.C. suggested she go in and get dressed for bed, and he would fix them a nightcap. They both went to the bathroom with Sandy going first. After she came out and was dressing for bed, J.C. went in, and while he was in there he took a couple of Melatonin out of the bottle and put them in his pocket.

In a few minutes, Sandy came out, and J.C. had her drink ready for her. He had put two, 10mg Melatonin pills in it, stirred it, and it was completely tasteless. She drank it, and J.C. made a toast. He held his drink up for the toast, but he had failed to put any alcoholic beverage in his. He fixed one more after that, and at that point, Sandy was pretty well gone. He went into the bedroom with her, and they had one last fling before they went to bed to sleep. It wasn't long before Sandy was past the point of loving or anything else, and J.C. laid her down in the bed and tucked her in. She went to sleep immediately, and he kissed her on the cheek.

He couldn't afford to go to sleep, so he went into the kitchen and made a pot of strong coffee. It was already midnight, and he was going to have to get up at three, so he thought he just wouldn't go to sleep. There would be plenty of time for sleep on the way to Managua.

Between nearly a full pot of coffee and occasional brief dozes, J.C. managed to stay awake all night. Sandy usually got up to go to the bathroom around three a.m., and J.C. was counting on the Melatonin he gave her to keep her from waking up, and his calculations were right on. He never undressed, so he didn't have to dress when he got ready to go. All he did was wash his face, brush his teeth, and comb his hair.

The cab pulled up precisely at four thirty, and J.C. saw it coming and went to the street to meet it when it got there. The driver knew they were going to the airport without J.C. telling him, but he told him anyway. They talked on the way, and when they got to the Qatar Airways terminal, J.C. got out. The driver had been such a help, he tipped him with an extra heavy tip and shook his hand as he got out of the car.

His flight was scheduled to leave at seven thirty-five, and by the time he got checked in and went through security, it was six fifteen, so he had some time to kill before he boarded his flight. He did the same thing he did before his flight from Atlanta to Tokyo; he went to a gate that was not his and waited until time to board his plane before going to his gate. Not wanting to get on the plane too early, he waited until the last minute before boarding, and by then, it was almost seven fifteen.

About two minutes before he got on the plane the loudspeaker at the airport announced, "Would Mr. J.C. Hodges please go to the airport information counter, and they announced that twice," and his heart was beating out of his chest. Then, in a minute, another announcement was made, and that time it paged Mr. D.W. Handy to go to the airport information counter. He thought, *how in the world did she come up with that? I hope this plane takes off in a hurry.* By then, he was a nervous wreck. Almost immediately after he took his seat, the engines started, and in about five minutes, they were taxiing down the runway, getting ready to lift off.

He felt a ton of relief when they took off, but he was still in nervous shock about his real name being called over the intercom. How could Sandy find out that his name was really D.W. and not J.C.? Then it came to him; the folder holding his passport had been carelessly left open, and when she went up to the bathroom, she found it.

Now, the question is, will she use it to try and hurt him? He was weighing both sides of the question. First, they had had a great time together for several months, and that should account for something, but he ran off and left her without telling her he was leaving, and that didn't bode well. The only thing he could think of was to completely disappear in Nicaragua as J.C. Hodges, and maybe, sometime, try to find another counterfeiter and have new papers made, using another name. It had been almost a year since he killed Coco, and he had hoped he would be able to put it behind him, but due to his own carelessness, he was still in trouble, and it was all because of a woman. With all of his careful planning, how could he have been so stupid?

All he could do was hope she wouldn't pursue trying to find him, and if she didn't, then he might be okay, but if she tried to cause him trouble, then he may have a problem.

He thought of every scenario that he could think of, and the one thing he always came back to was the fact that there was only a limited number of flights leaving Denpasar that morning, and for a good private investigator, it probably wouldn't be too hard to find out who was on the passenger lists. All these thoughts went through his mind, and he knew there was nothing he could do about it while he was on an airplane, seven miles up, on the way to a strange country, so as hard as it was, he tried to relax. He had bought a Bud Fussell novel at the airport, before he left, and he thought he would try to get his mind on it instead of on what may happen later.

His flight was to take almost twenty hours, and it had only been three since they took off from Denpasar, and there was a long way to go before they would reach Managua, so he might as well try to make the best of it. Maybe he could come up with another scenario to use when they landed.

The next seventeen hours were taken up with reading, napping, eating lunch and dinner, and having a couple of Margaritas in the upstairs cocktail lounge. After the Margaritas, he returned to his seat and was relaxed enough to go to sleep. He fell into a deep sleep, and after about four hours, he was awakened by the Captain announcing that they were beginning their approach to the Augusto C Sandino International Airport in Managua, Nicaragua. The airport was called the ACS Airport for short.

J.C. began to get his things together in preparation for landing, and he had already decided to use his J.C. Hodges passport when he went through Customs, and he just hoped there would be no problem.

After the plane landed and the passengers were going through Customs, there was some kind of disturbance at the head of the line, and several Policemen were involved, and more were coming. Then one officer came back almost to where J.C. was and began telling the passengers to come another way, and the other way allowed them to enter the country without presenting their passports, other than holding them up to show the officer as they walked pass. How lucky was that?"

J.C. went straight to the ticket counter of the Aerotaxis La Costeno Airline. Aerotaxis La Costeno was a small regional airline that served primarily Managua and Bluefields. He bought a one-way ticket to Bluefields, and he couldn't wait to get there. He had read about a hotel there, named Hotel Tranquilo, and he thought he would try to get a room there.

Fortunately, there was a vacancy, and he checked in for an undetermined amount of time. He wanted time to explore and to decide if he would stay there or move on to somewhere else because his first impression was anything but good. When he first arrived, he thought the area looked as if it was total poverty, but he was there, and there wasn't anywhere else for him to go at the time, so he decided to at least give Bluefields a chance. Maybe there were some nicer places that he would just have to find. He hoped so, anyway.

Chapter Sixteen

Spring was beautiful, especially around Lake Tanisi. The trees had gained their fresh new leaves, for the most part, and many of the early species of flowers were blooming, and the entire area was showing signs of new life. Sally Jo thought that was what spring should be, new life. Easter was in the spring, and that's when Jesus came back to life after being crucified. He was the ultimate example of a new life, and Christians, everywhere celebrated that.

It was Sally Jo and Buddy's little boy, Joey's first Easter, and they couldn't wait to teach him about Jesus. It seemed as if everybody was ready for winter to be over, and some had bigger plans than others. One such couple was Donald Lee Mathis and Jean Shelton.

They had been going together for almost a year, and finally, they decided to get married, and the wedding was to be on June second, however, Jean had begun to have some health problems, and Donald Lee was concerned about her, as were her parents.

Jean was normally a ball of fire, when it came to energy, but lately, she didn't seem to be able to do anywhere near what she would usually do. Donald Lee would sometimes make fun of her because of her huge appetite, but in the last few weeks, she hardly had any appetite at all, and she had to make herself eat, and as a result, she had lost a lot of weight.

One day, at breakfast, Sarah, Jean's mother noticed that Jean looked kind of yellow. She said, "Honey, look at me."

Jean asked, "Why? What's going on?"

Sarah told her, "You look a little jaundiced, and your eyes look a little yellow. I'm going to call Dr. Kerley and see if he can see you this afternoon. I think you might have something wrong."

"I don't want to go to the doctor, Mom," Jean said.

"Well, I think you need to. I hope he can see you right away."

Jean said, "I hear people talking about trying to get into a doctor's office and having to wait two or three months. Dr. Kerley is so popular, it will probably be at least that long before he can see me."

"Well, if he can't see you, then I'll call someone else because I feel sure you need to see somebody."

She went to the phone and dialed Dr. Kerley's office and asked to speak to Dr. Kerley or his nurse. Kathy, Dr. Kerley's nurse answered, and Sarah told her what was going on with Jean, and that she felt she should see the doctor as soon as possible. Kathy told her, "Mrs. Shelton, Dr. Kerley is completely booked up for the foreseeable future, so I don't know what to tell you. I'll tell him you called and I'll tell him what you told me about Jean, and I'll call you back. Okay?"

"Okay, Kathy. Please call me as soon as you can because if Dr. K can't see her, I'll call someone else.

I'm pretty sure she needs to see someone right now."

"Alright. Dr. Kerley is with a patient right now, and as soon as he's through with them, I'll talk to him, and I'll call you back after I've talked to him.

"Thank you, Kathy."

In less than fifteen minutes, Sarah's phone rang, and when she answered, Dr. Kerley was on the line. "Mrs. Shelton, from the way you described Jean's symptoms, I think she needs to come into my office as soon as you can get her here. Can you bring her in first thing after lunch at one o'clock?"

"Yes, I can have her there then."

"Good. I'll see y'all then."

When she hung up and told Jean that they were going to see Dr. Kerley right after lunch, she said, "I think I'll call Donald Lee."

Sarah said, "I don't think I'd bother him at work because you don't know what to tell him. Why don't you wait and see what the doctor says before you talk to him about it?"

"I guess you're right. Mom, have you ever had anything like this?"

"No, Sweetie, I haven't."

"What do you think is wrong with me?"

"Darling, I don't know, but Dr. Kerley will probably know, so try not to worry about it until we see him."

They were at Dr. Kerley's office a little before one for their one o'clock appointment, and Jean was kind of nervous.

Dr. K took her in first thing after they reopened after lunch and began examining her. He had the lab take what looked like a gallon of blood as well as a urine specimen. He appeared to be very serious during the examination, and finally, he said, "Will y'all come into my office for a couple of minutes? I think we need to talk about a couple of things."

Jean and Sarah followed him into his office, and after they had sat down he said, "Jean, it's too early to tell until we've done more tests, but from what I see now, it looks as if you've got some sort of a problem with your liver, and I want you to have what is called a Hepatic Screening. That will give us much more detail and should tell us how we should treat you. Will you agree to the screening, Jean?"

"Of course, if you think it's necessary. I need to tell you this Doctor, I hardly drink at all, so I don't see how I can have sclerosis, or whatever it's called."

"It's called cirrhosis, and that's not what you have. What you may have is not caused by drinking."

"What do I have?"

"It's a long word. It's called *Hepatic Encephalopathy.* Okay, Miss Jean, we're through for today. My nurse will set up the appointment for the screening, and we'll call you. In the meantime, I'm going to prescribe a round of Antibiotics, and they should help get rid of the jaundice. Do you have any questions?"

"Yes sir. I have a couple."

"Okay, shoot."

"First, will the screening be done here in your office?"

"No. It will be done at the hospital. Next question."

"I'm supposed to get married June second. Do you think that what I have will interfere with my wedding?"

"I sincerely hope not, but let's get through this screening and see where we are. Anything else?"

"No sir. I guess that's all. Will the screening be done pretty soon?"

"I'm going to try and get it done within the week."

They told Dr. K goodbye and headed to the pharmacy to get the prescription filled and then home. Jean said, "I'm anxious to talk to Donald Lee. It's so late in the day now, I guess I'll just wait 'til he comes over tonight to tell him."

Since Sarah was busy with Jean most of the day, she didn't try to cook dinner. She talked to Monty after they got home from Dr. Kerley's, and they planned to eat out that evening. Donald Lee, of course, would be included.

Before Donald Lee and Jean met, Donald Lee stayed in his apartment in Huntsville during the week and came home and spent the weekends with his dad, Carl, but since he and Jean became serious in their relationship, he had been coming home nearly every night, plus, since his mother died, he felt like he should be with his dad more. That evening, he didn't take time to go home and shower after work. He left

Huntsville and went straight to Jean's.

When he got to her house, Monty had already come home, and they were waiting on him, so they could go eat, and he noticed the mood was sort of somber when he walked in. He didn't say anything about it. He just figured Jean was having a hard time during her usual three or four days each month, but then he noticed Sarah and Monty. They, too, were not their usual happy selves, and finally, he asked, "What's going on? Y'all seem to be so sad. What's wrong?

Several seconds went by, and finally, Jean said, "Honey, I'm sick."

The color went out of his face, and he asked, "What do you mean you're sick? Have you got a bug or something?"

"No. It's not that kind of sick," and then Sarah interrupted.

"Don, Jean went to the doctor today, and while he doesn't know exactly what's wrong until they do more tests, he thinks she may have something wrong with her liver. He's setting up a screening later this week, and hopefully it will tell us what's wrong, but in the meantime, we need to pray that it won't be something serious."

Monty asked, "Is anybody hungry besides me?"

And Donald Lee said, "I am. I had an early lunch today, and I'm starving."

Then, Monty said, "Well let's go eat. Maybe that will make everybody feel better. Is the Dinner Party okay with everyone?"

Sarah said, "That will be fine," and Jean and Donald Lee didn't say anything; they just walked out to Monty's car.

At the restaurant, after they had ordered, Monty tried to lighten the mood by telling some of the things that happened at Southern, that day, and then Donald Lee told about some interesting things that were going on at the Space Center. Sarah seemed to be interested in the things happening at the Space Center, and she kept the conversation going, but Jean didn't say a word the whole time they were there except to answer a couple of questions. When they left the restaurant, they went back to Monty and Sarah's, and even though Donald Lee was there with Jean, she didn't have much to say, so out of respect for her mood, he didn't stay long. Sarah had hoped that his being there with Jean would help her mood, but she was so down that not even Donald Lee's company did any good.

Kathy Simpson, Dr. Kerley's nurse called Thursday afternoon, and told Sarah an appointment for Jean's screening was set up for Friday morning at the Belmont Memorial Hospital at seven a.m.

Sarah told Jean, and she immediately called Donald Lee to tell him. She was hoping that he would take off work to go to the hospital with her and her parents the next day, and of course, he did.

They all arrived at the hospital before seven, the next morning, and someone took Jean back almost immediately after they got there. Monty checked her in and gave them the insurance cards, and then they were told to go to a waiting room down the hall, and someone would be out to talk to them when the procedure was finished.

Jean was gone for about an hour, and then she came out to the waiting room. A nurse came out and told them the procedure went well, and when they asked what they found, the nurse said, "It will be two or three business days before the results are known, and Dr. Kerley will be in touch when he receives the results."

Monty said, "You said two or three business days. This is Friday. Do you mean that we won't know anything until sometime next week?"

The nurse replied, "I'm afraid not. If Dr. Kerley pushes them to start working on it today, we might be able to find out something by Monday, but the lab is closed on the weekend."

Monday went by, and they didn't hear anything, and Monty was getting a little irritated. Late, Monday afternoon, he called Dr. Kerley's office and spoke with Kathy, and in no uncertain terms, he told her he wanted the results of Jean's screening ASAP. She explained that they would call the minute they heard something, and it might be necessary for Jean to come into the office, depending on what was found. She seemed to satisfy him with her explanation, and he thanked her and hung up.

At nine thirty, Tuesday morning, Kathy, from Dr. Kerley's office called Jean and said. "Good morning, Jean. This is Kathy at Dr. Kerley's office. Listen, we have received the results of your screening, and Dr. Karley wanted me to call you to see if you can come in sometime this afternoon. Can you?"

"Yes ma'am, I can come. What time?"

"Can you be here while we're closed for lunch at twelve thirty?"

"Yes ma'am. I can be there at twelve thirty."

"Great. That will give Dr. Kerley some extra time to spend with you. We'll look for you then."

She hung up and yelled for Sarah. When Sarah acknowledged her, she said, "That was Dr. Kerley's office. They want me to come in at twelve thirty. Can you go with me?"

When they got to the doctor's office at twelve thirty, Dr. K. was waiting for them. Kathy led them to his office and told them to have a seat. He had several papers on his desk, and he held on to what Jean thought must be the main one.

The first thing the doctor did was to look into her eyes and then look at her abdomen. He said, the jaundice looks better., then, he said, "Jean, Honey, I've always been one to think positive, and I'm trying to think positive about your situation.

"I told you the other day that I think you may have what is called Hepatic Encephalopathy, and according to the screening, that's what you have."

"Is it serious, Dr. K?"

"I'm afraid it is."

"Can you give me some medicine that will cure it?"

"I'm sorry, but no."

"Am I going to die?"

He said, "Not if I can help it. We're going to try to find you a donor that will give you part of their liver."

"You mean a transplant?"

"That's what I mean. I'll tell you what we need to do. We need to get the word out that you need a liver transplant, and hopefully, we can find one real soon and get this taken care of. Are you from Belmont?"

"No sir. We're from Burlington, North Carolina."

"Here's what I suggest. Go home and make a list of everybody you know, and then make a list of your Church, your school, your clubs, and anything else you can think of to make people aware of your situation. When you talk with someone, just come out and ask them if they would be willing to give you part of their liver if they match. You can't afford to beat around the bush. Just ask them.

"Now, if anybody tells you they will give you part of their liver, they must be tested to see if they're a match. You can't accept any liver that's not a perfect match."

Jean asked, "Dr. Kerley, how long can I live if I can't find a donor/"

"We're not going to think about that. We're going to find one."

All at once, Jean perked up and asked, "Dr. Kerley, I have a sister that's a year younger than I am. Do you think she could be a match?"

"She sure could be. Why don't you ask her to get tested?"

"I will."

June was not a match, and several of Jean's friends were tested, but no one matched. She was getting really low when nobody was a match, and then, in a couple of days, Kathy, from Doctor Kerley's office called and said, "Jean, guess what."

"What?"

"We've found a match, and you're not going to believe who it is."

Jean screamed, "You've found a match? That's wonderful. Who is it?"

Kathy said, "It's none other than your boyfriend, Don. He's a perfect match."

Jean said in a low voice, as if she was talking to herself, *"Thank you, God. I just knew you would take care of me, and God, thank you for bringing Donald Lee into my life. Thank you so much."*

As soon as she had thanked God, she asked Kathy, "What do I do now?"

Kathy said, "I'm not sure. I'll have Dr. Kerley call you and go over all the details. I'm sure he'll have to see Don also. That's all I wanted, Jean. I knew you have been on pins and needles, and I just wanted to ease your mind. Congratulations."

"Thank you so much."

Immediately after talking to Kathy, Jean called Donald Lee at work. When he answered, she said, "Guess what. You're a match for my liver, now, we'll

314

truly be one, won't we?"

Excited, he said, "I'm a match? Wonderful. Yeah, we'll truly be one now. Honey, I'm thrilled with this news. What do we do now?"

"I'm not sure. I haven't talked to the doctor, yet, but I'm expecting him to call anytime. I'll let you know when he calls. I just wanted you to know about our being a match and to let you know that you're my hero. I'll talk to you later. Love ya."

"Love you too."

A little later, Dr. Kerley called. He said, "Jean, this is Dr, Kerley. Sorry to have been so long calling, but I've been talking to several of my colleagues about who would be best to do your surgery, and I feel we have come up with the perfect surgeon. His name is Dr. Chris Key, and he is recognized as one of the foremost surgeons in the country in the transplantation field. Luckily, he's located here in Belmont, and you have an appointment with him tomorrow morning at eight thirty. Do you think your fiancé can go with you?"

"I feel sure he can."

"That's great. Jean, you're a lucky lady. Not many people find donors this quickly, and some people don't find one at all, so you should give thanks for your blessings."

"I already have, Doctor. Doctor, do you think Don and I can still get married in June?"

"That's something you need to ask Dr. Key when you see him. I can't answer that. My guess is that you might possibly have to postpone it for a little while, but he can tell you more than I can."

She called Donald Lee again, after she talked to Dr. Kerley and told him that she had an appointment with a Dr. Chris Key the next morning. "Dr. Kerley said that if you can, you need to go with me. Do you think you can?"

"Yeah, I'll go with you. Is he in Belmont?"

"He is. Dr. Kerley said he's across the street from the hospital. I'm getting nervous. Are you?"

"Not yet, but I'm sure I will at some point. What time do we have to go?"

"Eight thirty. Is that alright?"

"That's good. Maybe I can come to work when we finish. Did Dr. K say how long we would be there?"

"No, but with all they're going to do, I'll bet it will take a long time."

Jean drove to Dr. Key's office the next morning and met Donald Lee a little before eight thirty. She told the receptionist, "I'm Jean Shelton, and I have an appointment with Dr. Key at eight thirty."

The receptionist said, "Yes, Jean. Dr. Kerley's office sent us all your paperwork, so we have everything we need. Just have a seat and the doctor will be with you in just a few minutes."

In a few minutes a nurse came out and called Jean's name. She and Donald Lee got up and followed her to Dr. Key's office.

When they got there, Dr. Key stood up, held out his hand and said, "I'm Chris Key."

Jean held out her hand and said, "I'm Jean Shelton, and this is my fiancé, Don Mathis."

Don shook his hand and said, "It's nice to see you, Doctor Key."

Dr. Key said, "Please, have a seat, and let's see what's going on here."

They sat down, and Dr. Key began going through what looked to be x-ray pictures, and then he picked up a paper, put it down and picked up another paper, and then looked at the x-rays again, all without saying a word. After he had looked at everything, he said, "Jean, may I call you Jean?

"Yes sir."

"Jean, I spoke with Dr. Kerley yesterday, and he told me about your problem, and in looking over your x-rays and lab reports, I can see that he was right in his diagnosis. Jeannie, it looks as though you're going to have to have a liver transplant, and I see that Don will be your donor, and that he is a match for you." He smiled and asked, "Am I right so far?"

Don and Jean both smiled and said, "You're right."

"Okay. Let me tell you a little about your liver and what we are going to do. First, your liver is the largest organ on your body, and it's the only organ that can regenerate itself. Now, Jean, your liver is no good anymore, so we need to remove it, completely, and replace it with something else. This is where your friend Don comes in.

"After we remove your liver, we will then take a

portion of Don's liver and attach it to where your liver was originally. We only need a portion of Don's to do the trick. When we attach the piece of Don's liver to you, it will then begin to grow, and at some point, it should grow to full size, and you will then have a normal, healthy liver.

Don, we will probably take less than half your liver to put in Jean, and when we're through, and you heal, you won't know you're missing some of yours. Like Jean, your liver will regenerate itself and grow to its normal size and act in a normal way. Do either of you have any questions?"

They both said they did, and Dr. Key said, "Jean, you first."

Jean said, "I don't know if Dr. K told you or not, but Don and I are scheduled to get married on June second, and now that we're both going to have surgery, will we be well in time to get married on June two?"

"I think you will need to postpone it until a little later. It's going to be two weeks before I can do your surgery, and then afterwards, you will have to do absolutely nothing for three months, and Don, your healing time is going to be from four to six weeks. I know this is a problem for you, but we're talking saving your life here, and a short postponement shouldn't be that big of a deal when you put everything in perspective. Oh, by the way, are you going to invite me to your wedding?"

Don said, "Doc, if you save my girl's life here, I

may let you be my best man. Of course, you will be invited."

Dr. Key said, "Don, you said you had some questions. Wanna ask me?"

"Well, you've answered part of it. You said my healing time will be from four to six weeks. Will I be off from work that long?"

"What do you do, Don?"

"I work for the Air and Space Center in Huntsville."

"What do you do with them?"

"I'm an engineer."

"You probably work inside most of the time, don't you?"

"Yeah. Just about all the time."

"You know, Don, many people are working from home nowadays. They do most of their work on their computer. Could your job be one of those?"

"I'm not sure. I'll have to talk to my supervisor. That might work. Thanks, Doc. By the way, what do Jean and I have to do until our surgery?"

"Nothing. Just wait until somebody contacts you, and then they'll give you instructions on what to do. You both look pretty healthy. Do either of you take any prescription medicines?"

They both said no. Dr. Key told them to not take anything, except if they had a headache or something like that, they could take Tylenol, but otherwise, their system should be free from any meds when they did the surgery.

Don said, "One more question: how long will we be in the hospital?"

Dr. Key said, "About a week. Maybe a little less or maybe a little more, but I'd count on about a week. This could change, but let's schedule you for two weeks from today, okay?"

Don said, "Okay. Thank you very much, Dr. Key. We'll see you in a couple of weeks."

The surgery was scheduled for Tuesday, two weeks from that day, and on Friday, the weekend before surgery, Jean and Don were told to come to the hospital for what was called pre-op. It was a simple thing. Their blood pressure, heart beat, and pulse were checked, just to be sure nothing had changed, and that they were both ready for the transplant. They were told not to eat anything after midnight on Monday, and to report at six thirty on Tuesday morning.

Don asked the nurse doing the pre-op how long the operation would take, and she told him about ten hours.

Over the weekend, Jean and Donald Lee called the people important to them and told them what time the surgery was going to be done. On Tuesday morning, Jean's mother, daddy, and sister were at the hospital, along with her mother's sister and her husband from Burlington, North Carolina. Don's dad, Carl, was there with his lady friend, Martha Von Steen, and surprisingly, Don's Supervisor came. Don told him how much he appreciated him coming and introduced him to everybody.

Before they took them back to the operating room, Jean and Don excused themselves from the others and went a little ways away for a private talk.

Donald Lee told Jean, "Sweetheart, everything's going to be good after this is over, and we'll be very, very happy together. I love you, and I'll see you later."

Jean said, "You know you're my hero, don't you? I love you so much, and I can hardly wait 'til we're married. Are you ready for this?"

Donald Lee said, "Let's do it," and they went back to where their people were.

Two orderlies or nurses, or whatever they were soon came with two wheelchairs and took them somewhere to dress for surgery. They left all their valuables with their folks to hold on to. When they were taken to surgery, the whole group went to the waiting room and sat down.

Every two or three hours, a nurse would come to the waiting room to tell everybody how the surgery was going and how the patients were doing. During the day, some of them read, some just talked, and Monty spent time on the phone to Southern. Different ones went to lunch at different times, but Sarah, Jean's mother never left the waiting room, except to go to the rest room a couple of times. Carl did pretty much the same, except he did go down for a cup of coffee a time or two, and the only times he would leave were right after they got a fresh report on the surgery's progress. He didn't think he would miss anything if he left then.

At five thirty, Tuesday afternoon, Dr. Key came to the waiting room and told everyone the surgery was over, and both Jean and Don were doing well. They would be in recovery for two or three hours, and he suggested they go get something to eat in the meantime. Some went and some didn't. Don's Supervisor decided to go back to Huntsville after he found out that Don was going to be okay, and Carl thanked him profusely for coming. Sarah's sister and her husband went back to Sarah's, and they said they would see Jean the next day.

That left Jean's parents and Carl and Martha, and they decided to all go to a small Mexican restaurant down the street from the hospital. They were all tired from being at the hospital all day, but they wanted to see their children before they went home. They took their time eating, and after a while, Monty said, "It's been about two hours since we saw Dr. Key. Do you think it's time to go back?

Carl said, "I'm ready. Are you ready, Martha?"

She said she was, so they headed back. As soon as they got back to the waiting room, a nurse came in and said, "You all can see the patients now," and she led Jean's parents to one room and Don's Dad and Martha to another. The first thing Jean said when they work her up was, "Is Don alright?"

They assured her he was, and they didn't try to make her talk because she was still groggy from the Anesthesia.

The same was true with Donald Lee. Like Jean,

the first thing he said when they woke him up was "How's Jean?" and they told him she was good.

Sarah wanted to spend the night with Jean, but Monty and the nurse convinced her that it would be better if she went home and came back the next morning. She was not happy about it, but she acquiesced to their wishes and went home to get a good night's rest.

No one had to talk Carl into leaving. He was bushed, and he knew Martha was tired, so they left shortly after seeing Donald Lee. He took Martha home and then went to his house and just fell into bed.

When he got to the hospital the next morning, he found that Donald Lee and Jean were next door neighbors. Jean was in three 0 five and Don in three 0 six. He stuck his head in Jean's door, and Sarah, Monty, and June were already there. Jean was awake and spoke to him, but she drifted off almost as soon as he got there.

Donald Lee was asleep when he got into his room, but he woke up soon after he sat down and said, "Hey, Dad."

Carl said, "Hey. Do you know how you're feeling yet?"

"Not really, but they tell me I'm doing fine."

"I stuck my head in Jean's door a few minutes ago, and it looks like she's doing okay, too. It won't be long until you guys are ready to get up and conquer the world."

Donald Lee said, "I'm ready."

The first day after their surgery was really rough. All either one could think about was getting something to ease the pain. Therapists got them up, but their time up was a horrible ordeal.

The second day was a little better. The pain was still there, but it wasn't quite as bad as the day before, and one time, when they had Don up walking, he stuck his head in Jean's door and asked, "How're ya doing, pretty lady?"

"Good. How about you?"

That was the extent of their contact that day, but the third day was better. They both really hurt that day, and the Therapists still got them up to walk. After Don's walk, he asked the Therapist to take him into Jean's room, which they did, and when he got in there, he sat down for a few minutes and visited with her. After about five minutes, the Therapist said, "Don, this is nice, but you need to get back to your room. Are you ready?"

"Not really. Can't I stay a few more minutes?"

"The Therapist said, "I'm afraid not. I have more patients, and I can't leave you in here."

"Okay, Party Pooper. Let's go. Bye Sweetie. If I can get away from the Stalag Guard here tomorrow, I'll try to spend some time with you. Love ya."

"Love you, too."

By the fifth day, both their pains were considerably better, and they spent quite a bit of time in each other's rooms. They even had the cafeteria lady take Don's lunch into Jean's room, and they ate together. Their conversation was sort of concentrated on their surgery, but mainly, they just enjoyed being together. From then on, they were both back to pretty close to normal, and they began to try and decide when they would get married.

Jean wanted to set the date for late July or August, and Donald Lee wanted to wait until September or early October. After much haggling, they decided on September first, and they hoped that day wouldn't interfere with anything that either of their families had planned.

That afternoon. Dr. Key came by to see them, and he told them that they were doing so well, that if nothing happened, they could go home next Monday. He gave them instructions on what they could and couldn't do, and one of them was they couldn't under any circumstances drive for about six weeks.

That hit them like a two by four because they were both planning to start back with their regular activities in about two weeks, but not being able to drive for six weeks really put a damper on that. Don asked Dr. Key, "Man, that's going to make it tough. If we can't drive, can we ride in a car?"

"Yes. You can ride, as long as it's not too far. Just don't try to drive."

Carl was at the hospital Monday around noon, and Sarah was already there. Like most hospitals, the patients are scheduled to be released, but a doctor has to sign off on the papers. That was true with Jean and

Donald Lee. It took until after two o'clock for their release to take place. Neither of them was impatient because they knew they would be stranded at home and couldn't see each other as much as they would like, so the hold up at the hospital just gave them more time together.

Before they left the hospital, they made plans to see each other as best as they could, but they were going to have to depend on others for transportation, plus, Donald Lee would be working from home every day, and that would limit his time to be with Jean. She thought she would be able to depend on June to take her to his house after he finished working every day. They would just have to wait and see how things would work out. They kissed each other bye when they left and told each other they loved them, and they went home for a rest of nearly three months.

Chapter Seventeen

Two Months Later

D.W. or J.C. as he was now known as, had settled in in Bluefields, Nicaragua. Bluefields was located at the mouth of the Escondido River and Caribbean Sea and had a population of almost sixty thousand, with two thirds of them black. There was a limited number of what D.W. described as nice houses, such as he was used to, and he didn't want something that would make him stand out, but he did want something that looked better than some of the houses in poverty-stricken areas in Bluefields.

After going through about three different realtors, he was able to find what he considered an acceptable place, and he moved in. He wanted to blend in with the general population, and he didn't want anything that would call attention to him or where he lived.

After searching for several days after he arrived in Bluefields, he found one restaurant, in particular, that he liked. There were others, but he liked the Galeria Aberdeen best because they served breakfast, lunch, and dinner, as well as brunch, plus they had a bar that really knew how to make a Margarita. He began to frequent the Galeria Aberdeen, and soon, he found some people who, like him, were there just about every day, and he became acquainted with several of them.

Most of the time, he would have brunch, because it would take the place of two meals, and then he would go back around five o'clock for a Margarita or two.

After living in Bluefields for a little more than two months, he became convinced that he had found the perfect spot to spend the rest of his life.

One day a man went into the American Embassy in Managua and asked to speak to the Ambassador. He handed the lady his card, and in just a minute, the Ambassador had the man escorted into his office.

The Ambassador's name was Peter Blackford, and the man shook his hand and said, "Ambassador Blackford, I am Special Agent Phillip Hines with the Federal Bureau of Investigation."

Ambassador Blackford said, "It's nice to see you, Agent Hines. What can we do for you today?"

"Ambassador Blackford, we…"

He interrupted Agent Hines and said, "Please call me Peter. Ambassador Blackford is so much."

Agent Hines said, "Okay, Peter. As I started to say, we have reason to believe that a wanted felon is in Nicaragua, and we'd like your help finding him."

"Tell me more about this felon. What do you have on him, and why do you think he's in Nicaragua?"

"That's an interesting story. His name is D.W. Handy, and he's wanted for the murder of a wealthy widow in Belmont, Alabama. D.W. disappeared about a year ago and left no trace. Then, four or five months ago, a British television company did a

Travelogue type program and showed the beautiful vacation paradise of Bali, Indonesia. During the program, it showed the inside of one of the local watering holes and panned the crowd inside, and D.W.'s girlfriend, whom he had left when he disappeared, recognized him. She called some of her friends and told them she thought she saw him, and a week or so later, the program was rerun. That time three or four people recognized him. His girlfriend hired a private investigator in Bali to look for him, but he never found anything. There was no trace of a D.W. Handy in Bali, so the trail went cold.

"A few weeks after the TV show, a woman who D.W. had met on his flight from the U.S. to Tokyo, on his way to Bali had also seen the Travelogue and recognized him. She was taken with him when they met on the flight, and she wanted to rekindle their acquaintance, so being freshly divorced and free, she went to Bali to look for this guy. After several days of searching the bars in Bali, she finally found him. He was living on the beach in a small bungalow, and she moved in with him and stayed three or four months.

She knew him as J.C. Hodges of Tampa, Florida, and one day, she saw a folder sticking out of his case and she looked at it. There were two Passports. One with the name J.C. Hodges, and the other, D.W. Handy. He got antsy about that time and disappeared from Bali. This lady knew when he left, but she didn't know where. She knew there could only have been a few flights out of Bali that day, so she became her own detective and found that he had boarded a flight to Managua, using his D.W. Handy Passport. She was pissed off because he left her and reported him to the local Bali authorities. She had no idea why he had two passports, but she knew he must have been running. That was truly an example of the old saying about a woman scorned."

"Agent Hines, you do know that the United States and Nicaragua don't have an extradition treaty, don't you?"

"Yes sir, but I also know that many times, when one country has something the other country wants, trades are made, and I'm hoping that's what will happen here if we can find this guy."

"You've done your homework, haven't you?"

"Yes sir, I have. Peter, I have a picture of this man, and I wonder if there's any way we could have it made into a wanted poster and have it posted around the country and possibly have it shown on TV."

"I don't know. Since this man is not a native Nicaraguan, and as far as we know hasn't committed any crime in Nicaragua, it's hard to say what the authorities here will say about that. I'll have to talk to them and see."

"Mr. Ambassador, when you talk to them, you might mention that our law enforcement people have three of your wanted felons in one of our prisons in South Florida, and if this D.W. Handy is found and captured in Nicaragua, it might be possible to make a trade."

"Are you going to be in Nicaragua overnight Agent Hines?"

"I can be if you think you'll be talking to the right people later today or tomorrow."

"I'll have to talk to Nicaragua's Attorney General, and sometimes he's hard to reach, but we have guest quarters here at the embassy, and you can stay here if you would like."

"I'd like that. Thank you, sir."

"You seem like an easy to get along with person, so why don't you have dinner with my wife and I here at the Embassy tonight?"

"That sounds wonderful. Thanks again."

At dinner, Peter told Phillip, "I tried to reach the Attorney General this afternoon, but he was not in. His assistant said he would be in the office in the morning, and he would tell him I had called."

"Good. Are you on good terms with him?"

"Fairly good, as good as you can get with a semi-honest government official."

"Oh, one of those, hunh?"

"Yep. He's one of those."

The next morning, after breakfast, when the Attorney General had had time to come into work, Ambassador Blackford called his office.

After the greetings and small talk, Peter told him why he was calling, and explained that he would be doing the United States a great favor if he would help. They talked for quite a while, and then Phillip heard Peter say, "Okay. Thank you, sir. I'll call you back."

After he hung up, the Ambassador told Phillip, "Well. It went pretty much like I thought it would. The Attorney General said he would be glad to distribute 'Wanted' posters throughout the country, but he wants you to know that it will be expensive."

"How expensive," Phillip asked.

"He said the Nicaraguan government will print the posters and distribute them, but the Untied States will have to pay for it. He also said he would have to have twenty thousand dollars for himself as a handling fee. He first said twenty-five thousand, but I told him I was sure you wouldn't go that high, and that's when he said twenty. I told him I would call him back, so what do you think?"

"I can't authorize something like that. I can probably get the printing and distributing paid for, but there's no way my people will pay that guy twenty thousand dollars for a handling fee. He probably won't let us handle it ourselves, will he?"

"His way is the only way, I'm afraid."

"Peter, do you have a way I can call my superior?"

"Yeah, we have a phone that we can use to call the states. Do you know the number?"

"Yes sir."

"Okay. Let me place the call for you. Give me the number and the person you want to talk to."

Phillip gave him the name and number, and in a minute, someone answered. Peter identified himself and gave the extension and who he wanted to speak to. Shortly, a voice answered, "This is Charles Crane."

Phillip said, "Charlie, this is Phillip Hines. Look, I'm in Managua, Nicaragua, and I need your help." He explained the situation to Charlie and told him how important it was to do what he asked, and after arguing back and forth for quite a while, Charlie finally relented and agreed to pay the Attorney General the twenty thousand dollars he asked for.

A week later

D.W. left his house and headed to the Galeria for brunch. When he got close, he looked up, and on a telephone pole right out front of the restaurant was a picture of him that read, 'Have you seen this man?', and it gave instructions what to do and a telephone number. His heart sank, and he looked around to see if anybody was looking. When he was satisfied that nobody was, he tore the poster down and stuck it in his pocket.

He had been seeing one particular individual every couple of days ever since he had been going into the Galeria, and he suspected that the guy was not exactly 'kosher' every time he saw him. A couple of guys had become his friends since he started coming in, and after seeing the poster, he knew he had to do something. While drinking his Margarita, he asked one of them who the guy was, and his friend told him that his name was Brian McGregor. He was thought to be one of the biggest drug lords in the whole country, and he was exactly who D.W. needed right then.

He knew there was a risk to getting acquainted

with Brian, but. he was desperate, and so he went over to him and introduced himself. He asked Brian if he could buy him a drink, and he said no. Then, out of desperation, D.W. told him that he really needed to get to Florida on the QT, and did he know anybody that could help him.

At first, Brian said, "No, I don't know anybody that could help you. Why would you think I would know somebody?"

D.W. said, "Oh, no reason. I just thought you might. Let me show you something," and he pulled the poster out of his pocket and showed him low, below the top of the bar. He said, "I took this off a pole in front of the restaurant."

Brian looked at the poster, and then he looked D.W. over carefully, and then he asked, "Do you have any money?"

D.W. said "Yes."

"What would it be worth to you if you could get to Florida?"

"A whole lot. What are you talking about?"

"Do you have twenty five hundred dollars, American?"

"I do."

"Be at the Bluefields airport tomorrow morning at two thirty, and I'll take you to Florida City. Come to the area where the private and business planes are parked. Be sure to bring the money with you."

D.W. asked, "Two thirty in the morning?"

"Yes. I want to be in Florida before it gets

daylight. Do you have a problem with that?"

"Oh no. I just wanted to be sure you were talking about morning instead of afternoon. Morning is fine with me. I'll see you then."

Instead of walking to his house, he took a cab because he didn't want to pass a lot of people and take a chance on someone recognizing him from a poster. When they pulled up at his house, he did the same thing he did in Bali the night before he left. He arranged for the cab to pick him up the next morning at one forty-five to take him to the airport. He wanted to get there early, just in case Brian decided to leave earlier than he said. He waited around the airport until he saw Brian coming in about two fifteen. He walked over to meet him and said, "Good morning."

Brian didn't say good morning back to him. His first words were, "Did you bring the money?"

"Yeah, I did." He made a move to reach in his bag and said, "Let me get it out for you," and Brian said, "Wait 'til we get on the plane."

He led him out to a nice-looking twin-engine Beechcraft and said, "This is it. You can sit in the right seat. After they were on the plane and before they took off, Brian said, "Okay, I'll take the money now, and D.W. handed it to him.

They took off for the three-hour flight to Florida City, and D.W. felt relief to get away from the wanted posters. He looked around and saw a lot of boxes in the back of the plane. He thought he knew what was inside them, but he dared not ask. A tailwind let them fly faster, and they reached Florida City a few minutes after five.

The landing was smooth, and Brian taxied up to the small terminal. He had barely shut off the engines before what looked like an army of Police and DEA agents surrounded the plane.

They dragged D.W. and Brian off the plane and handcuffed them both. It seemed that the Drug Enforcement Agency had been working to catch Brian for several months, but they didn't know anything about D.W. When they asked him who he was, he said his name was J.C. Holmes, and he didn't have anything to do with Brian or his cargo. He said he simply caught a ride with him for a fee. One of the police officers called in to see if there was anything outstanding on a J.C. Holmes, and he was told they had no record of a J.C. Holmes, so they took him to jail along with Brian.

D.W. didn't see Brian anymore after their arrest, and the police kept him pretty busy with their constant interrogation, which lasted until later that afternoon.

The lead DEA agent said, "This J.C. Holmes guy must have left some traces of his activities in Nicaragua. How about calling the Embassy down there to see if they know anything about him.

One of the agents called the Embassy and spoke to Ambassador Blackford. He told the Ambassador, "Sir, we apprehended a drug dealer named Brian McGregor this morning in Florida City, Florida after a flight from Bluefields, Nicaragua. He had an American passenger that calls himself, J.C. Holmes, and there is no record of a J.C. Holmes, and we're wondering if you have any knowledge of a person by that name."

"No sir. I don't recall ever having a J.C. Holmes on our radar, but I have a hunch. You say he goes by J.C., which are two initials. The FBI was down here about a week ago looking for an American national named D.W. Handy, which are two initials. This may not be the man, but I'm going to send you a picture of him, and you let me know if this is the same person."

"Thank you, sir. I'll let you know just as soon as we get the picture.

It wasn't but about ten minutes before a picture came into the police in Florida City, and everybody in the office gathered around and looked at it. It was a picture of D.W., and as soon as they saw it, they let Ambassador Blackford know that J.C. Holmes was in fact, D.W. Handy. They thanked him for his help and immediately got on the wire to see what kinds of warrants D.W. had against him. Instantly, it showed that he had a warrant out for him for murder in Belmont, Alabama.

They brought him back into an interrogation room and confronted him with the picture, and he admitted that he was D W. Handy. As soon as he admitted who he was, they called the FBI and told them they had him in custody. Before the FBI got there, they talked to him about him having to go back to Belmont, and he agreed to waive extradition from Florida to Alabama.

That afternoon, Special Agent Phillip Hines and another Agent arrived in Florida City to pick D.W. up. After doing the necessary paperwork, they put a belt on him with handcuffs made onto it, and they put chains on his legs. Two police cars escorted them to the airport, where they boarded a small jet, belonging to the FBI, and they immediately took off for Belmont.

The flight was almost nine hundred miles, so it was going to take a while to get to Belmont; from start to finish, about four hours.

D.W. was not like the typical murderer. He was more like a classmate, and he wasn't short on speech. He talked to the Agents about everything, from the time they took off in Florida City, until they landed at Belmont.

The county jail in Madison County was undergoing renovations, and they couldn't put him there, so they put him in the Belmont City Jail. He had been such a hit with people before he fled to Bali, it was almost like a homecoming for a long lost relative when they brought him in.

Some of the policemen and jailers knew him from when he worked the funerals of some of their friends or relatives. He had even sung at the funerals of a couple of their loved ones, but still, he was an accused murderer, and they had to treat him as such.

Some of them considered him a friend, and they wanted to help him as much as they could.

Joseph Lowe, the District Attorney had been alerted that D.W. was on the way in, and he was there when he arrived. After the initial reception with his friends and acquaintances, Mr. Lowe wanted to talk to him. The District Attorney and two detectives took him into a room and told him to sit down. After he was seated, Mr. Lowe asked him if he had an attorney. D.W. said he did not and would appreciate it if the court would appoint one for him.

"Alright. I'll ask the judge to do that. Mr. Handy your arraignment is scheduled for nexr Monday at nine o'clock. If the judge appoints a lawyer for you, he or she should be by sometime before Monday to talk to you and discuss your plea with you."

D.W. said, "Thank you sir."

Things settled down at the police station after a while, but when someone like D.W., who's almost a celebrity, is caught for something, the news media has a heyday with it. In that afternoon's Belmont News-Free Press, large headlines on the front page read 'HANDY RETURNED TO BELMONT', with an accompanying story. Of course, nobody had the story of what he had been doing since he left. All they knew was that he was caught with a major drug smuggler in Florida after a trip from Nicaragua, but that was enough to get the people who knew him talking, and everybody wanted to know what everybody else knew.

Jolene called Buddy. "Have you seen this afternoon's paper?"

"Hi Jolene. No, we don't take the paper. Why, what's in it?"

"The headlines read 'HANDY RETURNED TO BELMONT'. I'm just flabbergasted."

Buddy said, "Wow. What about that? I figured D.W. was smart enough to elude the police and keep out of sight forever."

"I did too. You know I told you I thought I saw him on a TV program from Bali, Indonesia several months ago, but I guess I was wrong about that. The paper says he was caught in Florida with a major drug smuggler after a trip from Nicaragua. I wonder if he was selling drugs."

"I doubt it", Buddy said. "He always hated drugs so bad, I can't see him dealing."

"I just wonder what he's been doing all this time."

"Maybe we'll find out at his trial."

Jolene said, "Buddy, when they have his trial, I think I'm going to go to it every day."

"What about your job?"

"Well, it probably won't last too long, and I've got a lot of vacation built up, so I'll use that as long as it lasts."

"Good idea. I'll try to keep up with what's going on. Thanks for calling, Jolene. Let me know if you find out anything that we'd like to know."

"Okay, I will I'll talk to you later, Buddy."

Talk about D.W. was rampant that night.

Everybody that knew him had something to say, and even people who didn't know him put their two cents worth in. Of course, nobody knew anything other than what was in the paper.

The next morning, Benjamin Price, D.W.'s court appointed attorney went to the jail to see him. After a brief get acquainted time, Mr. Price asked D.W., "D.W., are you guilty of the charges being brought against you?"

D.W. answered, "Yes sir, I am."

Mr. Price said, "Wow. I don't have many clients who say they are guilty from the gitgo. Does this mean you want to plead guilty at trial?"

"Yes sir. It does."

"Are you sure that's what you want to do?"

"Yes sir."

"D.W., you know there are degrees of guilt. The charge against you is first degree murder, and that carries the harshest penalty. Did you have Mrs. Cochran's murder planned ahead of time?"

"No sir. I went there to actually do some things for her, but she was all upset about something and threatened to have me arrested for stealing from her. I couldn't calm her down, and things went from bad to worse, and I knew where her husband kept his pistol, and I got it and shot her before she called the police."

"So, you didn't go to her house planning to kill her?"

"Oh no. I had her Power of Attorney, and I went

341

there to look after some of her things when she jumped on me."

"D.W., what if we could get the charge reduced to Manslaughter. Would you rather do that than face a murder charge?"

"What's the difference?"

"There's a lot of difference. If you're guilty of murder, you can spend the rest of your life in prison, and I can tell you, that's no picnic. If you're guilty of manslaughter, you could face as little as two years. It'll be up to the District Attorney. Would you like for me to talk to him for you?"

"Absolutely. Yes. By all means."

"I thought you would. I had better get out of here if I'm going to see him before he leaves for the day. After I talk to him, I'll come back and let you know what he says, and oh yeah, your Judge will be the Honorable Regina Campbell. I'll see you later, D.W."

"Okay. See ya."

As usual, the newspaper picked up on the story, and in the afternoon paper, there was a short piece that headlined, 'HANDY TO PLEAD GUILTY'. There was still no story. Only the fact that he had been arrested and the guilty plea.

Benjamin Price came to see D.W. the following afternoon with information about his sentencing. He said, "D.W., I spoke with Judge Campbell, and she has set the date for your sentencing for April third. That's one month from tomorrow."

"Okay, Ben. Thank you. Did you talk with the District Attorney?"

"Yes, I did. He was open to the manslaughter charge, but he wants to talk to some people who know you to see what kind of danger you would be to society if you only do a short term, and from what I can find out, you're pretty much loved by about everybody, so let's hope the D.A. talks to some of the same people."

"Thanks, Ben. Will you do me a favor?"

"If I can. What is it?"

"Would you please call Jolene Fuller for me and tell her I'd like to see her. The people here said I could have visitors for two, twenty-minute visits per week, and I'd sure like to see Jolene. I need to apologize to her. I've been gone for over a year, so I don't know if she still has the same number, but if she does, it's 256-876-2377."

Mr. Price said, "I'll see if I can reach her and tell her."

"Thank you, Ben."

That evening, Ben Price called Jolene. When she answered, he said, "Ms. Fuller, my name is Benjamin Price, and I'm D.W. Handy's attorney. D.W. asked me to call you and tell you he wants to see you. I guess you know where he is, don't you?"

"Yes sir. He's in jail."

"Well, he can have two visits a week for no more than twenty minutes each time, and visits are only allowed on Mondays through Fridays. Okay?"

"Okay. Thank you, Mr. Price."

As soon as she hung up, she called Buddy. When he answered, she said, "Buddy, a man named Benjamin Price just called me and said he is D.W.'s lawyer, and that D.W. wants to see me. I hate to ask you, Buddy, but I would really like to see him, and I wonder if you would go with me to the jail to see him."

He hesitated for a couple of seconds and then said, "Of course, I'll go with you. When do you want to go?"

"I thought maybe Friday. Can you go Friday?"

"I should be able to, What time?"

"Well, visiting hours are only from three o'clock to five, so whenever you can go within that window will be good for me."

"Do you know where my office is?"

She said she did, and he told her, "Jolene, why don't you come to my office at three o'clock, Friday, and we'll go from there."

"Okay, thank you so much, Buddy."

On Friday afternoon, Jolene and Buddy went to the Belmont City Jail to see D.W. When they got inside, they had to go through several security checks, including a search of Jolene's purse and both of their shoes. After the jail was satisfied that they weren't a threat, they were led to an area in the back of the jail where there were what Buddy called Cubby Holes. Each cubby hole had a glass in front, with a partition on either side, and a straight chair in the middle. On the outside of the cubby hole were two chairs. The guard instructed them to sit down, and in a minute, another guard led D.W. in in handcuffs.

As he was being led into the room, all Buddy and Jolene could do was to look at each other. If they hadn't known they were there to see D.W., they would have thought they were visiting a stranger. He had lost quite a bit of weight, his face was gaunt, and his hair was long, and he didn't look anything like the old D.W., but as soon as he opened his mouth, they knew it was him.

He smiled through his unshaved beard and said "Hi Guys."

They both said, "Hi, D.W.", and Buddy said, "It sure is good to see you, padna."

Jolene asked, "Where have you been, D.W.?"

"Honey, I've been halfway around the world for several months. Have you ever heard of Bali?"

"Yeah, I've heard of it. Is that where you've been?"

"I was there for about ten months, then I went to Nicaragua. Things began to get hot for me down there, so I caught a ride to Florida with the wrong guy, and that's why I'm here. Gosh, It's sure good to see you guys. Buddy, do you still have the Suburban?"

"I do, and it has almost fifty thousand miles on it now."

"That's great. Jolene, you're not married yet?"

"Not yet and not even close."

"You know, I thought several times when I was gone that it would have been good if we had gotten married. Before I got in trouble, if I had asked you, would you have said yes?"

She said, "In a heartbeat."

Buddy changed the subject. D.W., you remember Donald Lee don't you?"

"Yeah, I remember Donald Lee. How is he?"

"Well, he met a girl named Jean Shelton, and they are planning to get married, but they ran into a problem. Jean got sick, and when she went to the doctor, they determined that she was going to have to have a liver transplant. Donald Lee turned out to be a match for her, and they took part of his liver and gave it to Jean. Right now, they're both still in the hospital, but it looks as though they're going to get out in a week or two. I heard they're going to get married in September."

"That's good to hear. Tell Donald Lee I said hello, and I wish him and his bride the best. Will you tell him that for me?"

"I sure will, and then he asked, "D.W., have they said what they're going to do to you yet?"

"My lawyer says I should plead guilty to manslaughter. He thinks the D.A. might go along with that. The penalty for manslaughter is from two to twenty years as opposed to life for a murder charge."

"If they accept the manslaughter charge, has your lawyer said how much time he thinks you'll get?"

"He doesn't know. He said the D.A. is going to talk to several people about me that may serve as character witnesses, and if he can find some character witnesses, then maybe the sentence will be shorter."

The twenty minutes flew by and the guard said visiting hours were over, and came to escort Jolene and Buddy back to the jail entrance.

As they started out, Jolene turned around and told D.W., "I'll try to come see you again next Friday. You'll still be here, won't you?"

"Yeah, I think I'll be here for two more weeks. I hope you can come."

She didn't wait until the next Friday. Since visiting days were Wednesday through Friday, she went back on the next Wednesday. When they brought D.W. out, and he looked like the old D.W., her heart melted. She wanted so much to get across the restraints and hug and kiss him, but of course, she couldn't. They talked about a lot of things in the short twenty minutes they had, and one of them was when D.W. brought up the subject of marriage when he gets out.

He said, "I know I don't have the right to ask you, but even though I'll be an ex-con when I get out, I feel like we would be happy together, don't you?"

"I don't know. D.W. There's a lot to think about. You know, you left me once, and I'd be afraid you would do it again if times got tough."

D.W. said, "Things shouldn't get tough. Most of the time when things get tough with people, they're because of finances, but Jolene, I have plenty for both of us to live on for the rest of our lives."

Then Jolene said, "Like you said, you'd be an ex-con, and I'd be the wife of an ex-con, and I don't know what my family would say about that. I'll have to do a lot of thinking."

"Fair enough. We have plenty of time, so you think about it, and we'll talk about it later. I hope you'll write me, but I'll have to send you my address because I don't know where I'll be."

The guard came to get her at the end of twenty minutes, and as she was leaving, D.W. called out to her, "I love you."

She turned around and said, "Love you, too."

The D.A. didn't have to look for people to talk to on D.W.'s behalf because ever since the people of Belmont found out that D.W. was back and was facing charges for killing Coco Cochran, the D.A.'s mailbox was overflowing, and his voice mail was stacked up until there could be no more messages taken. Every one of them was showing their love for him. It was a veritable love fest.

Ben Price went to see D.W. Saturday morning, and he told him about the large crowd coming to his rescue. He said the D.A. was extremely impressed by it, and he told the Judge about it. She told him she had heard about D.W. before he ran away, and she was inclined to help all she could.

His Arraignment was set for Tuesday at nine a.m., and normally, in cases like this, there is hardly anybody in the courtroom, but in D.W.'s case, there were probably twenty-five people there, including Jolene and Buddy. They were pleased to see that D.W. had cleaned up. His lawyer more than likely saw to it because he was clean shaven, his hair was cut, and he had on a nice suit and tie. Judge Regina Campbell was the Judge for D.W.'s case, and she told him to stand up. When he did, she said that the D.A. had informed her that he would plead guilty to manslaughter, and she asked him if that was correct, and D.W. said it was. She said, "Very well. The court will set Tuesday, two weeks from today, as the date for your sentencing. Does that work for you, Mr. Lowe?"

"Yes, your Honor."

"For you, Mr. Price?"

"Yes, your Honor."

"Good. Court is dismissed."

In two weeks, at his sentencing, there was a crowd. Normally, when a plaintiff pleads guilty, and there's only the sentencing, there is usually some members of the plaintiff's family and maybe a friend or two present, but not in D.W.'s case. The courtroom was packed, and everyone there was in support of him. Most, if not all, spoke to Ben Price, D.W.'s lawyer, as well as Joseph Lowe, the District Attorney on D.W.'s behalf, and when the court was called to order, and Judge Campbell asked the two lawyers if they had anything to say that the court should know, they both told her that the entire crowd in the courtroom was there in support of D.W.

She thanked them both, and then she told D.W., "Mr. Handy, please stand."

D.W. and his attorney stood up, and Judge Campbell said, "Donald Wayne Handy, it is the decision of this court, on the charge of manslaughter, to sentence you to two years in the St. Claire Correctional Facility in Springville, Alabama. Mr. Handy, you can thank all your friends for this short sentence. Normally, a charge like this would carry a much longer term, but it seems there were mitigating circumstances in this case, so again, I suggest you say thank you to your friends."

The guards came to cuff him and take him away, but before they had the chance to do it, D.W. called out to Judge Campbell.

"What is it, Mr. Handy?"

"Your Honor, you said I should thank my friends. Would you allow me to do that right now, while a lot of them are here?"

"I think that would be appropriate. Yes, you can address your friends."

"Thank you, Your Honor." He turned around and faced the crowd and said, "Judge Campbell said I should thank you for your help getting a shorter sentence for my crime."

He then called some of the people by name, such as Jolene and Buddy, and he brought up a thing or two that each of them had been a part of, and then he talked to the whole crowd and expressed his thanks to all of them, and when he finished, he simply said "Thank you all. I love you." He then held out his hands so they could cuff him, and they led him away.

Afterwards, a lot of the people who had come to support D.W. hung around to talk to each other because most of them had lost contact with most of the others, and they just wanted to bring some of their activities up to date with each other. Buddy and Sally Jo stayed until most of the crowd had dwindled down before they left. As they were getting ready to leave, Buddy asked Sally Jo, "While we're out, would you like to go see Donald Lee and Jean?"

"Yeah, I'd like to see 'em. I've talked to Jean, but I haven't seen her since her surgery."

"Okay, but I had better call to see where they are. If Donald Lee is working, I feel sure he's home, but it could be that he's over at Jeans, so let's see."

Donald Lee answered, and Jean was at his house. He was working, but he said he had worked late the day before, so he could take some time off for Jean. He invited Buddy and Sally Jo over, and they went, but they didn't stay long.

Buddy rang the doorbell, and he heard Donald Lee yell, "Come on in," and they did just that. The two guys shook hands and Buddy hugged Jean, and Sally Jo hugged them both.

"How are you guys doing?" Buddy asked.

We're doing great. We're almost ready to start driving, and neither one of us can hardly wait. Where have you all been this morning?"

Buddy said, "You remember D.W. Handy don't you?"

"Yeah, I remember D.W. How's he doing?"

"Okay, I guess. We've been to court to his sentencing this morning."

"To his sentencing?"

"Yeah, he killed a woman and has been on the run for over a year. They finally caught him in Florida and due to some ultra-clever work by his lawyer, he got off with only two years."

"I didn't know anything about that. Working in Huntsville, I miss out on a lot of stuff that goes on around here. Sometime, I'd like to hear more about all that."

"Okay, after your wedding and recuperation, we'll get together, and I'll fill you in on everything. D.W. told somebody that he was going to write a book about it while he is in prison. From what I know about it, if he tells everything, it should be a big seller."

"Wow. I always liked D.W. You say he killed a woman?"

"Yeah, and he admitted he did." Buddy said, "We didn't come over here to talk about D.W. We want to hear about you guys. Was the surgery pretty rough?"

Jean said, "Yeah, it was rough, but my hero here was by my side and he saved my life, and that made it all worth it."

Buddy smiled and said, "Yeah, I think he liked you."

Jean said, "I sure like him."

Sally Jo asked Jean, "Are y'all pretty well set for the wedding?"

Jean said, "I think so. Between Mother and June and Donald Lee's daddy, we're not going to have to do much more than just show up. We had everything pretty much planned before the surgery came up, and so, after the surgery, we just had to change the time."

Donald Lee said, "Buddy, you're still planning to be one of my groomsmen, aren't you?"

"I sure am," and smiling, he said, "I want to be there to make sure you go through with it."

Jean said laughingly, "He'll go through with it. I'll see to that."

After a few more minutes, Buddy said they needed to go, and he and Sally Jo told them how great it was to see them doing so well, and that they would see them at the wedding, if not before.

Six weeks later

Jean and Donald Lee were completely recovered from their liver transplant, and finally, their wedding day had arrived. Carl Mathis, with help from Martha Von Steen had planned a great rehearsal dinner at Coach's Restaurant. All of the wedding party as well as Don and Jean's family were there. In addition, there were several family members from out of town, making a total for the rehearsal around fifty.

The meal was outstanding, and due to Jean's close encounter with death and her life-saving surgery, thanks to Donald Lee, it was an extra special occasion, and the bride and groom both took the opportunity to thank everybody for their support. They both gave God the credit for their healing and promised to serve Him for the rest of their lives. Their speeches were so touching that nearly everybody in attendance had tears in their eyes. After their serious comments, they lightened the mood by telling some of the funny things that happened while they were hospitalized and at home recovering.

The gathering broke up with everybody feeling good and looking forward to the wedding service the next evening.

The wedding was very traditional, and Jean was beautiful in her dress with the long train. Donald Lee was a handsome man, and he looked especially handsome in his tuxedo. The pastor did a great job with the ceremony, and after it was over and the pictures were taken, everyone moved to the Fellowship Hall for the reception.

Sarah and Monty had outdone themselves with the beautiful wedding cake and other refreshments. The receiving line was also nice with all the attendants displaying their personalities and love for the newlyweds.

There was no band or dancing, since it was in the church, but they didn't need it. Everyone was happy just being together and sharing Donald Lee and Jean's happiness, after Jean's close call.

After most of the guests had left, and only the families were there, Carl asked the family members to gather around for a minute. When they had encircled him and Martha, he said, "Folks, I didn't know if this was the right time or not, but this is such a happy occasion, I wanted to add to it. I hope all of you are as happy as I am when I tell you that Martha and I have decided that we are going to get married. Donald Lee, I know this is a surprise to you, and I'd like to know what you might have to say. Anything?"

He said, "Wow. It just keeps getting better," and he went over and hugged his dad and Martha," and told them, "I love you both, and I'm very happy about this."